breaking
FREE

ADRIENNE
GIORDANO

STEELE RIDGE
www.SteeleRidgeSeries.com

Print Edition, April 2017, ISBN: 978-1-944898-13-7
For more information contact: adrienneg@adriennegiordano.com

Books available by Adrienne Giordano

PRIVATE PROTECTORS SERIES
Romantic suspense

Risking Trust
Man Law
A Just Deception

Negotiating Point
Relentless Pursuit
Opposing Forces

HARLEQUIN INTRIGUES
Romantic suspense

The Prosecutor
The Marshal

The Defender
The Detective

The Rebel

JUSTIFIABLE CAUSE SERIES
Romantic suspense novellas

The Chase
The Evasion
The Capture

LUCIE RIZZO SERIES
Mysteries

Dog Collar Crime
Dog Collar Limbo

Dog Collar Knockoff
Dog Collar Couture

CASINO FORTUNA SERIES
Romantic suspense

Deadly Odds

JUSTICE SERIES w/MISTY EVANS
Romantic suspense

Stealing Justice
Holiday Justice
Undercover Justice

Cheating Justice
Exposing Justice
Protecting Justice

Missing Justice

BOOKS AVAILABLE BY CO-AUTHORS OF
THE STEELE RIDGE SERIES

BOOKS AVAILABLE BY TRACEY DEVLYN

NEXUS SERIES
Historical romantic suspense
A Lady's Revenge
Checkmate, My Lord
A Lady's Secret Weapon
Latymer
Shev

BONES & GEMSTONES SERIES
Historical romantic mystery
Night Storm

TEA TIME SHORTS & NOVELLAS
Sweet historical romance
His Secret Desire

BOOKS AVAILABLE BY KELSEY BROWNING

PROPHECY OF LOVE SERIES
Sexy contemporary romance
A Love to Last
A Passion to Pursue

TEXAS NIGHTS SERIES
Sexy contemporary romance
Personal Assets
Running the Red Light
Problems in Paradise
Designed for Love

BY INVITATION ONLY SERIES
Sexy contemporary romance
Amazed by You

G TEAM SERIES w/NANCY NAIGLE
Southern cozy mysteries
In For a Penny
Fit to Be Tied
In High Cotton
Under the Gun
Gimme Some Sugar

JENNY & TEAGUE NOVELLAS
Contemporary romance
Always on My Mind
Come a Little Closer

NOVELLAS
Sexy contemporary romance
Love So Sweet
Amazed by You

breaking FREE

ADRIENNE
GIORDANO

CHAPTER ONE

SOME DAYS LIFE JUST SUCKED. And there wasn't much Micki Steele could do about it.

She sat at her desk in the bland, white-walled, just short of rundown and extremely un-Vegas-like offices of Phil Flynn and Associates staring at Tomas—aka Tommy, T-Man, Tomster, or whatever other nickname she could think of to annoy him.

For the past forty minutes he'd had his feet propped on his desk, one earbud in, listening to an illegally recorded conversation while Micki cruised the local cable company's network.

Happy Thanksgiving.

This life. She peeped through the window blinds to the street where morning traffic whipped by. With the Strip just blocks away, even on Thanksgiving morning they tended to get high traffic and on days like today, she wouldn't mind throwing herself in front of a truck or some other large vehicle that could free her from boredom. But in an effort to find the positive in any situation, she reminded herself that in a few hours Phil would be back from Mexico and she and Tommy would be sitting at his dining room table stuffing themselves with a feast fit for royalty. One thing about Phil, he didn't skimp on special occasions.

She gave up on the blinds and looked back at Tomster. "Anything?"

He shook his head and Micki managed to stifle her sigh.

Sure as hell burned hot, if they didn't get some kind of valuable information their boss could blackmail a judge with, Phil would not be happy.

A familiar sickness roiled inside. If Phil was here, he'd look at her with those hyper-focused eyes that screamed of death one minute and the next could soften like a baby's rear. All of it made her skin itch. Ten years she'd been playing this game with him. The anxiety, the drama, the *aggravation*. The special meals at his house, the latest-greatest electronics for her to play with, the birthday parties in her honor. It all added up to one monster game of love-hate she couldn't do a thing about.

This life.

Well, sitting around feeling sorry for herself wouldn't stave off Phil's pissiness.

She swiveled back to her laptop and sent her fingers flying across her keyboard. "I'll check his bank records again. Phil thinks this guy is taking payoffs and he's usually right about that stuff. There has to be something there."

"Go ahead. I'll be here. Listening to this douche have phone sex with his twenty-year-old assistant while he jerks off."

Micki made an ick face. "Ew. I'm glad it's you listening and not me."

Tommy propped his hands behind his head. "According to the shorty, he's being a *very* bad boy."

Then he flashed the smile that had opened all sorts of doors—and windows—for him.

At thirty-two, Tommy had reached that age where boyish good looks collided with maturity. His Hispanic heritage had blessed him with olive skin, inky black hair, and soft brown eyes that could turn hard in seconds.

Over the past ten years, he'd become her adopted brother and she'd seen women swoon over him thousands of times. Women were drawn to Tommy and he made it work for him. Personally and professionally.

His cell phone rang and he leaned in to check the screen, rolling his bottom lip out. At the second ring, he yanked his earbud free, replacing it with his phone.

"Hello?"

Whatever it was, it was important enough for him to dump the judge. Micki went back to her laptop, where their target's deposits for the past twelve months appeared in front of her.

"What?"

A sudden sheen of sweat pebbled his perfect forehead.

With the tasks they performed, Tommy suddenly looking like a crack addict in need of his next fix didn't happen a lot, and the *buhm, buhm, buhm* of her heartbeat echoed in her head.

Tommy flipped a page on his notepad, scrawling notes as he bit down on his lip. The lips were always the tell. Not much rattled Tommy, but when it did, his lips got active.

Buhm, buhm, buhm.

To alleviate the pressure, she stuck her fingers in her ears, pressed, and let go. *Press. Let go. Press. Let go.*

"Three o'clock?" Tommy checked his watch. "I can do that." He punched off the call and met Micki's gaze. "Big problem."

"What happened?"

Tomas smacked his desk drawer open, grabbed his keys and wallet, and hopped up. "Phil got pinched in Mexico."

What?

Phil. In his five-thousand-dollar Brioni suit, sitting in a filthy, rat-infested Mexican prison. Crazy.

On Thanksgiving. If ever there was a sign…

This is it.

She shook that off. Couldn't think about it now. Phil was in jail. They'd have to get him out.

"The goddamned passports," Tommy said.

The fake ones. The ones Phil was hand-delivering to

their client, an insanely wealthy network executive about to permanently relocate overseas to avoid a financial fraud charge.

"He got *caught* with them?"

Phil in a Mexican prison shocked her, but the thing that sent her mind zipping was the idea that Mr. Meticulous, Mr. Let's Stay Under the Radar, Mr. Anticipate Every Problem had actually gotten busted carrying forged government documents.

This is it.

Tomas made his way to the door, but detoured to Micki, holding his hand palm up. She smacked it and they did a quick fist bump, their usual hello-good-bye just for the heck of it sign of affection.

"I'm going down there," he said. "I'll call the lawyer on the way to the airport. See what you can do from here. I'll call his wife and make our apologies about today. Happy freaking Thanksgiving."

Micki watched him open the door, watched his habitual pat of his pockets before he left. For the first time in months, years maybe, she'd be completely alone in the office.

This is it.

All the planning and dashed hopes, the endless nights of imagining her hometown—her family—flashed in her mind.

Could she do it?

No. Too late now. Her life was here. In Vegas. With Phil and Tomas.

"Micki?"

She blinked twice, met Tomas's eyes and shook her head. "Sorry. I was…thinking. I'll see what I can do. I might be able to hack into the Policía Federal's system. I tried that a few months ago when the pop star got pinched on that nudity charge."

"Jesus, that kid. Unbelievable. At least you've done this before. Anything you can do." He gripped the edge of the open door, his long fingers wrapping around it.

He'd chewed his nails to the quick again, but she'd given up nagging him about it three years ago. He took a step out the door, then glanced at the empty desk where their receptionist normally sat. *Not on a holiday.*

It had finally hit him: When he left, she'd be alone. He brought the full weight of his focused attention to her. "Will you be all right?"

Really, what he wanted to know was could he trust her to stay alone. After all these years, Tommy, of all people, knew she longed for...something.

Something other than helping crappy people slither their way out of the even crappier situations they themselves created.

This is it.

"I'll be fine. Go help Phil."

He swung his head to the outer door, then back to her, obviously questioning his next move.

"Phil needs you," she said.

The ace in the hole, the thing that motivated them, always, was pleasing Phil. Their boss. Their pseudo stand-in parent. The one who made not only their health insurance payments but covered their medical bills and cell phones and cars. Phil took care of it all. To keep them happy.

Tommy jerked his head. "I'll call you later. Keep your phone close."

"I will." As he moved into the hallway, she added, "Tommy?"

He popped back in. "Micki, I have to go."

"I know. Just..." *What? Have a nice life? I'll miss you?* Her one chance and she was being stupid. "Don't forget your passport."

Now he cocked his head. "Are you sure you'll be okay? Don't make me worry about you. Not now."

She responded with a smile that was at best lazy and at worst halfhearted. "I'll be fine. Go."

The second Tommy was gone, Micki jumped from her chair and scanned the office.

What the hell am I doing?

She knew.

Sure did.

Ten years she'd been here, in this craptastic forty-year-old building waiting for this, anticipating the moment when she'd finally have the grand combination of nerve and opportunity. And here it was. The best she'd get, anyway.

She hustled to the rear window, peeped out the blinds, and watched the taillights of Tomas's Mercedes swing out of the tiny lot behind the squat brick building. Phil liked the finer things, but when it came to the office, he stuck with low-grade.

Nondescript, he called it. Whatever.

Don't. Thinking about Phil would kill the adrenaline buzz. She needed that buzz to push her out the door.

She ran back to her desk, slid the bottom drawer open, and grabbed her messenger bag, the expensive leather one with the hand-stitched skull on the corner. Phil had given it to her for Christmas the year before and she loved it. Used it every day, in fact. She ran her thumb over the worn edge and the rough surface dragged against her skin. Should she leave the bag? Make it a symbol of her final good-bye?

Oh, the drama. What a jerk I am.

Dammit. *Go.*

She shoved her phone and laptop—also from Phil—into the bag along with her wallet and slung it crossways across her body. At the door, she double-checked the lock.

Not knowing how long it would take to get Phil released, she didn't want the office sitting open. The hallway was empty, eerily quiet, and more than a little unnerving. Or maybe that was just her being creeped out by the lack of activity from the only other unit in the building. The mailbox said it was a lawyer's office, but she barely ever saw the guy and figured it was a front for something.

Like everything else under that roof.

She shook her head and inhaled the killer combo of stale, closed-in air and floral freshener. God, that smell always made her head spin.

Time to go.

Twenty feet away, the outer door beckoned. All she'd have to do was walk through it. Like she'd done every night for ten years. Just. Walk. Through.

"This is it," she said.

She pushed open the door, let the late November sun wash over her. Parked in the space next to the one Tomas had just vacated was her compact. The one Phil constantly wanted to upgrade, but she'd had it for five years and had barely put thirty thousand miles on it. Where did she ever go? Half the time, she was too afraid to move, much less take a road trip.

Phil, as he'd often said, could always find her. Including now, if she took her car. Knowing him, he had a GPS tracker on it somewhere.

The bus station was only two blocks over. She'd walk it, hop on the first bus heading to the airport, and wing it from there. Popping the trunk, she found her black gym bag with the Canyon Ridge High School logo.

Her go-bag.

The day she'd bought this car she'd put that bag, packed and ready for action, in her trunk. She thought about it every day, but somehow couldn't summon the nerve to actually go.

For years, her excuse for the go-bag was that she'd always have a change of clothes on hand. You know, just in case she got lucky one night, wink-wink. Whether Phil or Tomas believed that, she didn't know. Aside from some teasing, they'd never questioned the go-bag.

If she picked up that bag, after today, there'd be no more teasing. No more family dinners, no Thanksgivings with Phil's family.

Assuming he got out of Mexico.

And what about Tommy?

Her friend. Her confidant. He'd never forgive her.

If she ever saw him again. Because if she went, she'd have to disappear. Forever.

But she'd be free.

Her phone rang.

Dammit. The phone. Another thing Phil owned and could track. *Leave it.* But if it was Tomas, he'd wonder where she was and he couldn't be that far away yet. What if he'd forgotten something? He'd still have time to swing back to the office.

She dug the phone out. Mom. A squeak sounded in Micki's throat and panic, mixed with heartbreak, stormed her system, made her vision blur as she stared at the screen.

Mom.

Her second sign of the day. But there was no way she'd pick up that call now. Phil seeing an extended conversation with her mother right before Micki skipped on him would send him straight to her hometown.

No. She'd get another phone and download her contacts from her laptop. She tossed the phone in the trunk and before she thought too hard about it, grabbed her go-bag and slammed the lid shut.

She moved to the driver's side, popped the lock open, and dropped into the seat, closing the door behind her. She snagged a thumb drive from the inside pocket of her messenger bag, felt around the side of the seat for the port, and—*come on, where are you?* There. She rested her head back, anticipated the burst, slid the thumb drive in and waited one, two, three. *Poof.* The airbag from the side of her seat blew.

Please, please, please. She shoved open the door, checked the pocket attached to the back of the airbag— *yes*—for the fake driver's license and passport she'd obtained years ago. The sad part about grabbing someone's identity, other than living with the fact that she'd done it, was how easy it was to pull off. A simple online search of death notices to find someone about her age and a few days later, voilá, Micki Steele had become Stephanie Gimble. After that, all she'd needed was a safe, easy-access place to hide Stephanie's credentials. Enter Josh, the car/engineering whiz she'd met at the electronics show who'd helped her rig this little secret compartment. *Thank you, Josh.*

Exiting the car, she glanced back at the faded brick of the office and the torn awning that had once been a vibrant red, but which years of harsh Vegas sun had withered to a pale maroon.

At least ten times she'd e-mailed the landlord asking him to change it. Such a small request never granted. Add it to the list.

Today, she'd leave it all behind.

Finally.

"This time, I'm going."

CHAPTER TWO

IF GAGE HAD TO HEAR another minute of Reid's bitching about the contractor's schedule, he might slide his .45 from the drawer, prop that baby under his chin, and—*pow!*

"Dude," he said, "please. You're driving me batshit crazy. You come in here every day complaining about construction being two weeks behind. I know it's frustrating, but it is what it is. The weather sucks and certain things can't be done in the rain. And, oh, yeah, your *brother* is the contractor."

"Exactly! You need to talk to him. You're the admin guy."

Nuh-uh. No way. "I'm not getting into the middle of any family shit. If you're pissed, take it up with Britt."

Gage's cell phone rang. His mother's ringtone. By now, Reid knew that.

"Go ahead and take it."

"Sorry." He poked at the screen. "Hi, Mom."

"Good morning. Have you talked to your father yet?"

No preamble. No warm-up. No pleasantries. Just—bam.

Yesterday, when Gage had called to wish them a Happy Thanksgiving, she'd begged him to speak to his father about half a dozen things Dad was apparently too stubborn to listen to *her* about.

"Not yet. But I will. I'm in a meeting right now. Can I call you back this afternoon?"

His mother sighed as if his job were a major imposition. "Of course. You know where I'll be. Right here. Wondering when my boy is going to come see me."

Ah, the guilt. "I'll come soon."

"I love you."

"Love you, too. And don't worry about Dad. I'll talk to him. I promise."

Gage punched off and set the phone down. "Where were we?"

Reid pushed out of his chair, his long jean-clad legs eating up the length of the office Gage had claimed as president of the Steele Ridge Training Academy. Gage liked the view of the outdoor shooting range. The first time he'd seen it, he'd been taken by the bordering bright green grass and Callery pear trees loaded with leaves. All in all, not a bad view.

The building, originally designed as a sports complex, now housed the administrative offices Reid and Jonah Steele had hired Gage to oversee. All of it was in Steele Ridge, a tiny town ninety minutes from Asheville that Jonah, billionaire game developer and baby brother to Reid, had bailed out of bankruptcy and slapped their family name on.

When it came to the training center, Gage was the admin guy, handling all the paperwork and finer details that Reid couldn't manage to wrap his mind around. Just as well. Gage liked the quiet, analytical stuff. Even if it had become harder since his injury last spring, he'd still happily let Reid handle the tactical angles and design the courses.

"Tarzan is being a pain in the ass," Reid said. "He keeps hanging up on me."

Gage laughed at Reid's use of his brother's nickname. Hadn't he just sat at a table with the brothers celebrating Thanksgiving, laughing and just happily breaking balls? "Maybe because you call him ten times a day."

"We got shit to do here. A schedule to keep. We're opening doors February first and our shoot house isn't nearly complete."

"The shoot house is fine."

Wasn't it? He thought they were on schedule with that. He'd have to check it.

Refusing to make a note of it in front of Reid, he focused on that little detail, hoping if he thought about it hard enough, it would somehow get cemented in his brain.

Reid gripped two handfuls of his dark hair and tugged. "The shoot house is *not* fine. We don't have any walls!"

Wait. Walls? Crap. The shoot house. Right. Wrong building.

"Sorry. My mind left me for a sec."

"I guess."

"The walls are my fault. He wanted to do drywall. I told him plywood instead. Nobody'll be living there, and with the way the walls will get beat up, the plywood'll hold up better. Couple of days is all he needs. Let's get the outside stuff done first. The rain isn't helping."

Gage stood, moved too fast, and immediately regretted it. He set one hand on the edge of his desk and took a second to let his spinning head settle in.

"Whoa," Reid said. "You okay?"

He held up a hand. "I'm good. Stood up too fast." He swirled one finger. "My head spun."

"That happen often?"

"No."

"You sure?"

"Cut the shit, Gertrude." He waved one hand. "I'm just hungry. My body is getting pissy."

"Lunch," Reid said. He jerked his thumb toward the door. "Let's head up to the house. Mom said something about fried chicken today. After that, *you'll* call my brother. Who keeps hanging up on me."

Reid flashed a smile that had served him—and most

of his friends—well back in their Special Forces days. He might be a loudmouth, but he wasn't short on his own twisted brand of charm.

All these years later, though, Gage knew when he was being played. "I'm not calling him."

He followed the big man out the door, his mouth already watering over Miss Joan's fried chicken.

From the minute Gage had settled into his office two months ago, Miss Joan had treated him as one of her own, letting a stranger sleep in her guest room in the main house—Tupelo Hill—just up the drive from the training center. After renters moved out of the original Steele family home, Gage had moved in, leasing it from the family. But Miss Joan insisted on still feeding him and kept him in a steady supply of his favorite chocolate chip cookies.

And she refused to take money from him. For anything.

"Speaking of which," Gage said. "You gotta talk to your mom about letting me chip in for groceries. I may not be an ape like you, but I eat. She doesn't need to pay for it."

Reid waved it off. "Forget it. She'll be pissed if I say anything. Consider it part of the training center budget. Executive compensation. Plus, she's got a soft spot for military guys."

"Injured military guys?"

"Whatever."

They both knew he was right. First Reid had come home to Steele Ridge after blowing out his knee and now Gage had taken squatting rights after a paranoid villager decided he was done talking and put a bullet in his chest.

For both men, their injuries had been enough to earn them a ticket out of Special Forces, and now Gage couldn't face his own family. Not yet. He loved Iowa. Loved being on the farm, but he wasn't going back there until he was 100 percent in mind and body.

And that wasn't the case. Yet.

He followed Reid to the main entrance of the building. "At the rate we're going, the budget'll be decimated."

"Relax, Suds. We'll be fine."

Suds. Six months out of the Army and he couldn't leave behind the nickname his Green Beret comrades had leveled on him. The sons of bitches had slipped half a bottle of liquid soap into a hot tub and when Gage fired it up and got in? Suds. Lots of 'em.

"I hope so. February first can't come too soon. It'd be nice to have money coming in instead of going the other way."

Outside, the unrelenting rain had finally slowed to a drizzle and Reid hopped over a puddle. Gage wouldn't do any hopping. He sidestepped the water and his boot sank into mud.

Shit. He'd have to leave his boots on the porch, because he sure as hell wasn't tracking mud into Miss Joan's.

Just ahead, a taxi pulled around the long drive that led to the main house. A taxi. In the time he'd been here, Gage could count on one hand how many taxis he'd seen in town, never mind at the Hill.

Reid picked up his pace. "No idea who that is. My mother didn't say anything about visitors."

The cab came to a stop at the front porch and a few seconds later, the back passenger side door opened and a long—really long—leg appeared. A dark-haired woman slid out. She wore a black jacket with zippers on the side.

She hooked a messenger bag crosswise over her shoulder, then gave her shaggy hair a flip before grabbing a duffel from the backseat.

Whoever this was, she was a tall drink of water. Tight jeans wrapped around her lean body and the damned legs went on for miles, sparking something low and deep in Gage's belly.

Reid halted, and a fierce energy charged the air around them. That fucking fast, Reid's cheeks turned to cement.

The battle look.

Reid started walking again, his eyes on the porch where the brunette slowly climbed the steps.

"Jesus H. Christ," he said. "I have no idea if my mother knows she's here."

Well, this didn't sound good. The woman reached for the door, then paused. Waiting.

Unsure.

Hold up, here. His first night at Miss Joan's, he'd walked around the living room, taking in all the family photos. Reid and his siblings goofing off, school photos, Christmas. An entire life on display.

Miss Joan had remarked she had all her children back in Steele Ridge.

All but one.

Gage followed Reid up the drive. "Is that…her?"

Reid snorted, but kept his eyes on the woman lifting her fist to the door, about to knock. "That's her. Apparently, my sister has come home."

Micki stood on her mother's porch, the damp air closing in, pressing down, forcing her to raise her chin and lock her eyes on the door.

For nearly a day she'd been stressed about using fake credentials to hop flights that would get her back to Steele Ridge. She'd see her family for a quick visit and then be on her way again.

This time for good.

Before Phil caught up to her.

Now that she stood here, her beloved and missed mother just on the other side of the door, she didn't know what to do. Walk in? Knock?

Everything was different. When she left ten years ago, they'd lived in the three-bedroom ranch in town. Eight people sharing one and a half bathrooms. Now it would be two and half, since Britt added the second-floor master suite after the renters moved out. But back when they were kids, the boys fought over space while she, the edgy Goth-like nerd, and Evie, the girly-girl, tried to figure out what to do with each other.

If she could, she'd go back. In a heartbeat.

Back then the decisions had been easier. If only she'd realized.

Now she stood on the porch of Tupelo Hill, the home her mother had gushed about—dreamed about—for years. And it was hers. Not just the house. The property, too. All bought by Micki's billionaire twin.

Micki hadn't been involved in that move.

At all.

The time away, the loss, ripped at her and she sucked in a hard breath, fought a wave of tears. If she let them fly, that would be it. Over. Years of compartmentalized sorrow would erupt, all its poisonous venom pouring onto this newly painted and glossy porch.

Onto her mother's new life.

But she wouldn't let that happen. Wouldn't regret her decisions—right or wrong. She'd done it. Now it was over. Even if she couldn't stay here in Steele Ridge, she could visit and then move on before Phil found her.

Besides, why would her family even want her? After all the time away, she didn't fit anymore.

"Micki," a deep voice said from behind her.

Reid. She might have been gone a long time, but she'd always recognize her siblings' voices.

She steadied herself once more and turned to see her brother, all six foot three of him striding toward her and—*hello.* Accompanying Reid was a blond guy who looked like he should be in a Ralph Lauren ad.

Or a fairy tale.

But Micki didn't believe in fairy tales. Not anymore.

She'd get back to him in a second. Right now, she needed to deal with her brother, who wore the pissy look of judgment he'd obviously perfected. Reid had always been handsome. Man candy, her old friends would say.

In the years since she'd moved, his cheeks had molded into sharp, hardened angles. His hair was still that dark coffee brown bordering on black, much like hers, and his eyes were still as intense.

"Uh, hi," she said.

The side of Reid's mouth lifted into a smirk. Her brother taking enjoyment out of her not knowing what to do. Great start.

He climbed the porch stairs with the apple-cheeked guy trailing behind and came to a stop in front of her. Her longing to recapture the bond they'd shared as teenagers nearly doubled her over.

Don't.

Never one to allow her brothers an easy mental victory, she steadied herself, stood a little taller and met his gaze.

"Still a pisser, huh, Mick?"

"Well, when you stare at me like I'm a freak, what do you expect?"

He turned back to Mr. All-American, but jerked his thumb toward Micki. "Gage Barber, meet my ball-busting sister, Mikayla Steele. We call her Micki."

She slid her gaze to Mr. All-American, then held her hand out. "Hi."

"Hi," he said in a voice that was pure sex. Brandy straight from the cask. All deep and smooth and so very easy.

He shook her hand and his palm was warm, the skin a little rough. Work-hardened. Which made her wonder just what the Ralph Lauren model had done to earn those hands.

He pointed at the duffel in her other hand. "Let me grab that."

Tightening her hold, she shook her head. "That's okay. Thanks."

"Here we go," Reid said. "Forget it, Suds. She does what she wants. You learn to live with it."

If that were true, at least the part about her doing

what she pleased, she wouldn't have spent the past ten years in Vegas. Her brother didn't know that, though. From his vantage point, he saw a selfish young woman who'd walked out on her family and a college scholarship to work for a creep. Worse than a creep. A scumbag.

Reid pointed at the door. "Mom know you're here?"

When she walked through that door, there'd be explanations to be made. All these years, any trips home had been planned. She'd called ahead of time with an exact schedule of when she'd arrive and when she'd leave. All arranged by Phil to make sure she didn't get any funny ideas about doing what she'd done yesterday.

Leaving him.

"No," Micki said. "I thought I'd surprise her."

"You'll definitely accomplish that."

Micki laughed and her brother shot her a look, all those hard angles softening as he smiled. This was the Reid she remembered. Playful and sarcastic. Before things were…strained…between them and they had shared the same twisted humor.

Now? She didn't know what they shared. If anything.

"Seriously," Gage said, "your smiles are exactly the same. Are you sure *you're* not the twins?"

How many times had they heard that? Jonah may have been her twin, but she and Reid, in addition to the sibling resemblance, had always had that rebellious edginess to them.

"Unless the birth certificate is wrong," she said, "Jonah is my twin."

Reid let out a snort. "He's gonna shit a brick. As shocked as I am to see you standing on this porch, I can't wait to see his reaction."

He slid his keys from his pocket and unlocked the front door. What was that about? Her mother never locked the doors.

She eyeballed the key in his hand as he pushed the door open. "We've had some…incidents. We make her keep the front door locked now."

"What kind of incidents?"

"Later," he said. "Now, let's make our mother happy."

"Uh," Mr. All-American said, "I'll head back to my office. Give you guys some time."

Office.

That's who he was. On the last call to Mom, Micki had heard all about the training center erected out of a broken-down sports complex, and Britt and Reid nearly killing each other over the rebuild. Mom had mentioned Jonah hiring one of Reid's military buddies to help with the administrative side of the operation. Mr. All-American must be that guy.

Reid turned to his friend. "You said you were hungry. You need to eat."

"I'll grab something out."

"Screw that, Suds. You're family now. Besides, if I know my sister, we're not gonna be discussing any deep dark secrets."

Oh, he couldn't resist that shot, could he?

The hunk met Micki's gaze, as if...what? Was he really waiting for *her* to give him permission to stay? Huh. How about that. When Reid spoke, most people simply fell in line. It had been that way since their school days, when he'd threaten to maim anyone who came near his younger siblings. Even back then, he had that commanding way about him.

"It's fine with me." She locked eyes with her brother. "Like Reid said, we won't be sharing any deep dark secrets."

CHAPTER THREE

THE SECOND THEY WERE THROUGH the door, Reid was yelling for Mom. Could he not give Micki a second to settle in? To adjust to all those damned family photos scattered everywhere, hers included, and Mom's lavender scent lingering in the air. All of it, the yelling, the scent, the family photos came at her, making her head spin.

Micki stepped back, bumped straight into Mr. All-American. And who'd have thunk that under his loose, long-sleeved shirt she'd find a solid wall of muscle. From behind, he set his hands on her arms and steadied her.

"You're okay," he whispered.

His warm breath tickled her ear and stifled the panic revving inside her.

"Mom!" Reid hollered again. "Where are you?"

"Reid Sullivan Steele!" came a return shout. "You stop that yelling in this house! For the love of Pete, I was putting out the trash."

Their mother marched into the hallway leading from the back of the house, her eyes murderous as she approached her mouthy son. Then her gaze sliced to Micki and…she halted. Literally skidded to a stop, her Chuck Taylors squeaking against the hard wood and— wow—her mother now wore Chuck Taylors.

At some point in the past ten years, Mom had

obviously started wearing Micki's preferred brand of footwear, and the evidence of all that she'd missed crashed into her.

I can't do this.

What she'd been thinking, coming here on her way to who knew where, still eluded her. Astounded her, really. She should have just run. Left Vegas and the States and contacted her family when it was safe.

Mom threw her arms up. "My baby!"

Everything Micki had been holding in—anticipation, regret, fear—for the past day broke loose, unleashing a wave of relief that had her dropping her duffel, shoving past Reid, and slamming into her mother's open arms. Tears burned the back of her eyes and she squeezed them closed, willing the damned waterworks away.

You can't stay.

She knew it. Understood it in ways not many could, but still, to be surrounded by family, her true family, annoying as they might be, gave her hope. One day, she'd have a home again. One day.

Footsteps pounded on the oak stairs, echoing into the entry. "What the hell, Reid?" Jonah snapped. "I was on a conference call."

Micki broke free of her mother in time to see Reid point at her. "You might want to hang up."

Jonah's head dipped. "Whoa!" But then he, too, rushed to her, holding his arms wide and wrapping her up in a hug. "Jesus, Mick, way to surprise a guy."

"Hi."

She held on, squeezing tight, inhaling his clean, soapy smell. The Jonah smell. They'd always been a team, the two of them. Always. Even when no one else understood her, including him, he'd been patient and non-judgey. No matter what, they'd stuck together. At least before the ill-fated party ten years earlier. That party had changed her life, and the bitterness still ate at her.

She'd adjusted to the hacking and illegal transactions she didn't necessarily complete but had a part in. At times, she'd even enjoyed life with Phil. The good times, anyway. Times when he invited her on outings with his family because he knew she was lonely or when, years earlier, he started helping her navigate life as a grownup, getting a credit card to establish a credit rating, finding an apartment, a car—all of it, he'd done with her.

Now Jonah, like most of her family, didn't know what to think of her. She couldn't blame them, considering *she* didn't know what to think of her.

Her own fault, she supposed. She'd never been honest with them. She'd hidden so much, yet, if she had to do it over again, she wouldn't change anything. To keep Jonah safe, she'd do it again.

"In the kitchen." Mom waved her arms. "Everyone. I made chicken for lunch. And tonight we'll have a big family dinner. Oh, my goodness! Our first family dinner in years. All my babies under my roof. I have to call your father. Jonah, Reid, call your brothers. And Evie! She's running some errands for me. She might be on her way already, but make sure. I want everyone here."

"Mom," Jonah said, "calm down. You'll have a heart attack."

"You hush up. I'm happy. And I swear, if any of you start a fight, I'll strangle you."

Micki swung back to her brothers, laughing because—yes—no matter how much had changed, certain things never would.

"Y'all get settled," Mom said. "I'll call your father and we'll have lunch. And Jonah, when you go upstairs, take your sister's bag to her room."

Her room.

In reality, probably not *her* room, but a guest room. She wouldn't focus on that; what mattered was that her mother had a place for her.

In the kitchen, Gage pulled out a chair for her. She met his eyes, a beautiful crystalline blue that prompted thoughts of sunny days and hammocks. Next to her, this guy was all light and sunshine. Totally unattainable.

She shook off the rotten mood starting to swarm. It wasn't Mr. All-American's fault she'd allowed her life to turn into dark isolation.

She slid into the chair he offered. "Thank you, Gage. I like your name."

"Suds," Reid said, "you want a soda?"

"I'm good with water. Thanks."

No harsh chemicals for Mr. Perfect.

From the fridge, Reid tossed his friend a water bottle while Jonah got active on his phone. Most likely texting their siblings about her sudden appearance.

Reid held up a pitcher. "Mom's lemonade."

Her mother's lemonade. Another staple that hadn't changed. And Reid had remembered it was her favorite. "Ooh, that sounds good."

Jonah took the seat across from her. "Where's the rest of your luggage?"

"No luggage. Just the duffel."

Reid stalled his pouring and stared at her. "How long are you staying?"

"I'm not sure. Maybe till tomorrow."

"Tomorrow?" her brothers said in unison.

And here we go. The big homecoming already splattering to the pavement.

"Yes. Quick trip."

"Why? I mean, you can't stay a few days?" This from Jonah.

No. She couldn't. Twenty-four hours ago she'd run from Vegas, leaving everything, including her phone, behind. By now, Tomas might be heading back from Mexico, with or without Phil. She couldn't be sure. The Mexican penal system was wacky, to say the least. They might keep him in jail, but he'd send Tomas back to Vegas to handle the office.

To handle *her.*

She knew from checking her e-mail on the road that Tomas was concerned. He'd sent her four messages asking where she was and why she wasn't answering calls.

Sooner or later, he'd figure out she'd taken off and it wouldn't be a stretch for him to search for her in Steele Ridge. She just needed to be gone when he showed up.

"One day. Two at the most," she said to her brothers. "That's all I have."

Reid's sister was hiding something.

Then again, Gage was six months into healing from a traumatic brain injury that could be messing with him. The TBI, thanks to the boulder he'd slammed his head into after getting shot, left him questioning a lot lately.

His instincts were no exception.

Reid finished pouring Micki's lemonade, shoved it in front of her, and flattened his hands against the big farm table. "You come here, unannounced, which is totally unlike the *barely* handful of other times you showed up, and tell us you're staying one day. What's the rush?"

"I just...have to go."

"Why?"

"Cripes, Reid!" Micki said, getting more snippy than necessary.

Reid had a knack for doing that to people. Poking at buttons they didn't want poked. They'd served together long enough for Gage to recognize it. Luckily for Reid, and most of the people in his orbit, Gage had gotten good at defusing Reid-induced chaos.

Gage pointed at him. "Don't lose your shit. Give her a second."

As expected, Reid pushed off the table, folded his arms, and leaned back on Miss Joan's gleaming countertop.

"Wow." Micki looked over at Gage, eyebrows lifted. "Thank you."

"No problem. He means well, but he gets anxious."

"Damn straight I do," Reid said. "I know you, Micki.

After all this time, I *still* know you and you're lying."

"How am I lying? I said I can only stay one day. That's how long I can stay."

"Then you're hiding something."

Jonah leaned in, propped his chin in his hand. "Listen, knuckle-dragger. Give her a break. But Mick, as much as I hate saying this, he's right. What's going on with you? Aside from Mom's birthday party, every other time you've come back you were on a schedule and knew exactly when you had to leave. Did that scum you work for do something?"

"No."

Miss Joan entered the kitchen, all bright smiles and clapping hands. "I just spoke to your father. He's on his way. If I'd known getting him out of that cabin was this easy I'd tell him every week our girl was home."

Jonah's phone bleep-bleeped and he scooped it up.

Miss Joan glared at him. She hated phones at the table. "Jonah? Really?"

"Yes, really. You told me to let everyone know. I'm letting them know. Britt and Grif are on the way. Evie was at the bakery. She's leaving now."

"Wonderful! The whole family here. I'm so happy."

Gage glanced at Micki, who gnawed at her bottom lip. A damned nice bottom lip that was just the right amount of full. Miss Joan might be happy, but her daughter looked...spooked.

By her own family. What the hell?

"Boys," Miss Joan said, "give me ten minutes to get food on the table. Take Micki outside, show her the property. Ten minutes!"

Jonah jerked his head at Reid. "You do that. I'll take her bags upstairs."

"Mom," Micki said, "I can see the property later. Let me help you."

"Shoo! All of you. Get some air. For someone who lives in Las Vegas you look pale. And tired. You need to get outside more. I tell Jonah this all the time."

Reid headed toward the door. "Let's go, Mick. Suds, you coming?"

He pushed out of the chair. Yeah, he was going. Because something told him the minute Reid got his sister outside, he'd be all over her with questions and she didn't look ready for that battle. "I could use some air myself."

Micki shot him a brief glance and followed Reid outside. Apparently, she had a pattern when it came to her visits. Suddenly, she'd altered the pattern. He didn't need his tenure as an Intelligence and Operations sergeant to figure out something about this situation was off. In fact, right after lunch, he'd head back to his office and do a little snooping about Micki and whoever this guy was she worked for.

CHAPTER FOUR

IT LOOKED AS IF MIKAYLA Steele worked for an absolute asshole.

The Internet didn't have a whole lot on him, and in this day and age of rampant selfies and overexposure, that always made Gage suspicious. On any given day, he could Google someone and find a hefty list of accomplishments, photos, and mentions. Micki's boss? No company website, no LinkedIn listing, no Facebook. Nada. For a man in his fifties, the guy was a total ghost.

Except for the photos. Two to be exact. One that took over an hour's worth of digging to find because it was five years old and showed the man at a Vegas fundraiser. This guy looked all kinds of slick in his fancy suit, gelled hair, and sparkly white teeth. High end. Very high end.

The second photo, the one that really got Gage's thoughts churning, was the one that showed Phil Flynn walking behind some knucklehead pop star leaving a Los Angeles courtroom. Flynn's face was turned away, but it was him. No doubt. He'd been listed on the caption as an "associate" of the knucklehead. An associate?

"I don't think so," Gage said.

"Hi."

He snapped his gaze to the doorway where—shit—Micki stood, one shoulder propped on the frame. Her dark hair fell around a face with just a dusting of makeup, but enough to emphasize her perfectly proportioned cheekbones. She used two fingers to brush her bangs from her eyes. Hard eyes. But, damn, the woman got his attention. Feminine, yet…edgy.

Realizing his screen still held a photo of her boss, he clicked out and cursed his inability, once again, to fight distraction.

"Hi," he said.

She pointed at the computer. Had she seen what he'd been looking at? From that distance? No chance.

"Sorry to interrupt. I called out, but I guess you didn't hear me."

"No prob. The furnace is right below me. When it kicks on, it's loud."

And sometimes, his screwed-up brain didn't hear the door chime.

Son of a bitch.

She looked around the office, took in the bookshelf in the corner where he'd stacked all his files so he could keep his desktop clear. After a minute, she moved on to the framed photos Gage had found on his wall one morning. All from his Special Forces days showing him in BDUs, holding some sort of badass weapon or hamming it up with his teammates. Not one of those photos belonged to him. That was all Reid, who thought Gage's Special Forces experience would add to the training center's credibility. Whatever. To Gage it was just a bunch of pictures of a bunch of guys doing their jobs.

"Come in," he said.

She pushed off the wall and walked straight to the pictures. "You look different."

"I like to think I'm more civilized now."

She landed on one photo of Gage and Reid standing next to a Jeep—in Colombia maybe—the two of them decked out in full combat gear. BDUs, body armor, helmets, rifles, the works.

"You were Special Forces with Reid?"

"I was."

She lingered on the photo for a moment, then tapped it. "Can I get a copy of this? I never really got to see him this way. It's so strange to me."

"Now see, it's strange for me to *not* see him that way."

A small smile quirked the corners of her mouth. "Different worlds, I guess."

"It's Reid's photo, but I can tell him you want it."

"Well, I suppose I can ask him."

She didn't sound too enthusiastic about that. "Whatever you want, Micki."

"Ha," she said, meeting his gaze. "Don't say that. Who knows what I might ask for?"

Obviously, Reid's sister had inherited her brother's knack for laying on the charm. At this point, the way her skintight jeans cupped her ass, he might give her just about whatever she wanted. *Whatever* she wanted.

Going there could damage his relationship with Reid. And Jonah. All the Steeles really, because as a whole, no one seemed to know what the hell to do with Micki. She was different. An outsider in her own family. Gage just didn't know why.

Leaving the photos, she came closer to the desk. "Is Reid here?"

"No. He went to see Brynne."

"She's his girlfriend, right? Mom said something about her last month when I called."

Last *month*? Gage talked to his parents almost daily.

"I'm thinking she's more than a girlfriend, but yeah, that's her. She tends to settle him down."

"He needed to be settled down?"

Careful here, buddy. As much as the Steeles had welcomed him into their lives, he wasn't blood, and offering his opinions on their familial issues probably wouldn't win him any points.

He shrugged. "Or maybe he just wanted to see her."

She smiled again, clearly realizing he would not take her bait. "Is my brother in love? Seriously?"

"Micki?"

"Yes?"

"I don't know what your situation with Reid is, but I'm not discussing his life with you. If there are things you want to know, ask him. You of all people should know he'll tell you."

"He doesn't like me much."

"I don't think that's true."

She propped one hip against the desk, twisted her lips this way and that, so Gage waited her out. Let her get comfortable with whatever direction she wanted to take the conversation.

"Did you notice he didn't hug me when he saw me?"

Yeah. He'd noticed. Shitty, that, but Reid had reasons for the things he did. Right or wrong, it was his business.

"If it concerns you, ask him about it."

"Where are you from?"

"Iowa."

"Of course."

"What does that mean?"

"You probably grew up on a farm. The apple-cheeked, Mr. All-American boy who has life all figured out. The war hero adored by all."

What the—? Seriously, she, the mystery woman who'd taken off to work for a bastard, was coming into his office and making like she knew him?

He sat back, set his hands on the back of his head. "Sweetheart, you don't know me. Whatever crap you have going on isn't my fault. And I sure as hell won't let you turn your shit on me."

She broke eye contact, looking down at the shiny surface of his desk. "I'm sorry. That was...horrible." She met his gaze again, and in those few seconds some of the bitterness had stripped away. "I just got here and I'm already pissing people off."

Whatever this girl had been doing in Vegas had wrecked her. Made her...angry. Resentful.

"Take it easy. This has to be difficult for you. And, to be fair, your family, too. You surprised them, that's all. And me? I'm just a guy who works here. I don't matter."

"Everyone matters. And my family seems to love you, what with my mother stuffing you full of her fried chicken and fussing over you and Reid not kicking your ass when you told him to calm down."

"Your mother is a good woman."

"Yes. She is."

"Reid? He's just intense."

"That's for sure." She waved a hand toward the doorway. "Anyway, I wanted to talk to him. Will you tell him I was here?"

"Sure. This may not be my place, but I care about your family and they care about you. If you need to talk, or whatever, I'm around. I'm a good listener. I spent half my military career as a sounding board for my detachment. Besides, I'm not a Steele. I'm neutral ground."

She stayed quiet for a few seconds, then finally nodded. "Thanks. But I'll be leaving soon."

"You mentioned that. While you're here, though."

She headed for the door and Gage watched her trim little ass. And the legs? So long and fluid and...yep...something about the mysterious Micki Steele got him going.

"Micki," he said, "when Reid gets back, you might want to tell him you'd like to hit Triple B with everyone tonight."

Pausing, she swung back. "Triple B?"

"Blues, Brews, and Books. It's the bar in town. Britt's girlfriend—Randi—owns it."

"I know what it is. Is everyone going there? Mom said something about a family dinner."

"Yeah. After dinner. It's Friday night. It's a thing. Especially now that Evie is twenty-one. Everyone spends Friday nights there. Since you're leaving so soon, it'll give you time with your family."

"Bars aren't really my thing."

"It's more of a restaurant and bar. Not a pickup joint. But, hey, it's up to you."

If she wanted to get to know her family again, he was damned near handing it to her.

She gnawed on her lip again. "Are you going?"

Oh, what an opportunity this could be to strap on a cape. All because Micki Steele didn't want to face her siblings alone.

Well, hell, why not?

"I've been known to stop in for a beer."

Apparently Triple B was the place to be on a Friday night. Who'd have guessed this sleepy little town could, under Grif's slick, Los Angeles-loving tutelage, become a Friday night hot spot.

Over the years, the town hadn't changed much and still held that cozy, we're-all-neighbors feel. Since Micki had visited last, new iron light posts had been installed and the storefronts had definitely gotten facelifts. Amazing how fresh paint in neutral colors gave Steele Ridge an elegant Rockwell-esque feel. It all seemed, well, different. Not bad different, just not Mayberry.

After a death-defying ride into town with Evie, who had clearly inherited Reid's driving habits—those being fast, fast, and faster—Micki might need a drink after all.

Being the golden child, Evie found street parking. Right in front of the bar. Someone pulled out as they cruised by and Evie jammed the car into reverse and nearly gave Micki whiplash while nabbing the spot.

One good thing about being in Vegas all these years was that Micki didn't have to be Evie's passenger.

"Everything okay?" Micki asked.

"Fine. Why?"

"You seem quiet."

They sat in silence for a few seconds with Evie

staring out the windshield. Finally, she leaned back, resting her head on the headrest. "You left me."

"What?"

"First Dad, then you. What is it with our family?"

"I didn't leave *you*, Evie. I left Steele Ridge."

"But why? You had a family that loved you. Why would you abandon me—us?"

Micki reached for her, ready to lay a reassuring hand on Evie's arm, but at the last second, unsure if her sister even wanted to be touched, pulled back. "I know you have no reason to trust me, but I left for a good reason."

"Can't you tell me?"

"No. It's…complicated."

Evie studied her—no, dissected her. Whatever she uncovered made those intelligent blue eyes dim a little before she sent Micki a wan smile.

"If not me, find someone to confide in. Bottling that stuff up isn't good for the soul."

Huh. Her baby sister. All grown up. "When did you become so wise?"

"While fending off four brothers on my own, thank you very much. For that alone, I'm not letting you off the hook."

Chuckling, they exited the car and headed toward the B. A tall man with reddish hair nodded at them as he passed and Micki did a double take. "Was that—?"

"Jeremy Johnson? Yep."

"He tried to stick his hand down my pants in high school."

"Well, not a lot has changed, then. He's still handsy. He groped one of Randi's waitresses two weeks ago and Britt about killed him."

Good old Britt, still making sure everyone stayed on the straight and narrow. What must her brother think of her? If he knew everything, the way she spent her days trolling for dirt, he'd be disgusted. Ironic, really. She spent her life uncovering the secrets of others while she kept her own firmly buried.

A car honked and Micki looked up to see no less than a six-car traffic jam on Main Street.

"It's busy tonight."

"Grif implemented midnight madness on Fridays. He calls it booze and bucks. All the shops stay open late and offer deep discounts after nine o'clock. Patrons also get a discounted dinner at Triple B."

They pushed through the B's entrance and a burst of loud country music, music she'd stopped listening to the day she left North Carolina, hit her with the force of a hurricane. Worse, she was faced with a literal wall of people nudged into every available spot.

Crowds, she disliked.

Despised even.

"No," she said. "I can't do this."

Evie turned back. "Why?"

"I'm not in there yet and my throat is closing."

"Don't stress. Randi reserves us a table in the back by the wall. There's more room there. You just need to get through the crowd."

Evie grabbed hold of her arm, pulling her forward, and Micki threw her weight back, refusing to budge.

"Ladies," a man said from behind Micki, "how about we move out of the doorway?"

Micki turned and found Gage and his sparkling blue eyes smiling down at her and some of that clogged air squeaked free.

Cupping her hands around her mouth, Evie went up on tiptoes to reach Gage's ear and speak above the melding voices and music. Whatever Evie said caused a sideways glance in Micki's direction.

Evie stood back and he waved her into the crowd. "You go. I got this. We'll meet you at the table."

With that, Evie was gone. That fast, plunging right into the crowd. Without a doubt, Evie was the daughter their mother always wanted. Girly, sweet, and fearless in one stunningly feminine package.

Determined to avoid the crush, Micki faced Gage,

shaking her head to reinforce just how positive she was that she would not, in any way, enter the hell in front of her. "This isn't my thing. I'll go back to the house and catch up with everyone later."

"Not happening."

"*Excuse* me?" If being home meant getting pushed around, she hadn't missed that particular aspect of family life.

"Look," he said, "you told them you were coming. They're all in there. I know that because Reid texted me twenty minutes ago telling me to get my ass moving. If you turn tail…"

Wow. What a thing to say to a woman who'd been on her own since eighteen. Well, sorta. She'd had Phil. And Tomas. Her quasi-family stand-ins.

Wacky as it was, at least with Phil, she knew she had a place.

Except she'd run from that place. That comfort zone that represented the devil she knew.

A man stumbled, his beer sloshing over the top of the mug as he bumped her. Gage body blocked him, forming a barrier between her and the drunk. "Dude," he said, "really?"

"Sorry, man. I'm wasted."

As if that were a good excuse.

The guy pushed into the crowd again and Gage shook his head, laughing at the idiot. Such amusement from a man whose entire presence screamed of honor and goodness knocked Micki back, forcing her to acknowledge that resisting him might be futile.

In all manner of ways.

Plus, why give her family another reason to be disappointed? She had to do this.

She straightened her shoulders and focused on a straight line through the crowd. "You're right. I'll just push through."

Gage leaned in, his warm breath against her ear, sending an all-out alert to her barely-touched-by-a-man skin.

"I hate mob scenes like this, too. It makes my head spin. We'll go around back. There's an entrance Randi lets me use. She's knows I'm a freak."

At that, Micki laughed. "You're not a freak."

Far from it.

He swung the door open, stepped back, and made a show of waving her out.

"Thank you," she said.

Their eyes connected for a long second and suddenly the loud room, the pressed-in bodies, disappeared. Her mind went quiet and the panic from moments ago faded. God, that felt good. Afraid to lose the moment and the utter calm where her mind didn't race or question, she stood still, savoring the peace.

"You're welcome," Gage said. "Stop thinking so much."

Good one.

Once outside, a gust of wind blew her hair across her face and she tipped her head back just as Gage lifted his hand. The cold air drove away the inferno from the crush of the crowd and she inhaled. Let all that fresh oxygen circulate inside her.

His fingers skimmed her cheek, then moved to tuck her hair back, sending a surge of straight lust roaring.

Loneliness. That's all this was. A definite weakening of her system due to the years of isolation. She continued holding his gaze. "Too bad I can't stay."

He cocked his head and unleashed a smile. "Your plans could change."

If only she had that choice. "Unfortunately, they can't."

With that, he dropped his hand and she instantly regretted the loss of contact. Something about him settled her, offered shelter from self-torture.

"That is too bad, then."

He set his hand against the back of her jacket, leading her down the block, past the Mad Batter Bakery where the sign out front read "Trust. It's all around. If you allow it."

How very prophetic, but, as Micki had learned, a total crock.

Gage led her around the building to the rear entrance. The temperature had dipped into the forties and now that the heat of lust had vanished, she shivered.

"You cold?"

"Freezing. I guess I've gone soft after living in a warm climate for so long."

"Soft? I doubt it."

He held the back door open and nodded. "Welcome to Friday night at Triple B."

She eyed the door, pictured the crowd inside. All those voices and loud music. Total nightmare for a girl used to spending most of her adult life alone. And with Phil constantly checking on her, all of it combined to make her a seriously neurotic head case.

She looked back at Gage, so different from the men in her life. Mr. All-American. Squeaky-clean. That was him. She'd given up on fairy tales long ago, but he might be a real-life Prince Charming. Just not hers.

"We'll do this together," he said, "or we'll never hear the end of it from Reid. I'm more afraid of that than the crowd."

Captain America had a point there. On a quiet day, Reid was a pain in the ass. When he put a little effort into it? Forget it.

"Let's do this, Mr. All-American."

"All-American. Seriously?"

At that she laughed and feeling a little playful—Her? Playful?—she pinched his cheek, gathered her courage, and stepped into the nightmare of a crowd.

The closed in, air-sucking crush of people stopped her. So much for bravery.

"I'm on it." Gage grabbed her hand and pulled her through the pressed-tight bodies. He pointed to the right with his free hand. "We're going there."

Not twenty feet away, her family had shoved four tables together in the corner. Gage led her to them, keeping their joined hands out of sight until they reached the table, then casually let go. Who could blame him? This guy was so far above her she'd need the world's biggest ladder to touch his feet.

Jonah glanced up from whatever he was doing on his phone and met her gaze. Immediately, his face lit up. Her twin. Happy to see her.

He waved and that got Grif and Carlie Beth's attention. Wow, she'd gotten prettier with age. They, too, smiled and Micki's nerves finally settled.

Britt, being Britt, stood. God forbid he should stay seated when a woman approached.

But this was…home.

All her brothers. Here. Right now.

Smacking Reid on the back of the head, Gage snagged the chair beside Britt. Jonah pointed to the spot next to him. Beside the one Gage had claimed.

Cozy. But, truly, in this group, she and Gage were the oddballs, so they could keep each other company.

"Hey, guys," Evie said, pushing through the crowd.

"How did we beat you?"

"I stopped to talk to a couple of people. Britt, I think Deke just came in. Were you, um, expecting him?"

Deke? Another name Micki didn't recognize.

"He said he might stop in."

Before Micki could move around the table, Reid grabbed her wrist. "Hey. I want you to meet Brynne."

The girlfriend. Next to him, a curvy brunette stood, set her hand on his shoulder, and scooted behind him.

And oh, she could see why her brother fell for this one. Even if she wasn't his normal tall, skinny supermodel type, she looked young, maybe mid-twenties, with a stunning face and killer brown eyes. Looking into this girl's eyes brought Micki's shoulders down that last notch.

A few inches shorter, Brynne angled her head. "It's great to finally meet you. Reid talks about you a lot."

"Is it nice?"

She laughed, but before Micki could say she hadn't been joking, Brynne forged ahead, moving into her space so she could speak into her ear. Micki forced herself to be still. To not offend her prickly brother's girlfriend by backing away.

"It's very nice," Brynne said. "He'd never admit it, but he misses you. So I'm glad you're here and that I got to meet you."

Bam. Micki liked her. Immediately. "I can see why my brother wants to spend time with you. Thank you for telling me that."

The girl shrugged. "Sure. Just figured you'd want to know. He's a handful sometimes. Believe me, I get that. I think it's because he loves hard."

"You two about done whispering?"

"I'll give you whispering." Brynne bent low, said something in Reid's ear that brought a grin to her brother's face.

"I do love you, Brynnie," he said, pulling her onto his lap.

Yep. There was her answer. Reid was in love. Good for him.

"Micki," Jonah called, "come and sit."

She moved around the table and Gage scooted his chair in, giving her space to squeeze between him and the wall. There wasn't a whole lot of room and, skinny as she was, she brushed his back as she went by. "Sorry," she said, patting one rock-hard shoulder.

"Not a problem."

If only that were true.

The music died down and Reid smacked a hand on the table. "Everybody, listen up. Since we're all here, I got something to say."

Still on his lap, Brynne elbowed him.

"Sorry. *We* have something to say."

"Better."

"See," he said, "I listen." The two of them shared a laugh, then Reid brought his attention back to the table.

"We were going to wait until Christmas on this, but since Micki is here and we're all together, we thought…" He looked up at Brynne again, and the connection was so intense and pure and full of love that something inside Micki came apart, an absolute rupture that reminded her she'd never looked at someone that way.

No one had ever looked at *her* that way either.

Not a lot to ask. Or was it? For her? Probably. Her secrets created distance. Distance severed connections and there wasn't much she could do about that. Except hook up with someone in her line of work, and really, what kind of life would that make?

"Come on already," Britt said. "I'm turning gray here."

Reid held up a hand. "It's been a little while for Brynne and I now. And, well, she's apparently crazy enough to want to marry me. So, we're doing it. Getting hitched."

CHAPTER FIVE

ALL AT ONCE, THE STEELE clan erupted and Gage flinched at the sudden commotion. Even during happy times, the mix of so many loud, yelling voices hacked at his battered brain.

Damned, fucking injury.

Evie rushed to Reid and Brynne and threw her arms around them. "Group hug! Yay!"

Around the table, there were more smiles and when Evie let go of the newly engaged couple, Grif reached over and shook his brother's hand. "Best move you ever made, asshole."

Reid's face lit up. "I know!"

Reid gushing. Those were two words Gage never anticipated being used together. But, hey, good for him. The guy had been schlepping his ass into town every day to see Brynne. Maybe he added in a trip to the bank or the post office, but Brynne was the reason he went and he never hid it.

She was good for him. Grounded and reasonable and more importantly, patient. According to Reid, Brynne saw through his asshole-ishness.

Across the table, Britt offered his congratulations. "Who'd ever have thought you'd be the first to get hitched? I figured it'd be Grif and Carlie Beth."

"Well, yeah," Carlie Beth said, "but since Grif wants

to invite half the universe and I don't, we seem to be at a marital impasse. And we're not even married."

Evie piped up again. "Did you tell Mom and Dad?"

"Yeah. We told them after dinner. Mom's already talking about a tent in the yard for the reception. Why am I feeling like Vegas might be the way to go?"

From the corner of his eye, Gage caught Micki stiffen. Everyone at the table was too keyed in to Reid and Brynne to notice, but Gage? He didn't necessarily have a dog in this race and his curiosity about Micki was growing.

He nudged her elbow, only to have her jerk away. What was up with this girl? "Pretty sure he was kidding about the Vegas crack. I don't think Brynne is a Vegas-wedding sort of girl and Reid wouldn't do that to your mom. First wedding in the family and all that."

Micki's gaze shot to the happy couple, then back. "That would devastate her. She'd love a wedding on her lawn."

"Will you come in for that?"

Why he asked, he wasn't sure. Really not his business, but what the hell? Might as well throw it out there. At least get her thinking about it.

From across the bar, a young woman called—shrieked really—Evie's name. "Ooh," Evie said. "Crystal is here! Be right back."

Evie flipped her long hair back and darted into the crowd, shoving through like a runaway bulldozer, and Micki's face transformed into a wide-eyed look of awe. Awe and something else, something in her hollowed-out cheeks.

Sadness maybe. But he was no shrink.

"She's so fearless," Micki said.

"That she is. Nice subject change, too, but"—Gage made a buzzer noise—"no dice. Are you coming back for Reid's wedding?"

"I...I'm not sure."

"I'll talk to Reid. See when they're thinking. Maybe you can work it into your schedule."

"Suds," Reid said, "I'm warning you now, after this wedding, I'm going on a honeymoon. We might be a couple of weeks. You'll have to man the fort on your own while I'm doing wicked things to my new bride."

"Jesus, Reid," Britt said.

But Brynne laughed and added an eye roll as she pushed off his lap. "Lord, you're a pig. I can't believe I'm marrying you."

"Too late now, sweetheart. You're committed."

"Before this is over," Gage cracked, "she might be committed all right."

Next to him, Micki snorted and—wait for it—was that, could it be? Yep. The corner of her mouth lifted into, if Gage wasn't mistaken, a Micki version of a smile.

Micki Steele didn't smile much. She simply sat, owl-eyed, taking in her surroundings like a kid waiting for the next beating.

Why that was, he didn't know. But more and more, with every second spent in this woman's presence, the niggling inside his damaged brain grew.

Whatever her secrets were, he wanted to know. The hint of attraction was there and his ignored baser needs could only stand so much. The lack of sex was his own doing, considering a few of the single females—Cherlyn Marstin for one—had made it clear they wouldn't mind losing their clothes in front of him. But Steele Ridge was a small town, and building a new life after his injuries had been his main focus. Dating someone from town meant seeing that person whether the relationship went anywhere or not.

And he wasn't ready. Not while his injuries made him less of the man he expected of himself.

Even going home to Iowa right now was out of the question. He could hide his impairment from the Steeles. From his family? No way.

But the mystery of Micki might be a good exercise in challenging his brain.

As she sat looking beyond his shoulder, that nearly-there smile disappeared. Tracking her gaze, he swung his head to the bar where a dark-haired guy wearing jeans and a black graphic T-shirt bent low and whispered into Evie's ear.

The dude straightened up, scanning Evie's body from head to toe, nodding his approval with a heavy-eye-contact kicker.

If the Steele boys caught this, they'd go insane.

Gage didn't like the look of this guy. Not even a little.

Just as he decided he'd make a quick trip to the john by way of Evie's admirer and break that shit up, Evie whipped out her phone and grinned up at the dude. *Maybe she knows him.*

But then the guy leaned over and whispered in her ear again, this time looking over her shoulder.

At Micki.

What. The. Fuck?

Did *Micki* know him? His clothing choices, dark and edgy with a skull and crossbones on his T-shirt, reminded him of Micki. Her messenger bag had that same skull and crossbones. Maybe they were friends from years ago? This guy had to be in his thirties, though. Definitely at least a few years older than Micki.

Beside him, she set her hands on the table and dug her fingertips into the scarred wood until her unpainted nails went white.

Not happy.

Gage's shit meter blew apart. "You know him?"

Pushing herself up, she set her shoulders and let out a long breath. "I sure do."

Micki's heart slammed so hard it should have bruised her spine.

Standing at the bar, in the middle of the Triple B, in

her hometown, where her family lived, was Tomas—
Tommy.

Basically having sex with her sister.

Maybe that sex thing was over the top, but she knew
exactly how Tommy operated. The way he wormed his
way next to Evie and whispered in her ear, he knew
exactly what he was doing.

Of all the women in all the towns in North Carolina,
Tommy didn't accidentally show up in Steele Ridge and
meet her sister.

He wanted Micki's attention.

Well, he'd gotten it and the rage, the absolute
devouring of her nervous system, made her limbs
tremble.

Dammit. Knowing it would be the first place Phil
would look, Micki shouldn't have come back. Even for a
quick stop. Her plan to stay just ahead of him and be
gone by the time he'd scammed himself out of that
Mexican prison was an epic fail.

Phil. Was he here, too? Or was this the proverbial
shot across her bow? The warning that she should get
back to Vegas where, if she did what she was told and
didn't make a fuss, she'd be rewarded.

No. If he were in the area, he'd be in the Triple B.
Either with Tommy or alone. Simply to unnerve her. To
get under her skin, to *control* her, by dropping hint
bombs of what would happen if she tried to run or
distance herself. The evidence. Always the evidence.

"Excuse me," she said to Gage.

When he grabbed her wrist, her already tense body
stiffened and he let go, holding his hands up.

"No," she said. "It's not…"

"It's okay. I shouldn't have touched you."

Now she'd insulted him. Great. She'd pushed away
the one person, a near stranger and bona fide war hero,
who didn't pepper her with questions or judgment.

"It's not you," she said. "I need to talk to someone."

"The idiot with Evie?"

"I'll take care of it. Please don't call attention to him."

Before Gage could comment, she pushed through the crowd, all that simmering rage moving her forward. Compared to what she'd experienced when she'd first arrived, diving into the center of this crowd to get to Tommy didn't seem like such torture. All she knew now was that she needed to reason with him. And get him away from Evie.

Away from Jonah.

Away from all of them.

As she approached, he met her gaze, cocked one eyebrow and held up his beer in toast. At the very least, he seemed amused. A good sign.

She could work with amused. Which, given their history together, he knew all too well. And that cut both ways. As coworkers and friends, they'd shared years of inside jokes, not to mention an affection for sarcastic humor.

Right now, he was screwing with her. Trying and succeeding in unnerving her by pulling Evie into this hot-ass mess of a scenario.

I can do this.

After ten years of being too afraid to break free, now suddenly she grew a backbone?

"Well, hello," he said, feigning surprise at Micki's appearance.

Evie swatted Micki's shoulder. "You didn't tell me your friend was coming."

I didn't know.

"Yep," Micki said. "I see you two are getting acquainted."

"You know me"—Tommy let his gaze linger over Evie again—"always a sucker for beautiful women."

Evie rolled her eyes. "We met in town earlier. I was at Brynne's shop and he came in looking for a gift."

Or following my sister.

Micki inserted herself in the minimal space separating her sister and Tommy and wound up bumping a woman attempting to divert Tommy's attention with her giant boobs.

Girlfriend, you don't want any part of this.

Micki ignored the woman and met Tommy's stare. "Talk about a surprise."

"Yes. Let's talk about it." He leaned in. "I guess I don't need to tell you that you left your phone in your car. Your *trunk*, of all places. And, hey, your emergency bag was gone."

He'd actually broken into her car. A slow-moving panic sparked in Micki's brain as Evie watched—and listened to—the exchange.

Get her out of here.

"Evie," she said, "give us a second, please."

"Sure." Evie waggled her phone. "Call me!"

Her little sister wandered off, her adorable butt swinging as she went. Something feral ignited in Tommy's eyes, and Micki's panic exploded. This was her friend. Years and years together. She'd trusted him, shared secrets—some anyway—as well as her heartache over her family's estrangement. All of it confided to a friend, and loved one.

Yes, she could admit that. She loved him. Maybe not the way she loved Jonah or her real family, but they shared a connection. A tether to the strange world of Phil Flynn that only those in his inner circle could truly grasp. How pathetic was that? Phil manipulated her into his lowlife world, then slowly, over time, convinced her she belonged with him, that she could trust him and her family didn't understand. The truly sick part was that she knew. All this time, she'd understood he'd worked her into a corner. She couldn't put all the blame on him. She took part by allowing him to separate her from her family. And then he'd capitalized on her fear of being without that same family by convincing her he was the one to trust.

And now Tommy, too. The son of a bitch was using her sister as bait.

The betrayal alone made her burn. She'd process that later, after the anger wore off.

"Stop it," she said. "I know what you're doing and Evie's a good kid. I thought you and I were friends?"

"We are friends. But imagine what I thought when I saw your bag gone. I trusted you to do the right thing."

The right thing. They'd been crawling around in filth for so long they probably wouldn't know the right thing if it clocked either of them upside the head.

"I'm sorry. I…" She looked around the packed bar— *what am I doing?*—and shook her head. "I don't know. I was alone in the office. Thanksgiving day and I had a moment there. I figured I could see my family for a couple of days while you worked on getting Phil out. Then I'd just come back when it was time. Besides, as long as I have my laptop, I can work from here."

Liar, liar. But, oh well. If it bought her time to back Tommy off and get out of Steele Ridge, she'd be set. The short-term goal right now? Convince him her visit to Steele Ridge was just that. A visit. Like all the other times.

Short-term goal two: Make sure Evie's number disappeared from his phone.

Tommy made a tsk-tsk noise. "I might believe that if you hadn't ditched your cell."

"Not intentionally. I must have dropped it when I reached into the trunk. By the time I realized it, I was already on the road and figured I'd e-mail you."

"And yet, you didn't."

"I responded to you."

"Once."

Touché. She stood silently while the music blared and the crowd bunched in. If she waited long enough, Tommy would say something. One thing about her old friend, he needed to fill space.

He eyed a tall redhead passing by, then faced Micki. "Tell me you needed a break. Some downtime. A little R and R, whatever. But don't lie to *me*." He drove a finger into his chest. "Not to me."

He knew better. She should have anticipated that. Being home was short-circuiting her brain. Best to agree with him, let him believe he'd gotten it right.

She nodded. "I'm sorry. With Phil out of the picture, I wanted a few days to myself."

She set her hand on his arm, a gesture she'd made thousands of times. Each time done with affection, but now, after his little charade with Evie, all the warmth usually found with Tommy—Tomas—had been replaced with a cold numbness.

Tomas looked over at the redhead again. Micki had already lost him to a *Playboy* model. Well, she could have him. She could fuck him hanging from a chandelier if she wanted.

After Micki convinced him to go back to Vegas.

"Tomas, please. Phil knows where I am twenty-four/seven. I freaked a little. I grabbed my go-bag and headed out. Originally, I'd thought about LA. By the time I got to the bus, I changed my mind. My brother just got engaged and I wanted to be here. That's all."

Of course, Tomas wouldn't know Reid had just announced said engagement. She hoped.

"And what? You weren't coming back? Phil won't let that happen. You know you have to come back."

"Is he with you?"

"No. He's still in Mexico. Should be out tonight. He sent me to keep an eye on"—he checked on the *Playboy* model and came back to her—"things."

On her. But, phew, no Phil to deal with.

Yet.

"Did you tell him I was gone?"

He met her gaze, his lips tight for a second before they slithered into a grin. "Would I do that to you?"

No. He wouldn't. Not Tommy. But this was Tomas. Phil's soldier. The one relied on to do things they wouldn't share with her. For her own good, they'd said.

And truthfully, she didn't want to know. Didn't want to face it.

All these years, Tommy had been her friend. Her ally. Her confidant when living in the deceit of Phil's world consumed her.

Except, he'd just leered at Evie to provoke Micki.

Some friend.

Still, she had to roll with this. Get out of this current dustup and make a plan. She gripped his arm and squeezed. "Thank you."

"You're welcome. I figured you'd come here."

"See? That alone tells you I didn't intend on *not* coming back. Of course this is the first place you'd look. If I wanted to run, I wouldn't be dumb enough to hang around here."

Which was all true. He'd simply caught up with her before she could disappear.

Tomas glanced over at the table, where a burst of laughter from the Steele clan erupted. "That's your family?"

"Yes. My brothers and their girlfriends."

And Gage. She found him watching her, those observant eyes of his taking it all in. She needed to peel away from Tomas before suspicion grew and Gage, or her brothers, wandered over. Because right now, she didn't have a clue how to explain who Tomas might be.

Other than to say he was Phil's henchman and in Steele Ridge to make sure she returned to Vegas.

Her brothers would love that.

Sensing something, Gage stood and she turned back to Tomas. "Give me until tomorrow with them. Please. If Phil needs something, I have my laptop. Okay?"

The redhead nudged closer, and Tomas gave her a once-over similar to the one he'd given Evie. "Tomorrow," he said, keeping his hungry eyes on the woman. "Then we both get on a plane and go."

CHAPTER SIX

MORNING SUN BROKE THROUGH THE wooden blinds on the French door in Micki's bedroom and she groaned at the intrusion.

Still on Vegas time, her body had no interest in greeting the day. No matter what time it was. She rolled over and blinked until the red neon numbers on the clock came into focus: 7:30.

She buried her head under the pillow. "We need drapes on these windows."

We. Not *Mom*, but *we*. Did she have the right, after all these years, to assume she had a say in what went on the windows in her mother's house?

Could be she was tired and overthinking it. Another hour of sleep. That's all she needed. But today was the day. Tomas thought she'd be flying home with him and by now, Phil would be out of Mexico.

If she intended on getting away, on leaving her godforsaken, dirt-digging life behind, she needed to make her move now. Early.

Get it done.

Don't think too long or hard and just do it. Her motto for the past ten years. When it came to other people's lives, it was easier.

She tossed the pillow aside, stared up at the ceiling fan, slowly swirling above her.

What if she didn't go?

What *if* she stayed here and confessed everything to Jonah. Let him, for once, be involved in the process. They weren't scared teenagers anymore. And Jonah was loaded. So filthy, stinking rich that writing a check to hire attorneys—good attorneys—would end all of this.

These few days alone, out from under his control, had given her a taste of life as it should be. Freedom to move around and leave behind work she knew was wrong.

Maybe she could even strike a deal with Phil. She'd keep his secrets if he let her go.

But if it were that simple, she'd have done it years ago. Phil knew that. His plying her with gifts and a pseudo family proved it.

Too late now. With what she knew, he'd never let it happen. She needed to run. Draw Tomas away from Steele Ridge and her family. The plan wasn't great, but Phil's focus had always been her. Where she went, what she did, who she communicated with. Hopefully, that trend would continue when she left.

Whipping off the covers, she listened for any sign of movement in the house. Nothing. Not even Mom. Not wanting to wake anyone, she padded to the closet and grabbed her Canyon Ridge High School gym bag. She'd have to leave it. Too identifiable. She swapped it out for the backpack she'd picked up at the airport.

Even then she'd known she'd need to blend in at some point.

She shoved twenty dollars in the outside zipper pocket and stowed the remaining $800 inside, all she'd have until she landed somewhere and could find a job. A job she'd get using her Stephanie Gimble creds.

Micki ripped the zipper on the backpack closed and gritted her teeth against a wave of grief. Goddamned Phil. Always cornering her. Always making her decide whether she'd spend her entire adult life being controlled by him or running from him.

"Has to be done," she muttered.

Not wanting to wake the rest of the house with the loud pipes of the old Victorian, she opted out of a shower and gave herself a quick cleanup with the washrag. It would have to do until she got to a hotel somewhere. She dressed in her only other set of clothing. Jeans, a long-sleeved Henley, and her favorite Chuck Taylors. A vision of her mother in her own Chuck Taylors flashed.

Don't.

Thinking about her mother now, when she was about to disappear forever, wouldn't make this any easier.

Sorry, Mom.

Maybe someday she could come back. Or find a way to sneak her mother to her. That would be years, though. Phil wouldn't give up. He'd told her so hundreds, if not thousands, of times.

Bastard.

Time to go.

First though, she had a message to send. To Phil. She set her laptop on the antique desk and logged in to the website housing the folders she shared with Phil. She created a new folder, uploaded an mp4 file, and stopped.

If she shared it, even without a note, he'd understand. He'd get the message.

She dropped her hands, drummed her fingers against her thighs, and stared at the screen.

Now or never. *This* was the moment. Her chance to, for once, control the situation. To leave and build a life somewhere. A normal life with no shame or secrets.

She tapped the mousepad and a message popped up. *Your folder has been shared.* Soon he'd get the e-mail alerting him to the video. The one of him bribing a Vegas PD cop in their office. She'd managed to overhear part of that conversation when she'd returned from lunch one day four years earlier. On a whim, she'd snagged a copy of the video from the server before Phil could wipe it clean. She'd added it to the stash of other evidence she'd collected over the years, but the video had been the first documentation that wouldn't implicate her as well as Phil. As much as she liked to convince herself she didn't get into the truly nasty stuff, she knew the tasks she completed could land her in jail. When it came down to it, even if she found the nerve to squeal on Phil, she'd have just as much to lose.

The video, though, gave her an insurance policy that would convict him alone.

This was what she'd become? An extortionist. Just like her boss. Her mother would be so proud. All of her family, really.

But like every other time, she simply wouldn't tell them. She'd keep this shame all to herself.

Time to go.

She shoved her wool pageboy cap on and opened the bedroom door. Nothing. All quiet. Halfway down the steps, she heard the swish of water from the kitchen and froze. Her mother was up already. No shock there.

It didn't have to ruin her plan. The front door was just ahead. She'd sneak out, head to the barn, and borrow Jonah's mountain bike to get her into town. There, she'd lock the bike up and send him a text before she ditched her burner phone.

Problem solved.

At the bottom step, she glanced back at the kitchen where the faucet noise came to a sudden stop. She should say good-bye.

Or...go in there and confess everything. Finally be free of it.

But how to admit it? To her mother. A woman built on honesty and hard work, someone who taught her children, absolutely, the difference between right and wrong. Knowing her child did the things Micki had done would devastate her.

The door. Right there. If she walked out she wouldn't have to face it. The shame. Wouldn't have to see the heartbreak she'd caused.

Again.

Worse. If she went in there, she'd probably chicken out and decide to stay anyway. She knew it.

And Phil wouldn't allow it. He'd ruin them.

Her leaving would make things better for everyone. Especially Jonah and now Evie, who'd given Tomas her phone number. A detail Micki had already dealt with the night before by e-mailing him a virus. As soon as he refreshed his e-mail, bye-bye phone and bye-bye Evie's number.

The joke of it was, he'd just get the number again. That's how things went with Phil and Tomas; try, try again.

The front door seemed to grow wider. A big, giant opening that she should march right through. In the kitchen, her mother hummed to herself and Micki paused to close her eyes and file the lyrical sound away. Compartmentalized emotion kicked and clawed free, paralyzing her throat. All that nonsense was just stuck, buried inside where she couldn't rid herself of it.

I love you, Mama.

As always, she refocused her thoughts on the task ahead and moved quickly, silently unlocking the door and slipping out. As she walked, she gripped the backpack straps, squeezing until her knuckles popped.

She made her way to the barn, pushed the door open, and hopped on Jonah's bike. A dirt path led to the main driveway and she pedaled hard, wind slapping at her cheeks as she sucked cold air. It stung her throat and her eyes, but she kept her gaze on the end of the driveway.

Almost there. The underutilized muscles in her thighs groaned and she still had miles to go. Wherever she landed, she needed to start exercising. Get in shape and get healthy. Mind and body.

The end of the driveway grew closer and she pedaled harder, focusing on it, pushing herself to get there before she changed her mind and looked back.

Just go.

A black SUV pulled into the driveway. Dammit. Who

the hell could this be, so early on a Saturday morning?

Not one of her brothers. None of them drove black SUVs. Especially not Grif with that tricked-out minivan. Lord, what had he been thinking?

The vehicle slowed as it approached, but she kept peddling, intending to cruise right on by and be gone before the person could alert anyone in the house.

The SUV drew closer.

Mr. All-American. Purr-fect. Could she not get a break this morning?

Clearly realizing she intended to blow him off, he stuck his hand out the window and swung the SUV across the driveway, giving her enough room to stop. Of course he did. That's what heroes did. They timed everything.

She should just swoop right around him. That'd teach him.

Good thought, but he'd parked and now stood, hands on his lean hips, his jacket open and revealing a white T-shirt that fit loosely, but tightly enough for her to know there was probably something mostly spectacular underneath.

Just…crap.

She skidded to a stop, fully intending to employ the adage about the best offense being a good defense. "Are you nuts? You could have killed me!"

His response? To smile. The man was too darned good.

"Relax," he said. "You know you're not mad and you *know* I gave you enough room to stop. Besides, where the hell are you going in such a rush? Uh, and on Jonah's ten-thousand-dollar bike?"

Ten *thousand?* She gawked. First at Gage, then the bike. She'd borrowed a bike worth more than her car. Her old car, anyway.

Forget that. She straightened up. "I'm going for a ride. It's a nice morning."

"A little cold, I'd say."

"This from the Iowa farm boy?"

He grinned. "Guess I've gone soft."

Any other time, she'd appreciate his use of her line from the night before when complaining about the temperature. She angled the bike and adjusted her backpack. "I'm off for my ride. See you...later."

Not having any of her bullshit, he grabbed the handlebars. "Where are you going?"

She smacked at his hands. "Hey, hands off. I told you—"

"I know what you *told* me. Unfortunately for you, our government has trained me to recognize deception. And you, babe, are a liar."

She poked a finger at him, ready to argue, but she needed to not waste time and get out of there.

"First of all, I'm not your *babe*. Second of all, if we're stealing lines from each other, as you said to me yesterday, you don't know *me* at all. So screw you, Captain America. *Suds*. And what a stupid nickname *that* is." She swung her leg off the bike, started walking it around the SUV. "Why the hell would anyone call you Suds? Never mind. I don't have time for that. Later, *Suds*."

Micki Steele was a handful.

No doubt.

Luckily, he'd always enjoyed a woman with gumption. Despite all of that, underneath the sassy attitude, this girl was racked with some kind of terror he'd yet to figure out. She wasn't going anywhere until he did. He stepped in front of the bike, planted his feet and crossed his arms.

"Talk to me."

"No."

She made a move to go around him. These Steeles. So

fucking stubborn. Again, he grabbed the handlebars of Jonah's beloved bike only to receive another smack.

"Stop," he said. "Please."

"I'm going for a ride. Just let me go."

"No."

She pushed away from the bike, shook her fists at him and stomped down the driveway. "Damn you! Mind your own business!"

Now she wanted him to stay out of it? Way too late for that. Nine hours ago she was thanking him for his assistance. He swung to the side of the bike and gently set it on the ground. "When are you going to stop?"

"Stop what? Going for a bike ride?"

Smart-ass.

"No. With the secrets and lies? You're not going for a bike ride this early. It's forty frickin' degrees and last night you were complaining about the cold. You'd freeze your ass off."

She stopped walking. Damn near skidded to a stop right in Miss Joan's driveway. At least he didn't have to tackle her. Which, as much as he'd never put hands on a woman, he would have no problem doing. He wouldn't be the one to let her run off. Chances were, at barely eight in the morning and with her barreling down that driveway, she hadn't told anyone she was leaving. And she was most definitely leaving.

He sensed it. The backpack, the nervous tension. The short temper.

He took a few steps toward her and she backed away. Wow, this girl. Issues. Big ones.

"I'll stay right here," he said. "But please, let me help you. Whatever it is you're running from, I'll help. Your *family* will help. You need to come clean, though."

Come clean? Oh, he didn't want her to come clean. If

she did, that'd be it. The shame of it, the utter disgust, would send him running. He'd let her go then, wouldn't he? Captain America needed to be careful what he asked for, because he just might get it.

"Micki," he said, "whatever it is, let me help you."

He wanted to *help*. Of course he did. He wanted to *fix* her. Not happening.

She spun back, reached for the bike again. "You can't help me. Now get the fuck out of my way."

Vulgarity. Perfect. Captain America would definitely be repulsed by that.

Except, he pursed his lips and...snorted. "No."

Ohmigod. Was he kidding? Total hero complex, this one.

And stubborn.

And pushy.

And, and...She couldn't deal with it. She started down the driveway again, stomping so hard she might shatter a knee because she needed to go, just leave and be done with him and the rest of the people in her life. Her chest locked up, but she kept moving. The only way. For ten years she'd been pushing ahead, waiting for her break. This was it. As piss-poor as it was, this. Was. It.

He grabbed hold of her arm, and all the rolling anger inside of her, the years of isolation and loneliness and being separated from her family, came gushing up. What was she doing? She didn't know anymore. Just didn't know. *I'm going crazy.* The pressure inside her skull exploded and she pressed her free hand to the side of her head.

Gage held on and she whipped her arm free. "Don't touch me." She'd had enough of men controlling her. "I don't like men touching me. For God's sake! What don't you get about this? I'm leaving. I have to go!"

But dammit all to hell, why did her voice have to crack on that last part?

Still, he didn't move, just stood there, rock-solid Gage

Barber. He held one palm up. "Why? Tell me why you're leaving."

Unbelievable. She let out a huff of frustration. He wanted to know? *Fine*. If it would get her out of here, she'd do it. She shook her fists at him. "The shit I've done would horrify you, Captain America."

The horror she expected, the shocked disapproval, never materialized. He just stood there, looking at her with kind, soft eyes that hacked away at her anger. How could she be mad at him when he looked at her like that?

He pointed at the house behind them. "Whatever you're running from, whatever you did, you have a family that loves you."

"Oh please!" She flapped her arms. "If they knew, they'd toss me out in a second."

The events of the past few days hit her. Phil in jail, her going AWOL, Tomas and Evie. The virus.

The *video*.

What have I done?

She bent over, braced her hands against her thighs and breathed in. "Please, Gage. I know you're Reid's friend, but you can't help me. I've made a mess."

A hand touched her back. Stroking. From Gage. Up and down, up and down in a lovely, soothing motion that she hardly deserved.

"Micki," he said, "don't do this. Your family is here. Give them a chance to help."

She shook her head. "You don't understand."

"Maybe if you talk to me, I will."

It sounded so easy. She straightened up, adjusted her backpack, and flattened her hands over her face for a second. Just one little second to get her act together. "Gage, you can't help me." She slid her hands down. "And I won't drag you into this."

"You're not dragging me. I'm diving headfirst." He stepped forward. "So shut up and tell me what you need."

CHAPTER SEVEN

NOW THAT THE INITIAL PANIC fest had subsided, to be replaced by the humiliation fest—just another day in the life of Mikayla Steele, screwup—Micki drew a long breath of dewy morning air.

Any chance of walking away from this episode with her dignity intact loomed just out of her reach.

Behind Gage stood her mother's house and inside that house, Mom was probably getting breakfast ready. That's what her mother did. She took care of her children. In spite of an absentee husband and four boys who fought like crazy and a daughter who'd run out on her, she'd never failed them.

Inside that house lived sanctuary Micki didn't deserve.

Gage stepped closer. This time she let him. Fighting wouldn't work. He was too calm, too thoughtful, too determined.

The weight of her backpack tugged at her shoulders and she slid it off, let it hang from her fingertips for a second before it fell to the ground.

"That's a good start," Gage said. "Jonah will be glad you didn't steal his bike."

"I wasn't *stealing* it. I intended to lock it up in town and text him."

"Before you tossed your phone?"

Busted. He'd sliced and diced her plan, hadn't he? "Yes."

"Ah, Micki. What's tormenting you?"

Did he have ten years? It would take her that long to list everything. All of it though, could be encapsulated, boiled down to one word. "Phil."

"Your boss."

She nodded. "He was in a Mexican jail. He should have been released last night."

"A Mexican jail. From what I've heard, not a stellar place to be."

"With the things he's—*we've*—done, he deserves to be there."

No matter how she liked to distance herself, she'd done just about everything he'd told her to do.

"Why is he in jail?"

How did her once-promising future get to this? *Screw it.* If she intended to fix it, she'd have to admit what she'd done. Clear her conscience and just get rid of it. "He was smuggling fake passports to a client and got caught."

"I see. Who was the guy last night? It looked like you knew him."

"Tomas. He works for Phil. Until last night, I thought he was my friend. The day I left to come here, he went to Mexico to get Phil out. When he left, I bolted. And it was so stupid. I shouldn't have come, but I had to…say good-bye."

"Jesus, Micki. You were going off the grid and not telling your family?"

In her mind, it had been a great strategy. When *he* said it, when she heard it out loud, it sounded awful. "My plan was to stay a day and leave before Phil caught up with me."

"Why?"

His eyes were too much. Too honest and pure and she'd left honest and pure behind long ago. She looked away. Down at the ground and his sturdy work boots.

"Hey," he said, tipping her chin up. "It's okay. Believe

me, I've seen some brutal shit. You won't scare me off."

Then he did it, he wrapped his arms around her. She pressed her face into his chest, inhaled his clean, untainted scent, and a chunk of her resolve disintegrated.

Prince Charming might actually exist.

"You'll be okay," he said.

No. She wouldn't. "I can't live this life anymore. I'm angry and disgusted and...vacant."

The words, ones she'd never spoken before, tumbled out and she prepped herself for the next wave of humiliation, that immense weight she could never seem to rid herself of.

Nothing.

Whatever she'd expected never materialized. What she felt now was a massive offload of dead weight, so she breathed through it and let him hold her. Why not? She rested her cheek against him, absorbing his good, solid energy.

"Tell me about Tomas. Did he threaten you?"

His chest rumbled as he spoke and she backed away to look him in the eye. That was the least she could do.

"No. He hit on Evie. He knows messing with my family will get to me. I got mad and blew up his phone."

Gage laughed. "You blew up his phone? How?"

"I e-mailed him a virus. As soon as he opens that sucker, bye-bye phone. Based on the way he was looking at some giant-boobed redhead, he probably didn't back his files up last night after getting Evie's number. Then this morning, I sent Phil a video that could create problems for him. I've basically declared war. On Phil. Who can be a scary guy."

"Well," Gage said, "lucky for you, you've got the Steele Army behind you."

Micki wasn't buying it. The I-don't-think-so shake of

her head told him so. No matter. He'd stand out here for a week if that's how long it took to convince her she wasn't alone. After the past months with Reid's family, he didn't doubt they'd help her.

"With everything I've put them through," she said, "I can't stay here. If I go, if I cut off all communication, Phil can't use them as pawns. There'd be no point. It'll be a twisted game, but he'll know what I'm doing."

In that respect, her logic was sound. Sound enough for Gage to know that Micki understood Phil's MO. Still, he cocked his head, thought it through some. "Honey, all due respect, is that the best plan? If this guy is off his stone, he'll take your family out so he can make a statement."

She slapped her hands on top of her head and squeezed her eyes closed while she chomped on her bottom lip, rolling it in, then dragging her perfect top teeth against it. If she kept that up, she'd tear the skin straight off.

"I didn't think about that. How did I miss that?"

"It's all right. You're all keyed up."

"I only have one choice."

Now she was getting on board. Running from this thing wouldn't help. She needed to attack it. Straight on. No prisoners. "Yeah. To stay here."

Micki's face stretched long, her eyes bugging out. "No! Are you insane? I have to leave. Even if it's just back to Vegas. I can throw myself on Phil's mercy. Tell him I screwed up by sending him that video. I don't know. Something. What a mess. I promise you, I'm smarter than this. I was working on emotion. If I'd stopped to think it through…"

"Forget that. No looking back. You went on instinct and that'll save your life. Whatever your setup is with these guys, you have to stay away. No deals. No compromising. If you want a change, make a clean break and deal with the fallout."

She dropped her hands and opened her eyes again. "They'll come after me."

"And you'll fight back. Whatever you think, you're not alone. Your family loves you and there are resources now." He waved back to the building housing his office. "Let's go to my office and call Reid. Bring him in the loop."

"Oh, God. I can't. He already thinks I'm a disaster."

"Sorry, but I'm involved now and Reid and I were teammates. We've been friends for years. If I called one of your other brothers, he'd fry my ass. And I'm not doing that. He gave me a chance with this training center."

"Great. Now you're loyal, too?"

He smiled. "Above all else."

"Leave it to me to find Captain Perfect."

Far from it. At one time, he'd have sucked that up, gotten a high from it. All his life, he'd strived for that one unattainable thing. Perfection. Somehow it always landed just...out...of...his...reach.

At least until he'd gone off to the Army and figured out the hard way that perfection was overrated. And he'd learned to adjust. To accept less than perfect and make it work anyway.

A gift, really.

"Far from it," he said. "But if believing that will get you to call Reid, then have at it."

She stared at him for a long time. No problem there. He'd wait her out. Puffs of her warm breath hit the cold morning air, and it occurred to him that the weather might be his friend right now. A girl used to a warm climate wouldn't want to be out here long.

"Okay," she said. "But if he starts screaming, I'm not promising it won't be a war."

He leaned in, got right into her space, and this time she didn't flinch or step back. This time, she stayed put. "That's fine. Besides, it's aces when he makes an idiot of himself."

She gave him a wilting smile. He'd take it. Coming from her, the stoic one, he'd call it a win.

He gestured to his truck. "Hop in. We'll deal with the bike after I call Reid."

It took twenty minutes for Reid to leave his fiancé's warm bed and get his ass back to the Hill. Micki peered out the window as the big man tore up the driveway in his white F-150, parked in front of the training center, and hopped out, slamming the door behind him.

"He looks mad."

Whatever he and Brynne were doing—cough, cough—on this early Saturday morning, Reid wasn't happy about being dragged away. Gage couldn't blame him. Particularly since it had been months since he'd started a weekend with a warm, willing woman under him.

Looking at the alluring Micki Steele might have him ready to change that. "Eh. He'll get over it."

Micki snorted. "You're not afraid of anything, are you?"

"I'm afraid of a lot of things. Your brother isn't one of them. He was supposed to meet me here at eight thirty anyway, to check a couple of weapons. We just moved up his timeline."

From the main entrance, the alarm bell chimed, announcing someone's arrival. That was Gage's handiwork because he didn't like locking the door all the time, but didn't necessarily want people surprising him. His goal these past few months had been to keep his nervous system steady. No high drama, no surprises, no fast movements. Basically, nothing that would hype him up and set back his recovery.

"Suds!" Reid called from the entrance.

"Office!" Gage hollered back.

"Why *does* he call you that?"

Yeah, he wouldn't be telling her that just yet. No

chance. Reid swung in the door and stopped short at the sight of Micki sitting on the windowsill.

"What's this now? Why the hell is Jonah's bike sitting by the driveway?"

The bike. Right.

Micki jumped up. "I need to get that back to the barn before he sees it."

Gage held up a hand. "I got it."

"Suds, what's this about?"

On his way by, he clapped Reid on the shoulder. "I'll grab the bike before Jonah throws a fit. Talk to your sister. *Don't* interrupt. I nearly had to sit on her to keep her from taking off."

"*That's* why Jonah's bike is in the driveway?" Reid whipped back to his sister. "Are you out of your mind? He loves that bike."

Leave it to Reid. Gage shook his head, blew air through his lips, and waved a hand at Micki on his way to the door. "Ignore him."

On his way by, Gage gave Micki a little extended eye contact. Clearly, he hadn't forgotten their conversation about the lack of a hello hug and the emotional distance between her and Reid. As if a hug would cure her problems.

That aside, Captain Perfect had just handed her the chance to confide in her brother. To, as he'd put it, come clean. Perhaps smooth out the edges that had plagued their relationship these past years.

As much as she wanted privacy while dealing with Reid, the second Gage left, she wanted him back. What was that about? She'd been on her own for ten years and now suddenly she needed a man? Not likely. Considering the men in her life had brought about her current circumstances.

Still, something about Gage settled her, brought everything into sharper focus. He was so...so...calm. Strategic. *Thoughtful.*

Clearly suspicious, Reid leaned against the wall and crossed his arms. "What's up?"

Ha. She'd need a year to bring him up to speed. Certain things, she couldn't—wouldn't—admit. Not yet. The past needed to be worked out with Jonah. But right now, she'd be honest about today and moving forward. She met her brother's gaze. "A lot."

His stiff shoulders relaxed a fraction. He pushed off the wall, waved her to one of the guest chairs, then sat on the edge of Gage's desk, his long legs stretched in front of him. "I've got time. Brynne tells me I need to talk less and listen more. Which, who the hell knows? Maybe I do. Are you in trouble?"

Of course he'd go there. And of course he'd be right. "I have to leave today."

"Yeah. You said that yesterday."

"I don't expect you to understand."

"Then we've got no beef because I don't."

Micki stared down at her feet and tapped them. "I don't want to fight."

"We never fight. In order to do that, we'd have to talk."

"Exactly."

"So talk."

"If I could stay, I would. I just didn't want to go with us being unsettled. I guess."

If that admission was supposed to soften him, she might have failed, because all it earned her was a throbbing muscle in his jaw.

"Mikayla, I really don't get you. Suds didn't drag me out here so you and I could have a Kumbaya moment. What I think this is about is you and whatever is going on in Vegas. We know this guy you work for is an asshole. You don't think Jonah looked around on the deep Web for intel on him? Give us some credit. To say your boss's business dealings are suspect is a monstrous fucking understatement. He's probably dangerous to boot."

Deny it.

The thing she'd been so good at for ten years. "I don't get involved with any violence. I'm a...researcher. He tells me what he needs and I see if I can find it."

"A researcher. Okay. If that's what you're going with, it's your life."

Her life. It had never been her life. Her family just didn't know that. "Yep. My life. One I'm trying to fix by leaving. That's what I was doing when Gage busted me."

"You were stealing Jonah's bike to leave here?"

Again with the stealing? "No! I planned on locking it up in town and telling him where it was. I needed a way to get to the bus station. That's all."

"Where were you going?"

"I don't know."

Reid let out a long sigh and rubbed his cheek hard enough to leave red marks on his unshaved face. "God save me from women."

From somewhere inside, Micki laughed and it brought her back ten years when she'd spend half her time laughing at stupid things Reid said.

The memory should have made her smile. Should have. Not this time. All it brought was sadness. Loss. Her solid, loving relationships with her siblings, all those years, gone. "I want you to know I'm sorry for doing things that changed us. We always got along and you took care of me. I'm sorry I blew that. Believe me, it wasn't easy."

"You didn't *blow* it. Maybe I can't figure you out anymore, but you're my sister and I'll always love and take care of you."

But would he like her? And that's what she wanted. Brynne was right—when Reid loved, he loved hard. But loving *and* liking someone, well, that was the true accomplishment. One Micki hadn't achieved.

"I want…"

"What?"

She looked up at him, at her big brother. The one who'd kept the bullies at bay during middle school. The one who'd kicked the crap out of that creep in the seventh grade who'd grabbed her boob in the hallway. After that, no one bothered her.

Ever.

Until Phil. When he'd come along, she'd been complacent, a little too used to her brothers stepping in and taking care of her. As a result, she'd made one critical mistake. She'd never learned the art of battle.

The one thing she needed to know when Phil Flynn showed up.

"I don't expect help. This was my doing and I'll take care of it. I just don't want to hide things from my family anymore."

"Seriously, I'd welcome that. Look, start at the beginning. I'm not gonna judge or scream or do any of the shit you expect. All I know is I don't want you running from whatever this is. Not if we can stop it. We're your family. You're stuck with us. And if this douchebag in Vegas is hassling you, it'll get taken care of. You will always have a home here."

Pressure built in Micki's chest, trapping her air. Could it be that easy? She didn't want to believe that. Not after all the time spent at a job that left her with zero self-respect. And fear. She couldn't forget about the fear. She clutched at her belly and folded herself forward. A home. Here.

Thankfully, Reid stayed quiet while she clamped on to her composure, willing him not to come near her. *Please don't, please don't, please don't.* When she heard him get up, she raised one hand. If he tried to console her, she'd come apart. Just an emotional mess that she didn't want to be.

"Okay." He sat back down and set his hands on his thighs. "Whenever you're ready. I'm here."

For a few seconds, the only noise in the room was the *thunk* of the furnace Gage had warned her about the day before. Micki didn't mind. It gave her a tiny distraction while she got her thoughts together. Where to begin? Phil in jail. That's what had kicked this off.

Finally, she sat up, gripped the handles of the chair and focused on her brother. Now or never. "I ran from Vegas on Thursday."

"Ran?"

"Yes. Phil was arrested in Mexico and Tomas, the other guy who works for Phil, went down there to try and get him released. I was alone in the office and, I don't know, I'd had enough and I had the chance to leave so"—she shrugged—"I did."

"You said you ran. Running and leaving are two different things."

She met his eyes. "I ran."

Three or four seconds of silence passed between them and she hoped—prayed even—he wouldn't ask too many questions.

"Has he contacted you?"

"Not him. Tomas, though. He found me here. He was in the B last night and I caught him talking to Evie."

"Son of a bitch."

"I handled it. I told him I wanted a few days with my family, but that I'd go back. I don't want to, though. Not if I can help it. The work is—"

Reid held his hands up. "I have an idea of what the work is. I never understood that choice of profession."

"I had my reasons. Good ones."

"But you won't tell me."

"No. Not yet anyway."

Not until she told Jonah. He deserved to hear it first.

She stood, walked to the window, and stared out as Gage hopped on Jonah's bike and rode it to the barn. Such a good guy. Captain America. That was him.

"My thought," she said, "was to leave this morning and disappear. Phil won't stop looking for me." She faced

Reid again. "Over the years, Phil insisted on wiping my laptop clean. There are some files I keep on a remote server. Just in case. My own vault of information that would help build a case against Phil Flynn."

"Smart."

It was until she e-mailed the most damning of one of those files and tipped him off that her leaving was permanent. Now he'd come after her. After all of them, and the shame whipped at her. "Tomas getting Evie's number last night was the warning shot."

"He got her number? What the hell was she thinking?"

"Don't blame her. He told her he was a friend of mine. Tomas is an operator. Plus, he's good-looking."

"Damn, Evie is too trusting. I swear that girl is gonna send me to an early grave. How do we get this guy to lose her number?"

"I took care of it already. I blew up his phone. As long as he didn't do a backup last night, the number is gone. It's a temporary solution, though. He'll be back."

"Then I guess we'll have to be ready."

After killing time returning Jonah's bike to the barn and grabbing a mug of Miss Joan's famous pecan coffee, Gage wandered back to what would soon be the Steele Ridge Training Academy and spotted Reid heading up to the house.

Were he and Micki done? Ten years of distance and they'd wrapped that mess up already? No way.

Reid detoured and they met in the expanse of grass midway between the house and the training center. "Everything okay?"

"Hell," Reid said, "I don't know. She fill you in?"

Tricky business right here. Admitting too much might not be good for sibling relations. Really, this was

Micki's problem and she needed to handle it the way she saw fit. "Not everything. She was hauling ass when I pulled in, though. I figured something was up and stopped her."

"I can't believe she'd do that to us. To our *mother*. Even for her, that's a stretch. Usually she says goodbye." Reid leaned in, brought his face close to the mug Gage held. "Damn, that smells good."

"Take it. I'll get another one."

Clearly not feeling guilty about relieving Gage of his coffee, Reid snatched the mug up and took a healthy swig.

"Micki is scared," Gage said. "She thought leaving would draw her boss's fire away from here. Her logic is twisted, but she meant well."

"So she thinks she's gonna take this guy on herself? She's delusional." Reid shook his head. "When we were younger, I was crazy about her. She was edgy and smart and funny. Total badass with a computer. Then something happened during her and Jonah's senior year and the Micki we knew disappeared. Not physically, but she was *gone*. Now I don't know who the fuck she is."

"But she needs help."

"And my mother wants her back in Steele Ridge."

Two exceptional reasons to make sure she stayed. "What do you want to do?"

Reid took another long, enviable swig of coffee, making Gage regret handing it over.

Coffee now drained, Reid casually waved the mug. "I don't know. She wanted a few minutes. I'm giving her space while I talk to Jonah. She's sitting on Mom's bench."

Gage swung back to the glass and gray stone building that housed his office and spotted Micki, head down, hands braced against the marble bench that welcomed visitors. The front of the building needed additional landscaping, but they'd gotten things rolling with the bench and the plaque dedicating the training center to Miss Joan.

"Listen," Reid said, "thanks for helping with Micki. If you hadn't shown up this morning, she'd have bolted on us and we'd be wondering what the hell happened. And, Christ on a cracker, she was gonna leave a ten-thousand-dollar bike locked up to a lamppost. Jonah would have shit himself."

Gage snorted. "No problem."

"Dude, I hate to drag your ass into our family drama, but I may need your strategic mind to deal with Phil Flynn. This guy is all kinds of an asshole."

A sweet burst of dopamine that Gage had learned to thrive on flooded his system. His entire life, he'd been addicted to that feeling, that high that no drug would ever give him.

"No sweat. Whatever you need."

"Thanks. Right now I want breakfast and to think this through. I'm sensing a family meeting happening. Soon."

Taking the mug with him, Reid marched up the back steps leading to his mother's kitchen and Gage decided he was one hell of a friend for giving up his coffee on a morning like this. Having been away from his own family and their issues, phone calls aside, the drama had drained him. Already he needed a damned nap. Or a few mindless minutes in his office to close his eyes and let his brain rest. To recharge.

First he had to get by Micki.

From her spot on the bench, she watched him approach, her hazel eyes more than a little spooked. "I wanted to see Mom's bench. It's beautiful." She dragged a gentle hand over the surface of the marble. "Beautiful and strong. Just like her."

"Exactly what the guys were going for."

"They did well. As usual."

And, oh boy. He wouldn't comment on the unveiled bitterness in her tone. "Uh-huh."

Micki seemed to shift. *Wait.* No. Not her. Him. *Whoa.* His body swayed and he drove his heels into the ground for balance. If he fell over, he'd freaking kill himself. Right here. Damned dizziness. He closed his eyes, drew a breath. *Come on. Not right now.* A few seconds. That's all this would last. But if he didn't get ten minutes alone to shut his brain down, the dizziness would go on all day.

He opened his eyes, thankful for a seemingly stationary Micki. She stared up at him with that head-cocked, studious gaze people had employed around him lately. Everyone wanted to know what the hell was wrong with him.

"Are you okay?"

"I'm good. I get dizzy sometimes."

What? For months he'd been hiding the brain injury, telling no one. Not his family, not even Reid. How fair that was to the guy, Gage constantly asked himself. Reid had given him a job, a chance to rebound from his blown career, and in return he'd lied about his mental condition. A lie by omission, but a lie was a lie was a lie.

Sure, Reid had caught him plenty of times with his head back and eyes closed. Being the man he was, he didn't press it. He'd simply asked if he felt all right and invited Gage to talk anytime.

Gage didn't want to talk. He wanted his brain in working order so he could see his family and still be the son and brother they knew.

Until then, he'd stay away.

"Gage?"

He hit her with a flashing smile. "Sorry. Tired today. How'd it go with Reid?"

"I guess okay."

"Forgive me if I don't believe you. What with that enthusiastic answer."

"I said what I needed to. It's a process with him."

"Everything is."

"You *do* know him," she said.

"When you go into battle with someone you learn a lot. Fast."

He wouldn't talk war stories, though. War stories led to his purple heart and a gunshot wound that had healed and a brain that hadn't.

Micki stood, stared down at the bench a second, then faced him. "Thank you."

"For?"

"Trying to help. You don't even know me, and yet it feels like we're old friends."

"Your brother and I are old friends. And I'm nuts about your mother. I'll do whatever I can for anyone in this family."

"I'm afraid they'll get hurt."

"I get that. Believe me. From the time I was a kid, my dad pummeled it into my head that I needed to take care of my sisters. In a lot of ways, it's what drives me. But the thing is, they're adults now. As adults, they're entitled to make their own decisions. If they decide they'll help you, you should let them. That's what family does."

She looked up at him, holding her hand over her eyes to block the shifting sun. "I guess I've been on my own too long."

"Maybe that needs to change."

CHAPTER EIGHT

MICKI HAD LEFT HER BACKPACK in Gage's office and since her entire life—currently anyway—was in that bag, she didn't want to leave it lying around.

He ushered her into his office, holding the door open for her, a gesture she found wildly unnecessary but kinda cute.

For years, the men in her life had consisted of Tomas and Phil, and the day one of them would hold a door open for her would be the day she'd check her sanity. Or theirs.

Even so, that door-holding thing made her feel...feminine. Not like the nerdy cyber whiz who opted for ripped jeans and skull T-shirts.

Gage dropped into his chair and rested his head back. Something was off with him. Something in his eyes and the way they'd just glazed over.

"Are you sure you're okay? You don't look great."

Still with his eyes closed, he waved her off. "I'm good. Thanks."

She picked up her backpack and hooked it over her shoulder. "I'm heading up to the house. Reid said something about maybe calling everyone together. Big family meeting."

Gage opened his eyes, but kept his head back against his chair. "Are you comfortable with that?"

Did she have a choice? After years on her own, she'd have to readjust to having her family poking at her business. At her secrets. Right now, she wasn't sure what her options were. If she intended on staying in Steele Ridge, her family might be at risk, and they didn't deserve Mikayla-related hassles.

But leaving meant going off the grid. Possibly never seeing them again. Could she do that? To her mother? Whom she spoke with at least once a month. Connecting with her brothers hadn't happened much, but she counted on Mom to keep her updated. Those monthly calls were her oxygen. Her lifeline to an existence, a connection, she'd left behind.

She shrugged. "I guess I have to be."

Gage continued to rest his head back, but his eyes zoomed to hers. "Reid asked me to sit in."

Great. Mr. All-American—the extremely attractive Mr. All-American—having a front-row seat to her fucked-up life.

When Micki didn't respond, Gage sat forward. "It's your call. I'm an outsider. If you don't want me involved, I'll tell Reid I'm not coming."

An easy out. This guy truly was a superhero. A superhero who'd spent a lot of time around Reid, and more recently, her other brothers. In Gage, due to his lack of blood ties, she might have an ally. He hadn't experienced the disappointments and emotional carnage she'd caused.

If anything, Gage was neutral ground. He'd understand the level of stress created when going against such a determined bunch.

"No," she said, "I want you there." His eyebrows lifted slightly. She'd surprised him. Good. "You know how to control Reid. And"—how to say this?—"as weird as it sounds, I think you get me. I don't know why, but I don't feel like you judge me."

"I don't know you well enough to judge you. What I see is someone who made certain choices and the people around her don't know why. I have to assume you had reasons. Hopefully, damn good ones. Otherwise, you wouldn't have stayed away so long."

Just then, his cell phone rattled against the desk and he checked the screen. "Speaking of family. This is my dad."

"Should I leave?"

"Nah." He picked up the call before it went to voicemail. "Hey, Pop...What's up?"

She hadn't missed his giving her an opportunity to share her dirty little secrets. Not that she'd be taking him up on it, but she'd give him credit for being a master at the easy out. While he listened to his father, he smiled up at her, but slowly shifted his head back and forth. "I know," he said to his father, "but she's worried about you. You understand that, right?...Yup. I know. Where is she now?...Well, I'm in a meeting now. When she comes back, call me and the three of us are gonna talk this out...Pop, I get it. Don't worry."

After another minute, he said his good-byes and clicked off.

"Family problems everywhere," Micki said.

"Eh. No big deal. My parents are having communication issues." He laughed a little. "Meaning, she's talking and he doesn't want to hear it. We'll work it out."

"Thank you."

"For?"

"Not running screaming from me when you've got your own family to worry about."

"I try to make a habit of not running from beautiful women."

Beautiful. *Please.* "Listen, pal, back off on that charm or you might be in trouble. I may even start baking cookies again."

From the time she was seven, she'd stood by Mom's side in the kitchen, learning to crack eggs one-handed, stirring batter, getting just the right amount of dough on the cookie sheet, all of it supervised by her ever-patient mother.

Micki hadn't baked in ten years. Somehow, she didn't seem worthy of it.

"What kind of cookies?"

She brought her attention back to Gage. "Does it matter?"

"Bet your ass it does. I hate nuts in my cookies. I like them, but there's something about the texture of the nuts mixed with the cookie. Give me a gooey brownie, though, and there's no telling how far I'd go to say thank you."

She twisted her lips, fought the urge to take this conversation—this little flirtation—any further, but, hello, how many single women could resist Captain America with his muscles and protective instincts?

Oh, she could see it all right. He'd be the light in her darkness. The opposites that somehow, she hoped, made it work. Could she have that?

Not with Gage.

He knew too much for it to be organic. She wanted to start fresh with someone. Starting fresh with a stranger meant honesty and not being held hostage by her life in Vegas. Or feeling like a disappointment.

More than anything, that's what she wanted.

He popped out of his chair, took one step, and stopped. His body swayed and he grabbed hold of the edge of his desk just as she latched on to his arm, squeezing the corded muscles. "Are you dizzy again?"

"Need a second. That's all."

Interesting that he chose not to spew denials or convince her that he was fine.

"Do you want to sit?"

He leaned against the desk and clapped his hand over hers. His warm skin sent slow-moving tingles up her arm and...other places. Here she was asking what was wrong with him when she should ask what the hell was wrong with herself.

This was Reid's apple-cheeked, wholesome friend. With the life she'd lived, she had no business thinking about any sort of comfort from him.

"I'm okay." He patted her hand, then held on for a second. Not long enough to cross into let's-bang-each-other mode, but long enough for her to know he didn't mind her hands on him.

"Gage?"

"Yeah?"

"Why do I feel like I'm not the only one around here with secrets?"

Gage's phone buzzed. *Thank you.* Keeping his gaze on Micki, he pulled out of her grip and checked the text that had just saved his ass. Reid. Once again, his savior. He'd have to buy his buddy a beer.

"It's Reid," he said. "Your mother has breakfast going."

"That's better than a family meeting so early."

"I'm sure. At some point, if you want their help, you need to be honest."

"I know. I just feel…" She turned away, grabbed her backpack and slung it over her shoulder.

"What?"

"Nothing. You're Team Reid. I'm not throwing my ugliness into your friendship."

Team Reid? What the fuck did that mean? He leaned back on the desk, folded his arms. For a second there, he'd thought he'd actually gotten through to her. Cracked the stubborn barrier enough for her to confide in him.

You're dreaming, pal. "This has nothing to do with Reid. Two separate issues. Now, I ask again, you feel what?"

She gripped the strap of her backpack, squeezing her

fingers around it, then loosening her hold. Squeeze, flex, squeeze, flex. When she spotted him watching her, she dropped her hands, let them dangle at her sides. Finally, she looked at him and held his gaze.

He waited.

And waited.

And waited, until...

"I'm the disappointment."

Ah. Now they were carving into the meat. "Have they ever said that to you?"

"No. But—"

"Nuh-uh. I call bullshit."

She gawked and the look, that wide-eyed, mouth-agape astonishment forced him to absolutely not laugh.

"Excuse me," she said. "You call *bullshit?* On what?"

"If you haven't been honest with them, you can't know what they think."

Listen to him. Maybe he should take his own goddamn advice and talk to his family about his issues. About the fact that he didn't want to come home because of his TBI and his fear that his family couldn't handle him not being the dependable go-to one. No matter what. 1-800-Gage. That was the inside joke. Need a lift? Call Gage. Sibling drama? Call Gage. Someone's ass kicked? Call Gage.

Jesus, just thinking about it exhausted him.

But they weren't talking about him now. This was about Micki and her cluster.

His phone buzzed again, rattling against the desktop and Micki flapped her arms. "Is that him again?"

"He's probably watching. He's a pain in the ass that way."

At that, Micki smirked. "You *do* know him."

Slowly, he levered off the desk, got to his feet, and was rewarded with the lack of a dizzy spell. For now, he'd leave Micki be. She wasn't ready to talk and if she was anything like Reid, there'd be no convincing her. Damned bullheaded people.

Later. One step at a time. "Let's head up to the house," he said. "We can talk later."

After breakfast, Gage followed Reid into his office at the training center and waited while the big man situated himself by propping his feet on his desk. Had to give the guy credit for letting Brynne do some decorating in the place. His once white-walled empty office now housed a giant cherry desk, a shiny credenza, and some of the nicest leather guest chairs Gage had ever seen. Heck, sometimes he came in here just to sit in those damned chairs.

"Plant yourself," Reid said.

Gage gently lowered himself into one of the chairs. Moving too fast resulted in looking like a pansy and that would require explanations he wasn't willing to give.

His friend watched him, his dark blue gaze unrelenting, and a hiss of panic dogged Gage.

"Can I ask you something?" Reid asked.

Here it comes. If Reid asked him straight away about a possible TBI, he'd...he'd...Hell, he didn't know what he'd do. For months they'd been circling the weirdness, avoiding a direct conversation about his occasional balance issues and lack of focus.

Reid had never asked and Gage hadn't offered it up. Their own version of don't ask, don't tell.

"Reid, we've been friends a long time. Ask me anything you want."

"How do you feel about this Micki situation? I want your opinion. All of a sudden, she's running from this guy in Vegas. I don't know why."

"She's like a puzzle, your sister."

"That she is. She used to be..." He paused, squinted a little. "...I don't know, mischievous. When I was away at college, something changed. Then the day after she graduated from high school, she ran off to Vegas."

"Jesus, that fast?"

"Yep. She'd gotten a job with Flynn. At the time, we didn't know who the hell he was. Jonah looked into him and we realized he was"—Reid stared at the ceiling, choosing his words again—"a fixer."

"A fixer? As in, he cleans up the messes rich people create?"

"Pretty much. From what we can tell, he's the master. Gets the job done." Reid finally made eye contact. "Always."

"All these years you've all been wondering what she does for him."

"My mother doesn't know the half of it. She thinks he's a PR guy. Inside though, I have to believe my sister is telling the truth about her role as his"—he made air quotes—"researcher. She likes to break balls, but she doesn't have that killer instinct. Well, at least she didn't. Now? I don't know what I know."

The chime from the entrance sounded and Reid sat up, put his feet on the floor. "Hello?"

"It's me. Uh, Micki," came the reply.

Talk about timing.

"My office," Reid said.

A second later, Micki appeared in the doorway. She still wore the same jeans, black T-shirt and jacket from earlier, but she'd ditched the hat and her hair looked different—fuller at the top, but straight at chin level—and the whole look, edgy but feminine, gave Gage a yearning to touch it. To put it his hands in it.

While on top of her.

And, shit, that was wrong on so many levels. The first being he shouldn't be thinking disrespectful thoughts about the sister of a guy who'd given him an opportunity when he needed it. The second being she was vulnerable right now and if he was any kind of a decent guy, he wouldn't be contemplating getting into a physical relationship with her.

"Hi," he said.

She glanced at him, then to Reid. "Hi."

Reid propped his elbows on the desk. "What's up, Mick?"

"Are you going into town today?"

"Not until tonight. You need something?"

"Clothes."

"Clothes?"

After the morning they'd had, she wanted to go shopping? That one, he didn't see coming.

She nodded. "When I left Vegas, I only brought two days' worth. I thought I could go into town and see if I found anything. If not, I checked the bus schedule and there's one that goes into Asheville."

Asheville. By herself? After they'd just gotten done talking about what a prick her boss was? And what about this Tomas guy? He was probably still around.

"Uh," Gage said, "are you dealing with Tomas?"

She nodded. "I am. I sent him an e-mail and told him I'm not going back. He hasn't responded. Yet."

"Well, after you blew up his phone, it's probably taking him a minute to deal with getting a new one. Do you think it's smart to be wandering around by yourself?"

Reid eyed him for a second, clearly amused at Gage questioning his sister.

She gave him the stink eye. "Tomas wouldn't do anything."

"You sure?"

She spun to the door. "You know what, forget it. I'll ask Jonah."

"Hang on," Reid said, but Micki kept walking.

"Mikayla." Reid's voice stayed level, but with enough heat for his sister to know he wasn't screwing around. "Hold up a second."

Micki halted in the doorway and Reid rolled his eyes. "Suds asked you a legitimate question. This guy followed you here from Vegas. It's not unreasonable to ask if he's dangerous."

Micki turned back, the look on her face more fuck-off than you're-absolutely-right. "I need clothes. Can you help me?"

After a brutal stare down, Reid poked the speaker button on his desk phone, dialed, and waited while the line rang through. "Swear to God," he muttered, "the females in my life make me batshit crazy."

"Hey, babe," a female voice said.

Brynne. Perfect solution, considering she owned a boutique.

"Hey," Reid said. "I have you on speaker. With Suds and Micki."

"Thanks for the warning. I will refrain from dirty talk."

That brought a flashing smile to his buddy's pissed-off face. "You're too cute, Brynnie. I know you're about to open so I'll be quick. I'm gonna bring Micki down there. She needs some clothes."

"Oh, fun. I ordered some great T-shirts from that new designer I met. I'll have Evie pick a few things out."

"Thanks. I'll see you in a bit." Reid disconnected and sat back. "Check out Brynne's stuff first. If you have to go into Asheville, we'll figure it out. You are *not* taking the bus."

"That's just ridiculous. I can take the bus."

Reid's face turned stony again. *Here we go.* Knowing his friend, Gage held up a hand. "Before you lose your shit, I'll drive her into town after we check the weapons I wanted you to look at. I'm heading that way anyway." He looked back at Micki. "And, sorry, but I agree with him on the bus. Too risky right now. At least until we figure out what's happening with Flynn and this Tomas."

"Guys, I'm not an infant. I've been on my own for ten years."

"And look where that got you."

Micki turned a hard glare on her brother and—

yow—this girl didn't play. Before he had to bust up a sibling brawl—not uncommon between the males in this family—Gage put up two hands. "Both of you, take a second here and breathe. It's been a wild day. Everyone is on edge."

"No shit?" Reid snarked.

Gage faced Micki. "Let me take you into town. See what Brynne has. If that doesn't work, we'll tackle the bus situation. Let's deal with one thing at a time. Can we do that?"

Micki slid her gaze to her brother, but locked her jaw. *Oh, boy.* If he let them, they'd tear the place up.

"Great." She slapped a phony smile on. "Call me when you're ready to go. Reid has my number."

If being in Steele Ridge meant dealing with her pushy brothers, Micki wouldn't survive it.

She plopped on her bed, stared up at the ceiling fan and spewed a stream of swear words that would get her in trouble with her mother. What was it with the men in her life? Everyone wanted to control her.

Well, she was done with that. All around. She rolled sideways, grabbed her backpack from the floor, and pulled her laptop out. In need of something positive in her life, she'd been playing around with new software and now, given her holding pattern while waiting on Gage, she had time to get back to it. Besides, with her billionaire brother in residence, if she could get the last few bugs out, she might be able to sell it.

An appealing thought, considering her lack of current employment. If she intended to stay in Steele Ridge, sponging off of her family wouldn't do.

Nope. She needed a job. An honest one she didn't have to hide or feel shame over. For the first time in years, she had options. Freedom. An opportunity to decide what exactly she wanted to be when she grew up. All she'd ever been was a black hat.

The ding of her e-mail filled the quiet room and she watched the messages fire in like tiny missiles. Maybe Tomas had gotten back to her.

He'd be steaming mad, about a lot of things, but down deep, he'd understand her desire to move on. For years they'd talked about where they'd go, the places they wanted to experience, the people they'd like to meet. Underneath, they both yearned for something more than life with Phil. What that something was, they'd never quite hit on.

At least she hadn't.

Tomas had done a lot of listening and less talking during those revealing conversations, but she'd chalked it up to his DNA. Men weren't talkers. About anything.

She scanned the loading e-mails and—*dang it*—Phil's name popped up. An e-mail from his personal account. Out of jail. Had to be if he had access to his computer or phone. In which case, he'd probably already received her message.

But was he back in the States?

Panic bubbled inside. "No. Please. Not yet."

Her finger hovered over the mouse pad, ready to click on the e-mail. Wait. After she'd blown up Tomas's phone and, oh, right, sent the video, he could be retaliating by sending her a virus. Unlikely, given that this particular e-mail was from Phil's personal account. The one he communicated with friends and family from. He kept his business and personal accounts separate, but utilized software that allowed him to easily click from one to another and occasionally, he'd forget to click out of his personal account.

Something that might explain why she'd received a message from said personal account.

Still, anything from Phil, at this point, was suspect.

She clicked over to her online backup service. Last backup completed three hours earlier. If she opened

Phil's e-mail and it fried her laptop, she'd still have access to her files.

Why open it, though? Did it matter? If he were home, even if Tomas hadn't told him about her going AWOL, her absence meant she'd left Vegas.

Shoving the laptop away, she hopped off the bed, tugging on her fingers as she paced the room.

Just an e-mail with an attachment. That's all. Could be a simple note inquiring about her plans to return to Vegas. Phil was slick that way. She'd seen it hundreds, if not thousands, of times when he dealt with people.

Like any predator, he groomed his targets. At first he'd be unaggressive. Downright friendly. Supportive even. And then, *then*, when he'd cultivated the stirrings of a relationship and earned trust, he went for the kill. He'd manipulate and threaten, burying fear so deep inside his victim, they'd never be free.

She went back to her laptop and flexed her fingers. The attachment could be a problem. Dammit. One way to find out. She dropped to her knees beside the bed and clicked. A two-word message popped up.

See attached.

Her eyes snapped to the little paper clip where an mp4 file waited for her to fire it up. A video. Just as she'd sent him. This one titled "Jonah."

Tit for tat with the master of the kill.

Disregarding thoughts of viruses and logic bombs, she clicked the file. The little spinning wheel did its thing and a second later there was her brother. Ten years younger, coming out of a room and rushing down a hallway.

Instinctively, she knew what this was and she sucked in a hard breath. "Oh no."

All this time, she'd wondered about this video. If it actually existed or if Phil, in typical Phil fashion, had simply played her, giving her the ultimate mind screw, to keep control.

Four seconds of video from a security system. That's all Phil had sent.

He had more. At least that's what he'd told her. Twenty long minutes' worth. He'd never shown it to her, but now she didn't doubt it. If he needed evidence, he found it. If he couldn't find it, he created it.

This evidence, though? This was the real deal. No funky editing or splicing because on her screen Jonah wore his favorite Doctor Strange T-shirt. Back then, he'd lived in that shirt, and on this night she'd teased him about it. About maybe making more of an effort with his clothing choices, considering they'd be around the cool kids.

Her phone beeped, launching her from her mind travel. She whipped it from her back pocket and scanned the number on the text. Area code 563. Where the heck was that? This could be Phil or Tomas messing with her after sending the video. She tapped the screen and read the message.

Gage.

Letting her know he was ready to go.

Run. She dropped the phone on the bed and drove her fingers through her hair, massaging her scalp as the urge to escape, to just walk out the door, pounded her. If she went back to Vegas, maybe she could deal with Phil and everyone would be safe.

Jonah would be safe.

Vegas meant no Steele Ridge, though. And no more visits home. After this stunt, Phil—and Tomas—would never trust her again. In one swoop, she'd managed to deprive herself of her biological family and obliterate the twisted version of her makeshift Vegas one. Total isolation.

She glanced around the room, studied the warm beige of the walls, the bamboo ceiling fan, all of it meant to give comfort to whoever slept here.

Comfort.

Something she hadn't had since leaving for Vegas.

God, she'd left home so long ago. All this time she'd dealt with loneliness and shame and the tangled emotions that came with needing her mother's hugs that she couldn't have.

These thoughts. What good did they do? Other than to drag her down, make her wallow in unalterable circumstances.

On the other side of the bed, the French doors opened to property her mother had loved for years and now owned. All thanks to Jonah. Who'd made something of himself. For that she was grateful, but Micki had missed it all.

Now, on her screen, the paused video of Jonah sent its unspoken message.

Come back or the video gets released.

Her phone beeped again. Perfect distraction. She scooped it up and scanned the second text from Gage.

You're not plotting to overthrow a government, are you? Let's go.

Gage Barber. A man hotter than a Louisiana summer and more at home with her family than she was. Somehow, she'd found an ally in him. A bridge to her family.

To coming home.

And that's what she wanted. A safe place to land. A family, who, if she got really lucky, would hold her tight. Going back to Vegas wouldn't get that for her.

"No running," she said, loving the sound of it and the feeling, the absolute control, strengthening her spine.

If Phil wanted a war, she'd collected enough information to give him one. She wouldn't stop, either. The skills she'd learned in his employ not only worked for him, they could work against him. Her hacking skills, if she could get into his server, might uncover all sorts of additional dirt. How incredibly ironic.

But, Lord, using Phil's own tactics on him brought her to a new low. After this, there'd be no more denials, no more justifying how she stayed away from the ugliness of what they did.

After this, she wasn't a *researcher* anymore. Her family would be disgusted, but if it meant protecting them and reclaiming her life, she'd crawl into that nasty gutter and do it.

They just wouldn't need to know.

She tapped out of the e-mail from Phil, shut the lid on the laptop, and stowed it in her backpack. She'd deal with that later.

Right now, though, she had a ride into town with a hunky guy so she could buy new clothes.

CHAPTER NINE

AFTER DINNER, MOM HEADED INTO town to help man the Chamber of Commerce's hot cocoa booth at Novemberfest. According to Gage, big brother Grif's latest bright idea—literally—consisted of a tree-lighting ceremony to kick off the holiday season.

With Mom gone and the boys huddled around the television arguing over a basketball game, Micki grabbed a jacket and slipped out to the porch, plopping into one of Mom's Adirondacks.

Brotherly loudness took getting used to. Again.

According to Gage, the past two weeks had been filled with rain and cloudy skies, but beyond the trees, stars twinkled against a sheet of perfect black. Not one cloud.

Home.

To prove it, she puffed out a breath into the chilly air and watched the vapor disappear. Vegas got cold, but not like this. Not...peaceful.

Home.

"Micki!" Britt called from inside the house.

So much for peaceful. *Definitely home now.*

Already mourning her alone time, she pushed out of the chair, opened the storm door, and found her brother waving her inside. Could this be the dreaded family meeting she'd been anticipating? She slipped into the kitchen, her quickening pulse a giveaway that whatever this was, it wouldn't be easy.

In the dining room, Britt took his spot at the end of the table, sliding into his role as family leader. At least among the siblings. Why her father holed himself up in that cabin, Micki didn't know, but for years now, Britt had accepted the role of patriarch and no one seemed to mind.

"Huddle up. Since Mom is gone we can talk."

Reid dropped into the chair to Britt's right and met her gaze. Grif, wearing a crisp white dress shirt and gray slacks he'd managed to keep pristine throughout dinner, entered the room and commandeered the chair at the opposite end of the table. "What's going on that Mom can't hear?"

"And dragged me from my computer?"

Micki glanced at Jonah. Another thing that obviously hadn't changed was Jonah's habit of working late into the night and sleeping in when he could. As kids they'd joked that their brains didn't reach optimum speed until midnight.

Behind her, Gage, clearly waiting to make sure everyone had a seat, propped a shoulder against the doorframe. After being assured Britt would pick her up at Brynne's shop, Gage had gone home and then returned for dinner.

Not that she minded seeing him. Gage Barber was everything she'd never imagined finding attractive in a man. Wholesome, rugged, and outdoorsy. The blond hair and lean, rippling muscles didn't hurt either, but she was a girl with a sordid past and guys like Gage? They wouldn't understand. On the flip side, dating lowlifes who had no room to judge her wasn't an ideal option. Which left her stuck.

And alone.

"Suds," Reid said, pointing to the chair next to Micki, "have a seat."

"I was saving it for Evie."

"No Evie. She's helping Brynne at the store."

"Christ," Grif said, "she'll love being left out. But if it's that busy in town, maybe this goofy Novemberfest idea is working."

Reid sat back, his big shoulders smothering the chair. "According to Brynne, it's working, but we got things to deal with here. I talked to Micki earlier and she needs our help."

All eyes went to her and she froze. What? What could she possibly say right now? *Gee, guys, my boss has been blackmailing me for years and to save Jonah's reputation I broke about five million laws. And guess what? I'm actively trying to hack into his server and scrape up enough dirt to free us.*

Beside her, Gage jerked his chin, urging her to speak up.

"I...um..."

"Spit it out, kid," Reid said.

Gage eyeballed him. "Maybe you can give her a chance?"

Wow. Not even a sibling and he'd jumped to her defense.

He'd help her. He'd said it already. Only problem was, she'd gotten too used to being alone and not accepting help. All of this felt...off.

She looked at each of her brothers, pausing at Jonah, whose dark hair stuck straight up in the back. More than likely he'd been kicked back in his gaming chair, giving him a nice case of chairhead.

Annoyance at her brother aside, she had to tell them something. Even if it was only enough to get them off her case while she dealt with Phil.

"Okay," she said. "I'll start with leaving Vegas. I didn't tell anyone there my plans."

Britt narrowed his eyes. "Why?"

"Because I didn't want to be found. I can't do it anymore."

"Do what?" Grif shot back.

"The job. It's...a lot."

Jonah shrugged. "So stay here with us. Gage is bugging me about a cyber warfare class for the training center. I'd love to hand that off and you could do it in your sleep."

"Hold on there, Baby Billionaire," Reid said. "Twiggy isn't done."

At the time, she'd despised her childhood nickname. Now? Hearing it after all the years, it brought her a sense of stability, of belonging. A tight ball of emotion clogged her airway and she cleared her throat. *Get through it.* That's all she had to do.

"Phil—"

"That asshole," Britt said.

Well, yes. "He got arrested in Mexico."

"Ha," Grif said. "What he'd do?"

She shook her head. "It doesn't matter. While he was in jail, I took off. This trip isn't like the others. I knew when I left I didn't want to go back." She looked at Jonah again, stared into his eyes. The exact ones she saw in the mirror each day. "He won't let me go."

Jonah waved it off. "That's crap. He can't tell you where you can go."

Yes. He can.

"It's complicated and I can't talk about it. It's better for everyone if I don't. My plan when I left Vegas was to stop and see you and then leave. I didn't want to drag you into it."

"Into what?" Grif again.

"All of it."

"Mikayla," Britt said in that fatherly tone that sometimes annoyed her other brothers. "I'm confused."

She looked at Gage, still beside her, quiet and observant. She needed help and out of the group, oddly enough, he knew the most.

Taking her cue—or her silent pleading—he leaned forward. "Look, guys, I'm the outsider here."

"You're not an outsider," Reid argued.

"Whatever. My point is, I'm not family, but we're on a time crunch. At the B last night, I spotted a guy talking to Evie and then to Micki. I didn't recognize him, but then Micki walked away and that was the end of it. This morning, I found Micki hauling ass down the driveway trying to leave."

Reid muttered something at the same time Britt said, "I'm confused" and Jonah said something to Reid, apparently in response to whatever Reid had said and all of it melded together, squashing the quiet of the room.

"Shh," Micki said. "If you're all yammering, I can't talk."

"Fine," all four of her brothers said at once.

Sigh.

"I was sneaking out because the guy in the bar works for Phil. He came here to find me. Phil expects me back in Vegas and I'm not going. I was leaving because I refuse to drag you all into my problems."

"Why?" Britt asked. "Is Phil dangerous?"

Micki didn't answer.

"Shit," Jonah said. "We knew he was slime but dangerous? Seriously?"

Yes. Seriously. "I don't know what he'll do. Maybe nothing, but it's me he wants. I thought if I wasn't here and y'all didn't know where I was, he'd have no use for you. That was my original plan. I'm working on something else now. Something that will, hopefully, convince him to let me go."

"What does *that* mean?" Britt again.

Reid saved her from having to stretch the truth by popping out of his chair, the sudden movement stirring up the stillness. "This is bullshit. This guy can't hurt us."

If only that were true. "Tomas, the guy from the bar last night, is—or at least was—my friend. He said he wouldn't tell Phil where I was if I went back with him today." She looked at Jonah again, whose gaze had locked on to her. "I e-mailed him earlier and told him I'm not going back."

"Then," Reid said, "whatever this is, we'll deal with it together."

"But—"

Britt stood. "No buts. You've been running from us for ten years. If you want to stay, you'll stay. Now tell us what this guy has on you."

"I can't."

Grif ran a hand down the arm of his shirt, apparently smoothing away a wrinkle. "Here we go with the secrets again."

What her brothers couldn't grasp was that her secrets were meant to keep them safe. Giving them the full scope of her problem, the down-and-dirty truth, wouldn't accomplish that.

"It's better if you don't know everything. As long as I don't tell anyone, you will all be safe."

Jumping in, Grif smacked his knuckles against the table. "Guys like Flynn are a dime a dozen in LA. I had a client last year who wanted to hire him. Wanted *me* to hire him."

Oh, no. Please, God. As one of the premier sports agents in the country, Grif had many clients. She'd never heard his name thrown around the office, but that didn't mean anything. Phil often hid things from her. Or maybe she hid them from herself. Denial had become her friend. Her very close friend.

She leaned forward so she could see him on the other side of Gage. "What client?"

"Basketball player. Total party animal. Got wasted in a club one night with a twenty-one-year-old. He followed her to the ladies' room and had his security guy guard the door while he had sex with her. In the goddamn bathroom. When the girl sobered up, she claimed rape. My client came to me with it, wanted me to help him make it go away. I dropped him. I don't need a guy like him. I heard he hired Phil Flynn. And it sure as shit went away."

Sensing he had a question he wanted answered, Micki sat a little straighter. *Wait for it...*

But Grif simply stared at her, his jaw set. Questioning. Her own brother didn't trust her.

"No," she said, her voice only slightly pissy. "I wasn't involved."

"You're sure?"

For the love of... "*Yes.* I've never even heard of it."

"Are the cops after you?"

"No."

"The feds?"

Dear God. "*No!* I swear to you. I have never, ever, done the ugly stuff. And, gee, Grif, thanks so much for the support!"

"Christ, Mikayla," Britt said, scratching the back of his neck. "It all sounds ugly to me."

Point there. "I only did the research."

Jonah perked up. "Hacking?"

"Yes. And I never knew what exactly the cases were. He'd tell me he needed someone's credit history and I'd get it. Did they have any DUIs? Any sort of criminal history. I'd get the specific information. That's it. I swear to you."

Micki stood, walked around the table to where Reid now leaned against the wall. She gripped Reid's arm and faced all of her brothers and Gage. "I know you have no reason to trust me, but knowing the details of why I worked for Phil won't help. Please, just trust me."

A long few seconds passed with each of her brothers glancing around the table in silence. Men truly were apes the way they communicated.

As much as she wanted their acceptance, for them to believe in her, she knew they should toss her out. All these years she'd been gone and now she expected them to welcome her back? Not likely. Foolish girl.

"Fine," Britt said. "But we need a plan."

Reid, ever the tactician, held up a hand. "Where is Flynn now?"

"As far as I know, he's back in Vegas."

"Not good enough," Jonah said. "We need to know where he is. And this other guy, Tomas, he's probably still here."

"Which means," Grif said, "he's probably staying at one of the B and Bs in town. I'll call the owners and check that out."

"Good," Britt said. "And Micki doesn't go anywhere alone."

Wait. What? "No way," she said.

"Yes, way," Reid shot back. "You don't know what this guy is capable of."

Micki swung to Gage. The reasonable one. "Please, tell them I don't need to be in a prison."

"Ditch the drama," Reid said. "You are *not* a prisoner. If you were, I'd increase the security patrols on the property."

Slowly, she lifted her hand. And flipped him off.

Mr. All-American cleared his throat. "Micki," he said, "I'm sorry. I agree with your brothers on this. Until we know what Flynn is planning, I don't think it's safe."

Her final hope had just blown apart. Poof. Gone. She shook her head as frustration tore her up. She'd left one situation where she'd had no control and wound up in yet another.

She scanned the table, taking in the Steele stubbornness on full display. Arguing with them wouldn't help. There were too many of them. She'd just go about her business of dealing with Phil. Once that was settled, she'd be free to go where she wanted, when she wanted.

"It's settled," Britt said. "Mikayla, if things get dicey, you come to me. To *any* of us. *Immediately.*"

Having had more than his share of familial dynamics,

Gage excused himself and headed down to the training center to close up. As much as Reid rammed it into his head that he wasn't an outsider, Gage wasn't a relative and leaving them be might be a wise choice. It seemed to him they all needed to get reacquainted because, as of ten minutes ago, Micki Steele was officially staying.

God help him and his horny self, because she'd looked pretty damned steamed when he'd gone against her. Which might explain her high-tailing it from the room after the meeting. God knew where she'd run off to. She'd have to deal with her anger. In this instance, the Steele boys were dead on. Even if it did create mind-melting tension.

Right now, Grif's damned Novemberfest might provide the best distraction. Gage wasn't much for festivals, but since he worked for a soon-to-be-opening business and didn't have anything else to do on a Saturday night, he figured he'd swing by and avoid his growing attraction to Micki Steele. Damn, she had a spine. Her brothers weren't exactly easy and she'd faced them all.

He followed the worn path back to the training center, his boots crunching over the loose gravel as Miss Joan's porch light threw shadows from behind. A good thing, since the exterior lights on the training center hadn't clicked on yet. He'd have to adjust the timer, make sure the spotlights went on earlier.

He breathed in the cool night air, appreciating that the miserable weather had given them a break with clear skies, plenty of stars, and enough warmth to keep the temperature at a comfortable level.

A light wind rustled tree branches and all of it, the crisp air, the sounds of nature, surrounded him, gave him a sense of calm and peace. Exactly what he'd come to Steele Ridge for.

Nights like this, he wouldn't mind having someone by his side. Someone to hold and love and keep warm. But relationships required honesty and he couldn't give that.

Not yet. Honesty, in his current condition, meant weakness and he'd be damned if he'd willingly give that over. No way.

"Hi."

Twenty feet from the building, he jerked to a stop, his hands immediately at the ready, his brain spurting adrenaline. He squinted into the darkness at the outline—a lean, leggy outline—of someone sitting on Miss Joan's bench.

"Girl, you about gave me a stroke."

"I'm sorry," Micki said. "I thought you'd be up at the house with Reid."

"I was. We're done. I'm closing up and heading into town. Novemberfest."

A shaft of moonlight drifted around the corner of the building and Micki tilted her head up, the long column of her neck exposed and vulnerable. That neck. He wanted his mouth on it.

"You're going?" she asked.

"Since the center is about to open, I might as well put in an appearance."

She gave up on the moon and looked at him, her leather jacket—and the body in it—backlit and...nope...not going there.

"It sounds nice. Small-town nice. Not like Vegas, you know?"

"I do know." He stepped closer, lowered himself to the bench and his thigh brushed hers.

One of them should probably scoot over. Make room.

Except, no one did.

Ah, damn. Seconds ago, he'd lamented his lack of female company. Between him and Micki, they were a class A train wreck.

"Is it crazy that I'm sitting here in the dark?"

He shrugged. "Not to me."

"I like this bench. It's quiet and I get to think of my mom."

"We all need quiet sometimes. One of the guys in our

old unit was into meditation and all that Zen crap. He made all of us try it one night."

"Oh, Lord. Reid meditating?"

Gage laughed. "Yeah. That alone was worth it. It wasn't his thing, but I liked it. That chance to close my eyes. Settle my thoughts."

He liked it enough that he still did it every day. Whether it was actually meditation, he wasn't sure, but he'd take five or ten minutes and rest his brain.

A bird flapped overhead and he peered up. Micki did the same and there was all that soft creamy skin again, sparking an urge to drag his fingers down it.

He needed to get laid. Simple fact. The rotten part of it was he could make it happen. Cherlyn Marstin had been sending the signals for a month. Every time he saw her in town, she was all over him with the extended eye contact and brushing her hands over his arms.

She was pretty, for sure, but...

Hell, he didn't know. A quick screw with Cherlyn, for whatever reason, wouldn't cure what ailed him.

Not with the moon glistening off Micki's face. In profile, her sculpted cheekbones and stylishly messy hair falling around her face made his body hum, and he wasn't idiot enough to deny he liked it. "Damn, you're beautiful."

"It's dark. Everyone is beautiful in the dark."

"Not like you." He bumped her leg with his. "And that's just me being honest. I'm not hitting on you."

Not much.

"Well, that's a pity."

At that, he smiled. She definitely had that Steele wit.

She gave up on the moon, met his gaze, and held it while the previously cool air became charged and downright warm.

"I don't want to keep you," she said. "Novemberfest is calling."

The out. The escape hatch.

Smart man that his family professed him to be, he

stood. "Yeah, I should probably head down there. They're lighting the tree at nine o'clock." He took two steps, then paused.

Don't.

Being a smart man also meant not leaving desirable women sitting alone on benches. He turned back. "You wanna come?"

CHAPTER TEN

"INTO TOWN?"

Micki sat on Mom's bench, seriously paralyzed by Captain America asking her out.

Or maybe this was a sympathy thing to get her out of the house and away from the stress of the evening.

Did it matter? Either way, she wanted to go. Quite badly. Be normal for a while. Whatever normal might be.

Gage shook his head, laughing a little. "Yes, into town. But, hey, if you'd rather sit out here by yourself..."

"Yes. No. I mean—oy!" She laughed at herself. "I don't know."

"You're funny, Micki. Anyway, I wouldn't mind the company."

Her chest slamming, Micki stood. "Well, Mr. All-American, I wouldn't either."

In town, Micki strolled beside Gage under a canopy of Christmas lights while ducking around the growing crowd on Main Street. Her cousin, Sheriff Maggie, had barricaded the block to motor traffic, and a solid wall of people stretched from one side to the other.

All they needed was snow and Steele Ridge would be a holiday wonderland.

Pausing in front of La Belle Style, Micki peered in the window where Evie, Brynne, and another young woman dealt with customers. "They're busy."

"Yeah. Grif keeps coming up with ideas to increase foot traffic in town. He's pretty good at it and the business owners are all over it."

Brynne spotted the two of them at the window and waved. While she had her attention, Micki jabbed her finger at the gray cashmere V-neck sweater she wore under her jacket and received a double thumbs up for her choice.

Hours ago, Brynne had talked her into the sweater. At the time it felt way too classic. Cashmere? Seriously? But now that she had it on, it made her feel, what?

Grownup.

Feminine.

Pretty?

All of the above. And why not?

Brynne went back to her customer, and Gage and Micki moved on. "So," she said. "It's Thanksgiving weekend and you're here rather than in Iowa. Why is that?"

He shrugged. "We have a lot to do here. Training center opens February first."

Please. For every holiday she'd spent away from her home, she'd come up with a new reason she couldn't make it back. Everything from a burgeoning sinus infection, too much work, couldn't afford the flight, to…whatever. She'd used them all and the entire time, she'd known, down deep, that they'd never believed any of it. "Not buying it. All I've wanted for years was to spend a holiday with my family. And from what I saw with you mediating between your mom and dad, it seems like you're close to them."

"Just because I didn't go home for a holiday doesn't mean I don't miss them."

One thing Micki understood, better than most, was

secrets. Gage was hiding something and she was pretty sure it had something to do with those dizzy spells.

She wouldn't pressure him, though. Bottom line? Even heroes hid things. "I'm not bugging you about it—"

"Not much."

She smacked his arm. "*But* you've been nice to me. If you want to talk, I'm here."

He halted, right in the middle of the sidewalk, and hooked on to her elbow. "Shit."

"What is it?"

"Cherlyn. Twelve o'clock."

The hand on her elbow moved to her back, his fingers gliding up her spine and sending a happy zing to parts of her body that had definitely not experienced any recent happy zings. Yowza, yowza, yowza.

"Um, what are you doing?"

He leaned in, got close to her ear, his warm breath sending *you go, girl!* alerts to her extremely neglected private parts.

"Roll with me here."

Oh, she'd roll with him.

His fingers continued their climb until he reached her shoulder, where he casually draped that big hand and pulled her closer.

Whatever Gage had going on with Cherlyn, he clearly wanted the woman to believe he and Micki were playing House. Unable to resist, she reached up, linked her fingers with his, hanging on as they strolled.

"Gage Barber!"

Micki followed the voice, found a redhead who could be Cherlyn coming toward them, but Micki hadn't seen her since high school. Back then, Cherlyn's hair had been sandy blond and she'd worn heavy eye makeup. Her hair had changed, but the makeup hadn't and Cherlyn, sadly, resembled a trashy thirty-two-year-old grappling with—and losing—her fading youth.

"Hey, Cherlyn," Gage said, keeping his hand on Micki's shoulder.

Cherlyn turned her icy blue eyes on Micki. "And is this Micki Steele? I'd know you anywhere."

Micki wished she could say the same. "Hi, Cherlyn. How are you?"

"I'm good." Her eyes went to Gage's hand, then snapped back to Micki. "Are you visiting?"

"Sort of." She gazed lovingly up at Gage. "I think I'll stay a while. Maybe settle at home again."

"Well," she drawled, "you Steeles always did move quick."

Gage coughed and put his free hand in front of his mouth, turning away to hide the laugh. Apparently, he was unaccustomed to cats.

"Well," Micki mimicked, still gazing up at Gage, "when we see something we want, we don't dawdle."

The strum of a guitar streamed from speakers at the end of the block. Wanting to be rid of Cherlyn and have Captain America to herself, Micki patted Gage's hand. "Let's head over and listen to the music. Cherlyn, I guess I'll see you around town. You take care now."

Micki saved his ass.

Small-town living sometimes created awkward situations, and Cherlyn had become a full-blown man-eater. Hell, he'd run out of polite ways to turn her down. Growing up, he'd perfected the art of riding the line between accommodating versus total asshole, but this challenged him.

With Cherlyn, as much as he didn't want to, he might have to nudge into total asshole territory. The woman would not let up. If this had happened last year, his Special Forces buddies, guys who had stupid theories on women, would've told him to just do her and get it over with. The thought of that bunch of dumb-asses, him included, sitting around shooting the shit made him laugh, but the punch of loss was there. He didn't spend a lot of time lamenting his injuries or questioning the sudden directional change of his life. Why bother? Nothing would change and he'd still not be fit for duty. Still, he didn't mind admitting he missed his friends.

Micki bumped him with her elbow as they walked. "What's funny?"

"I was thinking about the guys in my unit. And, by the way, thank you."

Still with his arm around her shoulders, he squeezed her a wee bit closer. Really, he should take his mitts off of Reid's sister. He'd been in this town long enough to know that tongues would be wagging. As soon as word got back to the Steeles, they'd close ranks and expect answers on his intentions.

Which, at the moment, were far from pure.

Micki—the girl who didn't smile a lot—hit him with the trademark all-flash-and-glory Steele smile. That smile morphed her into a combination of Miss Joan, Jonah, and Reid. All in one. He saw bits of each of them in her—Jonah's eyes, Reid's carved face, Miss Joan's nose. When Micki smiled all of it came together in one fantastic package that made the extremely male parts of him roar.

"You're welcome," she said. "It's so odd to see some of these people now."

"Why?"

She shrugged. "I still picture them ten years ago. Cherlyn used to be…" She paused, thought about it a sec. "…softer. The girl next door. I don't see that now."

"From what I hear, she's had a rough few years. Her ex-husband worked her over pretty good. Word is he was abusive."

"That's a shame. But men can be jerks. Present company excluded."

A loud pop sounded—*behind the building*—and sent a warning blast straight to Gage's brain. He whipped around, dragging Micki closer, and an immediate *whoosh* rocked him. The street and the crowd swayed, then did a loop and he held his free hand out.

Focal point.

He locked on the first stationary thing he spotted, the now-lit Christmas tree, and let his overactive brain adjust.

Pop, pop. Pop. Three more went off and Micki gripped his forearm. "It's okay. Firecrackers."

Damned idiot kids. The Christmas tree anchored him and the spinning slowly subsided, but he'd almost fallen over in front of Micki.

He straightened up and forced out a laugh.

Yeah, he'd just blow this off. *Minimize it.* "I'm good," he said. "Moved too fast."

"That happens a lot, huh?"

"Not that much." He nudged his chin toward the tree, ignoring the post-whirl softness in his knees.

"You know," she said, strolling beside him, "I'm working on a software project."

Uh, okay. Could he get *that* lucky with a subject change? "Tell me about it."

"It's been in development for over a year, but I've really put some energy into it these last few months."

"What kind of software?"

"Educational. If I've done it right, it'll help people with ADD to focus."

Slick one. And, no, he hadn't gotten lucky with the subject change. He knew exactly where this was going. "You should ask Jonah about licensing."

"I will. When I finish it. The interesting part is all the research I've done. The brain is a fascinating thing."

Shit.

"I've heard that."

Now she stopped walking and peered up at him. The streetlamp illuminated tiny specks of green in her hazel eyes, giving them an un-Micki softness that caused his body to lock up. Total paralysis.

"I have files and files and files on brain research. In

fact, one of the websites I stumbled onto caught my interest."

"Why's that?"

"It talked about traumatic brain injuries."

To the left of the Christmas tree, the singer Grif had hired was doing a decent job with a Keith Urban song and Gage pulled his eyes from Micki, breaking the way-too-revealing eye contact. He pointed at the singer. "He's pretty good, this guy."

"He is. You have one, don't you? A TBI."

Now what, Ace? Leave it to Micki Steele to come right out and ask him. No one before had. Sure, Reid suspected. You don't spend that much time with a person and not notice changes. The mother of all telltales, at least for Gage, was the speed with which he processed things. The dizzy spells and lack of concentration Gage could, to a certain extent, hide. The processing thing? No chance.

"I don't—"

"Please don't lie to me," she said. "I may keep secrets, but I haven't lied to you. About anything."

She had him there.

Admitting his injury to her, rather than her brother, his employer and more than that, his friend, somehow didn't wash. If he had to admit it to someone, it should be Reid.

His extended silence must have clued her in to his dilemma, because she stepped back and held her hands up. "I'm sorry. I'm getting too personal. I shouldn't assume—"

Before she retreated another step, because Micki Steele, no doubt, was a runner, he wrapped his hand around hers. "I've been up in your business. You're entitled."

She glanced down at their joined hands, then squeezed his. "I didn't mean to pry. I thought, if you *did* have a TBI, maybe you could look at the software and tell me what you think. It's mainly memory exercises, putting things in order, that type of thing."

Man-oh-man. Brilliant. She'd turned this around on him, making it seem like he'd be helping her rather than the other way around.

A Steele to her core.

The singer switched to Little Big Town's "Bring It On Home" and Micki whirled to face him. "Ooh. I love this song."

A couple of teenagers crowded in and she sidestepped, winding up half in front of him, her back brushing against his chest. She peeped over her shoulder at him, those damned green flecks in her eyes once again flashing at him. "Can you see?"

I sure can. "I can see just fine."

The crowd continued to fill in, nudging her closer and even after she'd dinged him with the TBI discussion, he didn't mind. For months, his fear was that the injury had made him less of a man. Made him weak. With Micki, the old Gage, the go-to guy, started to bust free.

Of all the people who actually had the balls to confront him about his injury, it wound up being screwed-up Micki Steele. Go figure.

He stood for a second, listening to the lyrics, thinking about having someone to bring his troubles to. Something he didn't have. Had never had. Instead, everyone brought him their problems, conditioning him to believe that was how it should be.

God. How the hell did that happen? Micki turned and faced him, the front of her body flush against him and pressed way too close for his own personal comfort.

"I love this song," she said.

He grinned. "You said that."

She grinned back. "It's *very* romantic, wouldn't you say?"

"Couldn't agree more."

"Then, maybe you could kiss me?"

CHAPTER ELEVEN

MICKI HAD DONE SOME BOLD things in her lifetime, but begging a man to kiss her might top them all. She'd chalk it up to a mad crush, loneliness, and a newfound sense of freedom. For the first time in her adult life she'd been presented with the opportunity to wander aimlessly and enjoy a man who knew her secrets. Maybe Gage didn't know everything, but he knew enough and he'd invited her out anyway. For that alone, she would always be grateful.

Steele Ridge meant home and a place joyously lacking Phil and his paranoia. His constant watching. Between monitoring her phone bills and having the receptionist and Tomas keep tabs on where she went, Phil had kept her living in a bubble.

For ten years.

It took getting out of that bubble, for even a few days, to realize how invasive it had been. And how isolating.

A corner of Gage's mouth lifted and he dipped his head, hovering just over her lips. "This is probably a mistake."

Of all the mistakes she'd made, this one didn't crack the top fifty.

"Ask me if I care."

In response, he kissed her. Softly at first, testing, letting his warm lips glide over hers, then tentatively brushing his tongue against them. She gripped the front of his jacket, pulling herself closer. If she could crawl into that jacket with him, she'd do it. Just take shelter while she savored every bit of Mr. All-American. She'd experienced a fair number of kisses—some hot with plenty of craziness that landed her in a bed—but this? This *tenderness*, she'd never known. It reached right into her, casting light and warmth and peace. A perfect summer sunrise.

Gage Barber.

Who knew?

One of the milling teenagers bumped her and Gage settled his hands at her waist, holding her steady. Supporting her. From the second he'd walked into her life, he'd been shoring her up, helping her battle the chaos.

He pulled back slightly and dropped another quick kiss on her lips. His arms tightened, holding her against him, and everything inside—the heat, the want, the happy buzz—exploded.

By her own choice, she'd spent years without affection, holding people at bay, never opening up about her life or her job and now...Gage. He'd flipped her thinking in all kinds of ways. Ways that made her want to stay.

Getting lost in that idea wouldn't help her. Who knew where the battle with Phil would end and she couldn't leave her family—and Gage—in the rubble.

For now though, she'd enjoy a connection and some simple fun with someone. She burrowed her hand under his jacket and held on while he kissed the side of her head.

"You okay? You got quiet on me."

Tipping her head up, she nodded. "I'm...peaceful. That's something pretty darned special. So, thank you."

"Don't thank me. It was your brilliant idea. And it wasn't exactly hard labor."

"Micki! Is that you?"

Micki angled back, spotted a woman pushing through

the crowd, her long blond hair falling around her shoulders. Jenny Tichener. Another burst of excitement racked her and she tore away from Gage, bouncing off random strangers as she closed the distance to her childhood friend. They'd been inseparable from seventh grade, but lost touch after high school. When Micki left, she'd left. Nothing went with her. Friendships, mementos, all of it discarded. Emotionally, it had been easier than obsessing over the loss of a happy life obliterated by one night of partying.

"Jenny! Oh my gosh, how are you?"

Jenny launched herself at Micki. "I'm here visiting my parents for the weekend."

The two of them hugged tight enough to crack a rib and Micki's breath whooshed out. Two hugs in less than five minutes. *Home.*

Finally.

Simultaneously, the two women stepped back, each holding on to the other's arms, unwilling to break the contact. "It's so good to see you," Micki said. "Where do you live now?"

"Charlotte. I got married a few years ago. No babies yet, but we're working on it. How about you? Still in Vegas?"

"Yes. Well, no. I'm—wow—coming home."

"That's fantastic! I'm here a lot. We can get together and catch up."

"I'd like that."

She would. After things with Phil settled down, she'd work on getting her life together. Forming friendships. Maybe rekindling old ones while she made new ones.

Friends, like any relationship, created hazards. She'd been too fearful in Vegas. After all, friends talked about themselves, about their jobs, and what could Micki say? *I help my boss threaten people with their secrets.*

Jenny's gaze went to Gage, still standing behind Micki. Along with losing her friends, she'd clearly lost her manners. Her mother would kill her.

She reached back, touched his arm. "Jenny, this is Gage Barber. He's helping my brother with the training center."

Hellos were exchanged and Jenny half covered her lips with one hand. "Hottie," she mouthed.

Gage let loose on a laugh. "Uh, should I leave you two alone?"

Micki grinned up at him. "So we can talk about you? No."

But really, she wanted that. To gossip to a friend about the hot guy who'd just kissed her in the middle of town and—oh, boy—the busybodies at the Triple B would love this one.

Someone called Jenny's name and she gave a backward wave. "I have to go, but give me your number. I'll call you."

"I don't have my new number yet, but give me yours. I'll text you when I get set up. Can you e-mail it to me?"

"Sure."

Micki read off her e-mail address and Jenny sent her number through.

"I'm so glad I ran into you," Jenny said. "I can't wait to catch up and see what you've been doing. You disappeared on me! I've missed you."

And that tore it. Air stalled in her chest and the fierce grip choked her. Too much, too, too much. Kissing Gage, Jenny missing her. All of it. She hugged Jenny again as the wave of emotions hammered at her.

God, she was happy.

"Me too, Jenny. Me too."

Jenny gave her one last squeeze, disappeared into the crowd, and Gage dropped his arm over Micki's shoulder again. "I'm hoping that was a happy hug."

She inhaled long enough to corral her emotions. When she released the breath, the hammering in her head eased and the crazy tension broke apart.

So this was happiness?

"Absolutely."

"Good. And look at you getting all domestic tonight. First you're sucking face with me in the middle of town and now you're making friends."

Feeling playful, another anomaly, she shoved him just as the music stopped. Ten o'clock. Darn it. Novemberfest was officially over. In Vegas, the night would just be starting.

"It's late," she said. "Thank you for an amazing night."

"Thank you for coming with me. I had fun. I'll take you home."

"No."

His head dipped forward. "I'm sorry? You don't want me to take you?"

Don't screw this up.

"I do, but—" She waved a hand down the block. "If Evie is still at Brynne's shop, I'd like to ride home with her. I have a lot of lost time to catch up on with my sister."

"Ah," he said. "I thought I misread something there."

"Not a chance, Captain America."

"Good. But with everything going on, I'll follow you home. Make sure you get there okay. Please, don't argue. Humor me."

The babysitting thing irritated her. Absolutely. This was different, though. Having a man, this man, care enough to worry about her, to want to keep her safe, couldn't be bad.

He walked her to the shop where Brynne and Evie stood by the desk. The door was locked, but Micki knocked and Evie opened the door for her.

"Hi. Hi, Gage."

"Hey, Evie."

"Can I hitch a ride home with you?"

Evie eyed her, then Gage. "Sure."

"Okay, ladies, I'll say good night then. You two be careful. And Micki?"

"Yes?"

"Maybe tomorrow you could stop by my office with that software."

On Sunday morning Gage did his normal coffee run to the Triple B. Having just beat the church crowd, he snagged a corner table before Randi was forced to deal with overflow and open the connecting door to the bar.

If Gage had timed this right, in the next five minutes the activity level in the B would explode and he'd already have his spot.

He shifted the chairs, propping one against the wall before dropping into it. Life in Special Forces meant having a view of his surroundings, and those habits died hard. Plus, it never hurt to be cautious when some buttcrack terrorist or deranged psycho could slice and dice a man before he had time to get out of the chair.

Even in Steele Ridge.

Following his routine, he arranged his coffee and cinnamon roll to his right and spread the newspaper in front of him. As a kid, he'd watched his father read the daily newspaper. Every day. Three newspapers. For at least two hours. The man was a news junkie, but didn't go for television. He wanted it the old-fashioned way, with the written word.

Somewhere along the way, Gage had also developed an affinity for newspapers. Or maybe it was the tradition of it, the childhood memories of waking up and finding Dad at the table.

Whatever it was, he reserved Sunday mornings for reading the newspaper. Cover to cover.

The bells on the door jangled and he glanced up to see feisty Mr. Greene, a widower older than dirt, entering the shop. The man walked into town every morning for breakfast and to catch up on the day's gossip. If you wanted a direct pipeline to town drama, Mr. Greene was the man.

"Morning, Gage," the old man called.

He lifted his cane in greeting, nearly whacking a customer along the way, and Gage stifled a laugh.

"Morning, sir."

Gage eyed the cane, but had learned not to offer assistance. He'd tried that his first morning at the B and got smacked with said cane for his efforts. Mr. Greene preferred taking care of himself. Gage could relate.

"Nice day out there today," Mr. Greene said.

"Sure is."

"I heard tell that you and Micki Steele were carrying on last night."

And it begins. Hell, he hadn't even sipped his coffee yet. He'd expected it. Of course, he did. You didn't stand in the middle of Main Street kissing a woman known for her secrecy, a Steele no less, and not anticipate questions. A Micki sighting alone got Steele Ridge buzzing. Throw in her swapping spit with her brother's friend and it racked up to a good story.

From behind the counter, Randi, the owner of the Triple B and Britt Steele's significant other, eyed Gage for half a second, her lips dipping into a frown before she shook her head at the old man. "Starting already, Mr. Greene?"

"I'll call 'em like I see 'em, girlie." He shifted back to Gage. "Well?"

Gage grinned. "Well what, sir?"

"You want to tell me what's got everyone talking around here so early? And on the Lord's day no less!"

"Nope," Gage said.

He'd grown up in a small town, understood the intricacies of information flow. All he needed to do was shove a piece of dynamite somewhere to disrupt it.

In this case, the dynamite would be his absolute refusal to comment. And if Mr. Greene, the town crier, didn't have any intel, the clamor would die down.

Gage hoped.

Because in two hours he had to face his bosses. Both of whom were Micki's brothers. And by the way Randi had looked at him, he had no doubt Britt would be paying him a visit.

Shit. Should have thought with the proper brain last night. *Done now.* Wasting time stressing over it wouldn't help.

Mr. Greene shuffled by on his way to the next empty table and swatted Gage's chair with his cane. This town. These people. Too funny.

The bells jangled again, but if Gage wanted to get through the newspaper in his allotted two hours, he couldn't be looking up every time someone walked into the shop.

Instead, he focused on the article in front of him about the president's budget woes. What else was new? He scanned the article, the words blurring as he lost focus. What was that about national defense? He started over, this time not skimming. Slowly, he read each word, giving his brain the opportunity to absorb it. At this rate, he'd only get through main news, but if he could remember most of what he'd read, he'd consider it a win.

The empty chair beside him moved and he brought his gaze up. He found a dark-haired man wearing crisp jeans and a black-collared shirt dropping next to him.

What the hell?

But the guy looked familiar. Up close, his brown eyes screamed of…hardness. No warmth, no humor, no nothing.

Douchebag from the bar Friday night. Tomas. The guy whose phone Micki blew up.

Gage sat back, rested both hands on his thighs in case he needed them in a hurry.

"Good morning," Tomas said, his voice all kinds of friendly.

His eyes told the real story. This guy had blackness inside. An empty, dark well.

"Help you?"

He set an accordion folder on top of Gage's newspaper, blocking the article he'd been reading. For that alone he should kick his ass.

Tomas glanced over at Mr. Greene, then drew closer to Gage. "You know who I am?"

"I do. You should leave town."

"Not without her."

"Then we have a problem because she's not going anywhere. Whatever Phil Flynn wants, he's not getting."

Tomas offered up a pitying smile. The one where people looked at you like the fool you were. "Always the hero, aren't you?"

Bait. Dangling right there for Gage to take. Which he wouldn't. Why let this guy see him rattled? He sat, hands on his thighs, body still, facial features frozen.

"I get it," Tomas said. "Believe me. I saw you two last night."

Ah, shit. That kiss was creating all sorts of issues. "You didn't bother to say hello? How rude."

Tomas snorted and gave the expanding crowd in the shop a swooping scan. "You were *busy.* What's it like? To stick your tongue in that mouth?"

Gage didn't bother reacting.

"But hey, I don't blame you for wanting a piece of that. She's an attractive girl. And she's got those long legs. Imagine those wrapped around you? I sit ten feet from her every day and I think about it. Every. Day. For me, she's perfect. You? She's not the apple-pie type."

Bait. Bait. Bait. If Gage blew his stack, Tomas would win. And Gage didn't like to lose.

He rested his elbows on the table. Made direct eye contact. "You need to leave town. Don't make me say it again."

"Everything all right over there?" Mr. Greene asked.

Keeping his eyes on Tomas, Gage gave Mr. Greene a backhanded wave. "Fine, sir. My friend here was just leaving."

The old man picked up his cane, rapped it against the leg of the table. "Good. We're not big on strangers around here."

Which wasn't true, but Mr. Greene hadn't lived this long without learning a few things. Like pegging people who stank of bad news.

Tomas angled sideways, peeped around Gage to the old man. If he made a move, Gage would drop him. No question. As much as he refused to let this guy wind him up, old men were off-limits.

But Tomas only shrugged. Good thing. With the church crowd filing in, Gage wasn't in the mood to tear the place up. Plus he'd have to answer to Randi and then Britt, and that would surely suck.

Tomas stood, plucked a piece of lint off his shirt, held it in front of his face, and dropped it on Gage's newspaper.

This guy. Before the mess with Micki was done, Gage, TBI or not, would pummel him. Now wasn't the time. Later, though, he'd *own* him.

When Gage refused to acknowledge the taunt, Tomas tapped the folder. "Go through this. There are things you'll want to see."

CHAPTER TWELVE

MICKI SAT ON HER BED, laptop in front of her, while a light breeze slipped through the partially open French doors. When she'd woken up, she'd cracked the door, then hustled back to bed, snuggling under the covers for an extra few minutes while she fantasized about Gage slipping into bed with her.

Before long, the chilly air—and lack of hunky man—drove her from bed and into the shower. A hot shower because, as sexually frustrated as she was, a cold one wouldn't do.

Now, an hour later, she busied herself searching for a remote back door into Phil's office network. The one he constantly moved important files from and hid. If she found the back door, she'd get in and search for the files, adding them to the small stash of documents she kept as her insurance policy.

Her ajar bedroom door slowly came all the way open and she looked up, hoping to find Jonah. After her evening with Gage, she supposed it was time to clue her twin in on why she'd stayed with Phil for so long. She wouldn't give him the whole of it, but it involved him, and now that she'd made the decision to stay, he'd better get a lawyer. Only Jonah had gotten up early and headed out somewhere while she was in the shower.

Now she found Reid casually leaning against the doorframe.

Her brother's taut cheeks and pressed-tight mouth indicated he wasn't a happy camper.

"Good morning," she said. "You're here early."

Her brother seemed to spend more time in town with Brynne than in the bunkhouse he'd apparently claimed as his own. If he didn't plan on occupying it, she might want to move in there herself.

How things had changed in two days. Friday she'd shown up here ready to run. Now she pondered a turf war over a bunkhouse.

"Gage Barber," he said.

Alrighty then. Lovely greeting. Micki went back to her laptop, checking the scan currently running on Phil's server. "What about him?"

"I was just in town and talked to Bonnie Traughber."

"I don't know Bonnie Traughber."

"Bonnie talked to Danielle Santori."

Who the hell were these people? "I don't know her either."

"And Danielle talked to Cherlyn."

Uh-oh. Micki kept her eyes glued to her laptop. Dang it, she might need to tweak that code.

"Cherlyn told Danielle she saw you and Suds last night."

She saw us, all right. She waggled a hand at Reid. "She has a thing for Gage. I was helping him *discourage* her."

"Un-huh. Cherlyn mentioned that to Danielle."

Apparently Reid wasn't taking the hint that she was busy. "It's not a big deal. He put his arm around me to try and dissuade her. That's all."

Except for the smooching part.

Reid made snoring noises. "Nice try. Danielle told Bonnie she saw the two of you getting busy by the tree."

"Getting busy? Really?"

"Whatever."

Micki sighed and went back to her laptop. "It was a moment. Don't get your shorts in a twist."

"My shorts aren't *in* a twist. Gage is a good guy."

Well, that hadn't taken long. So much for giving her a chance. "And he's too good for me. Is that what you're saying?"

"Screw you. That's not what I meant. I wouldn't say—or think—that. He's my friend. He works for Jonah and me. Our new business that Jonah sunk a boatload of his billionaire cash into. *If* you're picking up what I'm putting down."

Now they were getting to the reason for this visit. Micki, in her brother's opinion, brought drama. Of course, the fact that she was trying a hack right in front of him only attested to that.

"It won't be an issue," she said.

"I don't want to be a dick about this."

"Yeah, you do."

"Look, he's been through a lot this last year. He got injured last spring. Shot by a villager in Mozambique. Damned near bled out."

She tried to picture it. Handsome Gage Barber on a stretcher, blood pouring from his body. But God, she didn't want to think about that. The injury, though, might explain the dizzy spells. "Was it a head injury?"

Reid eyed her. "No. Torso. But he hit his head when he fell. Got knocked out for twenty or thirty minutes. He's done a ton of rehab and he's back on his feet. I don't want him distracted. And I sure as shit don't want to see either of you hurt."

"*You* don't want? What about what he wants? Or what I want?"

"Whatever, Mikayla. You know what I mean."

Yes. She did. As always, her brother in alpha mode, being the master protector.

"I have no intention of hurting Gage. This might shock you, but I actually like the guy. Now, with all due respect, leave me alone and don't talk to me about this again. It's not your business."

He poked a finger at her. "Don't fuck this up."

Gage cut the turn into Tupelo Hill too damned sharp and the back end of his SUV fishtailed, almost slamming the post at the end of the driveway. He let up on the gas pedal, continuing at half-storming speed until he swung into the gravel lot in front of the training center.

He parked and grabbed the stupid fucking folder he didn't want to stupid fucking look at. Goddammit, he did *not* want to be in the middle of Steele family drama.

He'd been so good. For months. Just minding his own flipping business. Now? Not even ten a.m. and he had a headache.

What he needed was an ibuprofen—maybe the whole bottle—and Reid, for once in his life, to be quiet. No talking now. To anyone.

He'd read the stupid fucking file, assess the damage, and strategize. Read, assess, plan. A function with no emotional involvement.

No sweat.

If anything he read needed to be passed to Reid, he'd do it and remove himself. Or maybe talk to Micki first. Did he owe her that after the time they'd spent together? Where his loyalty should lie here, he didn't have an effing clue.

Just hell.

He checked the building entrance. Locked. Good. That meant no Reid. He tended not to lock the door behind him, but Gage would double-check before he opened this file. No sense in risking Reid busting in on him when his sister's nasty secrets were spilled out on his desk.

"Reid?" His voice echoed through the empty lobby,

bouncing off the walls and jabbing at his already pounding head.

All that echoing reminded him he needed to check on the furniture delivery for the reception area. He pulled his phone, typed in a quick note so he wouldn't forget.

"You here?" he called again, louder this time.

No answer.

Good. Chances were, if Reid was on the property, his spidey sense would tingle and as soon as he saw Gage's car, he'd wander in.

Gage needed to work quick.

He hustled into his office and tossed the folder on his desk. Without bothering to ditch his jacket, he shoved the three neat stacks requiring his attention to the side and fanned the folder's contents out. Mostly e-mails. Some photos of people he didn't know.

A thumb drive.

Those little bastards he hated. Thumb drives *always* contained potentially devastating information.

He sat back, ran his hands over the top of his head. Scrubbing enough to feel the irritation. He should forget about this file. Shove it all back into the folder and burn it. Whatever was in there was Micki's past. Her business. Not his.

But there was a reason Tomas gave this to him. Maybe he knew enough about Steele loyalty to anticipate they'd tell him to shove it up his ass. They'd protect their sister. Even if they didn't know what to think of her, down deep, they loved her. They were family.

Gage wasn't.

Given that nonbiological connection, Gage had the capacity to see beyond the emotional warfare.

And that's what Flynn was betting on.

Gage picked up the thumb drive, squeezed his fingers over it.

Don't.

Curiosity, though, was a persistent bitch. Particularly

for a guy who had built a military career on finding answers in the most minute details.

He swiveled his chair to the credenza and grabbed the cheap laptop he'd bought a few months back. Nothing personal had ever been entered on it and he'd never logged on to the Internet. Completely clean.

This laptop he used for documents he didn't trust.

Thumb drives included. Chances were, Tomas, given that Micki had most likely blown up his phone, wanted a little revenge. Revenge that came by unleashing a virus on the Steeles' network.

Plugging the potential minefield in, he fired up the laptop. Waited for it to blow.

Nothing. No burst screaming "surprise!" or exclamation point-laden warnings from his virus protection.

He typed in his password, waited for the spinning wheel to stop, and clicked on the thumb drive's folder.

A video.

"Shit."

He sat back, his fingers lightly tapping the edge of the keyboard. Did he really want to see this?

No.

Absolutely not. It sure as hell wouldn't be good. And…what if it was a sex tape or something twisted? Of Micki.

With this schmuck Tomas.

Or anyone, for that matter. He sat for a few seconds, weighing the options. After that kiss last night, the time they'd spent together, he wanted to trust her and help her build a life with her family. If that's what she truly wanted.

Who the hell was he kidding? His intentions weren't pure in all this. As much as he wanted to help her, he also wanted in her pants. All night he'd been distracted with thoughts of her. Under him, on top of him.

On her knees.

Goddammit.

He clicked the folder.

A grainy image popped up. Micki rushing from an office, waving one hand. Gage sat back, closed his eyes for half a second. He should stop. Just not look. Sex tape or not, Tomas wouldn't have given him this video if it were irrelevant. Tomas totally played him. And Gage let him.

"We'll get this woman." Micki's voice streamed from the computer. "I'm done messing around."

Gage opened his eyes.

On the video, Tomas rose from his desk, walked toward her. "Whatcha got?"

She dropped into a desk chair and banged away at a keyboard. "Yesterday I saw a bunch of charges from a pharmacy. Something is up with her. I got into the pharmacy records last night, but stopped. Now we're going for it."

"Don't get caught."

"I won't. I swiped one of the employees' passwords. Once I get in, I'll be able to see every prescription she fills."

"You are good," Tomas said.

The video went silent for a few seconds while Gage watched, transfixed, as a determined Micki hacked into a pharmacy's system. Jesus. Hacking, in Gage's world, was nothing new. In his mind, military operations were exempt from judgment. Watching Micki do it? Some reality he didn't need to see.

"I'm in," she said. "And look at that."

"What?"

"Oxy." Micki sat back, high-fived Tomas. "We've got her. She's going down."

The video ended and Gage sat forward. Not a sex tape at least, but it didn't play to Micki's virtue either.

He pressed his palms against his eye sockets and forced his thoughts to order. *One thing at a time here.*

Logic and control.

Gage shoved the laptop aside and moved on to the

documents still spread on his desk. E-mails to Phil Flynn. From Micki.

He skimmed them. Something about a custody battle. A local politician and his wife divorcing. Drug dependency. Unfit mother.

And—wait—a court transcript.

Criminal court.

He read the name of the defendant, checked the e-mails. The wife. Guilty of drug possession and child endangerment. Two-year sentence.

Yesterday, Micki had sworn, damned aggressively, she didn't get involved in the "ugly" stuff.

Sure as hell looked ugly.

The chime of the security alarm shattered the silence.

"Hello? Gage?"

Micki.

Quickly, he gathered up the pages, ready to shove them back into the folder. *Wait.* Now that he'd seen this and after last night—the kiss they'd shared, her suspicions about the TBI and his reluctance to deny it— he wanted answers. For no other reason than to know if he could trust her.

The woman he'd shared his deepest secret with.

A sharp blast of pain stabbed at the back of his eyes, and his stomach flipped. All this time, he'd been so careful, not confiding in anyone. Anyone. And now...

He set the pages back on the desk. "My office," he yelled back.

A minute later she appeared in the doorway wearing the same zippered jacket that wasn't nearly warm enough, a pair of stretchy leggings, and a fitted black shirt that hugged her lean torso. Her hair was poker straight today and a silver skull ring flashed under the glare of the overhead light.

In her arms she held a laptop. The software. He'd told her to come by and show him the program she'd designed.

Jesus, Gage. You screwed the pooch on this one.

"Hi," she said.

He locked his jaw and sat back, his movements tight. Stilted. The guys had always loved playing cards with him. His inability to present a poker face made him a sucker.

It seemed, by the way she cocked her head, Micki had figured that out. "You look mad—or something."

Stay calm. Logic and control. He wouldn't accuse. Not yet. "Or something."

Her gaze shot to the papers strewn across the desk. It took five seconds, at least, for her to face him again with that same hard-edged defiance he'd witnessed at their family meeting.

Micki Steele, whatever her secrets, was made of solid brick.

"What is it?"

"I had a visitor this morning." He gestured to his laptop. "Your friend Tomas. He isn't playing anymore."

From the middle of Gage's office, Micki contemplated the door. She could turn and walk out. Just leave whatever this was behind.

Whatever he'd been reading had irritated him. She saw it in the harsh angles of his perfect, honorable face and the glare in his eyes. All the heat—the longing—from that moment before he kissed her last night was now gone, replaced by a cold intensity that sent a shiver crawling along her arms.

Two hours ago she'd been fantasizing about this man. About making love to him on lazy Sunday mornings or dinner-and-a-movie dates. All those things normal couples with normal lives do. How, after the life she'd led, did she think normal could exist?

The door beckoned and she forced herself to be still. To not look back.

To not run.

Gage whirled the laptop toward her and poked the keyboard. "Take a look. It's a video."

The minute it went live, even before she heard, "We'll get this woman," she knew what it was. Remembered as if it were only yesterday, when, in fact, it had been years ago. Back when she'd still been young. Impressionable. *Moldable.*

She didn't speak or look at Gage. Couldn't. Not yet. She simply watched, tapping into her emotions from that day and her anger toward the woman who'd wasted her chance at being the kind, loving, protective mother Micki had left behind.

"You can turn it off," she said.

Gage studied her as if she were some bizarre lab experiment.

She rolled her shoulders, willing the growing knot there to disappear. "What?"

"I should be asking you that. You're the one who told your family you didn't get into the ugly stuff."

"Yes. But…"

"Jesus, Micki."

"She neglected her children!"

"She went to jail!"

That stopped her cold. She'd known about the jail sentence. Remembered it so clearly. Remembered the horror of overhearing Phil celebrating the big win.

It had been the first time, in her young mind anyway, she'd consciously confronted her own involvement. "I thought…"

He waited for her to continue and then tossed up his hands. "What? How can you possibly defend this?"

"I *thought* she was an abusive drug addict. Did you watch *that* part?"

"What part?"

Oh, Phil, you sneaky bastard. Standing there, in the dead center of Gage's office, she was caught. Stuck between two worlds. One where a foolish, loyal part of her had trusted Phil and the other, the new one that loomed just out of her reach and included a life with her family.

Sneaky, sneaky bastard. Later, she'd deal with her emotions. The betrayal.

"The part," she forced the wobble from her voice, "right before I came out of the office. Where Phil *told* me she was an abusive drug addict. You didn't see that part, did you?"

Gage went silent.

Unable to stop herself, she hit play again, let Phil's vindictiveness take hold. Let it really sink in. She laughed, but it came out as a sarcastic scoff.

Bastard. She waved one hand. "They clipped the video. That's not all of it."

"What's the rest?"

At least he had the decency to let her explain. Whether he'd believe her or not, they'd see.

"There was a part of me, a tiny little part, that wanted to believe Phil had a good heart. After all, he'd taken care of me for two years, set me up in a place to live, paid for my college courses, let me join his family parties so I wouldn't miss my own home too much. He was good. A total ace. Groomed me beautifully." She pointed to the laptop. "On *that* day, he'd called me into his office. He told me we had a client going through a nasty divorce. The wife was addicted to prescription meds and abusing their kids. For the children, he'd said, we had to prove the woman was an addict."

Gage pulled a face. "You took his word for it? Seriously?"

"Don't even look at me like that. Believe me, I've killed myself a hundred times over it. At the time, he knew exactly which buttons to push on me. He knew I had an exceptional mother. One that I missed." She gritted her teeth, bit back anger that tore at her throat. "He put his finger on that button and pressed and pressed and pressed. By the time he was done, as you can see by how hyped I was, he'd convinced me to get her pharmacy records. That's all I did. The pharmacy."

"Then how did she wind up in jail?"

"That's the horrifying part. Two years after this video was taken, I came back to the office after hours. I'd forgotten something in my desk. Phil and another guy I didn't know were there. They'd been slamming whiskey and were so drunk, they didn't hear me come in. God, they were wasted. Just carrying on about what a great team they were. How unstoppable. I was about to call out because I knew Phil had the place wired and I didn't want him thinking I was spying. Before I could say anything, that case came up. They were laughing and laughing and *laughing* about what they'd done."

Gage leaned in on his elbows, craning his neck. "I don't understand."

Of course he didn't. Neither had she.

"I gave Phil the pharmacy records."

Gage held up a stack of papers. "I have your e-mails."

"Yes. We talked about her being an unfit mother. That was it. I didn't e-mail the pharmacy records. I handed him hard copies. That was all I did. I swear to you. All the records showed was that she'd had a prescription for Oxy filled the year prior. A thirty-day supply. That was it."

"Then how did this woman wind up in jail for drug possession?"

"They set her up. Phil got one of his snitches to get him a bunch of black market Oxy. They put it in a brown paper bag, broke into her house and hid the bag. Then they told the husband where they hid it. The husband was a local politician and practically gave the cops a map. Suddenly, their juicy divorce became a criminal case because, at the very least, she was hiding a huge stash that made it look like she'd been dealing."

"You didn't say anything?"

Mr. All-American needed to get a grip on reality. He

wanted a twenty-two-year-old hiding secrets to go against Phil Flynn?

The man would have crushed her.

And her family.

"The case was two years old. She was out of jail by then. What was I supposed to do? Go to the police? The ones Phil has in his pocket? I couldn't do that."

"It was your chance to bring heat on him. To get away."

He didn't believe her. She could see it on his face. The narrow-eyed skepticism. No matter what she said, he'd still have doubts.

And she didn't want that.

She wanted him to look at her the way he had the night before. With hunger and want and…respect.

"Um, Gage? You might have noticed, me getting away from Phil isn't so easy."

Gage sat back and scrubbed both hands over his face. His attraction to Micki was fogging his brain. Smart Gage, the one who didn't fall for anyone's bullshit, would hand over all the documents and the thumb drive and walk her to the door. *Bye-bye, Trouble.*

He'd never been a fool or an enabler and he had no interest in starting. And yet, he hadn't shown Micki to the door.

Thinking with his dick, that's why.

She stood on the other side of his desk in that same spot, completely still except for a glance or two at the door. Ready to run. The squirrel factor with this girl was undeniable.

"I can see you don't trust me," she said.

Trust? Really? After this, he didn't know what to believe. "With what you have on this guy, you could expose him. The feds would eat him alive. Wiretapping alone would get the job done. Why won't you turn him in?"

"I can't talk about it."

Of course she couldn't. No wonder her family didn't understand her.

He shoved the stack of e-mails into the folder, ejected the thumb drive, and handed it all over. "Take this."

Her brows drew together, but she made no move for the folder. "You're not..."

"Handing it to your family? No. It's your business. I'm not the middleman. Get your shit together."

"Hey!"

Blood pressure kicking, he slapped the folder on his desk. "Tell me I'm wrong. This guy followed you to North Carolina. He's not going away. And every plan you've had so far has backfired. Spectacularly. Tell me, Micki, how am I supposed to help you if you won't be straight with me? With anyone!"

And holy shit he was *screaming*. When was the last time he'd hollered at someone like that? Years probably. Cool, calm Gage who never lost his temper was coming unglued. Excellent.

"Whoa," Reid said from the doorway, his eyes locked on him in the predatory way that meant he was about to kick some ass.

Shit. He'd missed the door chime. What a shocker, with the way he'd been hollering.

"Why the hell are you tearing into my sister?"

Micki spun back and faced Reid. "He's not tearing into me. We're talking."

"Mikayla, Suds doesn't raise his voice. I know when he's screaming."

The telltale folder still sat on the desk. A damned nuclear bomb ready to go off.

Gage could make it happen. Force Micki to come clean and allow her family to help her.

By showing Reid the file.

He reached for the folder, set his hand on it. For her

own good, he should. Before she fucked this thing up even more. The ramifications of that, without him knowing what kept this girl hostage, could devastate the Steeles. Something he wanted to avoid.

Reid broke eye contact with Micki and slid his gaze to Gage's hand on top of the folder. "What's that?"

Now or never. All of this could be over. Micki whipped back, color seeping from her cheeks, and a muscle in her jaw pulsed. Her pleading eyes though, they were the killer.

Don't. Gage picked up the folder, shoved it in a drawer. "Personal paperwork I need to deal with."

Reid angled his head to Micki. "You two gonna tell me what's going on?"

"Gage was asking me about Phil. I don't want to talk about it."

Finally moving, she pushed by Reid, who latched on to her jacket. "Where are you going?"

"Back to Mom's. I want some quiet."

"Don't disappear."

Good luck with that.

Still stewing over her conversation with Gage, Micki sat on her bed overseeing a scan of Phil's network for any available port she might sneak in through. Her mind wandered to the building just down the road.

To Gage.

And that blasted folder.

Rather than hand over the evidence, he'd hidden it from Reid. Something he clearly had issues with, yet...he'd protected her.

Most likely because he harbored his own secret. One Reid, who'd given him a job—an important job— wouldn't be happy about.

Micki and Gage. Two secretive liars.

She picked up her phone, checked her texts. Nothing. Even the house had gone silent. And where the hell had Jonah been when she'd finally raked up the courage to tell him, after all this time, what was going on with Phil?

A knock sounded. Probably Mom. "Come in, Mom."

The door swung open and Gage stood there, his perfect posture in place, his blond hair a little rumpled from the wind, and Micki's heart did a *whump, whump*. Even when mad she couldn't resist the pull of him.

In his hand he held what looked like the folder containing her telltale e-mails.

She sat taller and pushed her shoulders back. "Hi. Sorry. Thought you were my mom. Come in."

He gestured to the door. "Can I close this?"

"Sure. Jonah's not here. It's just Mom and I."

"I know. She was out on the porch when I came in." He held up the file. "I came to give you this."

He moved closer, that long body of his filling the space in the room, his presence alone giving comfort when just seconds before the isolation, the return to her own pathetic brand of normalcy, had offered that same calm.

Carefully, as if it was capable of inflicting great damage, he set the folder on the bed. He made a move to step away, but she grabbed his wrist and held on. The heat of his skin poured into her and her mind hissed.

You don't deserve him.

What else was new? "Thank you."

"It's yours. You should have it."

"Not for that. For not…telling."

He met her gaze and held it. "We all have secrets, don't we?"

"I suppose." She patted the bed. "Please sit."

When he took her up on it, she nodded. "You were right. Phil has something on me. I don't know what to do about it, but I've been living with it. I've been alone because of it."

"So talk to me. Talk to anyone in this house. Let us help you."

She nodded. It all sounded so easy. "I know I have to. Coming here made me realize what I've been missing. And last night, with you? It felt so good. You really have no idea." She stopped, let out a sigh. "Will you help me?"

"With what?"

"I need to tell my family everything. But I'm scared. And tired and...I don't want to live like this anymore."

There. She'd said it. Finally. After all this time, she'd finally admitted how vulnerable she felt.

He pulled out of her grasp and hauled her onto his lap. He met her eyes for a few long seconds, that intense crystal-blue gaze paralyzing her before it drifted lower, to her lips, making her yearn for things she shouldn't yearn for.

She wiggled closer, felt the growing bulge under her butt cheek and oh wow. He wanted her.

Someone *wanted* her.

She looped one arm around his neck, pressed her breasts into him and buried her head in his shoulder.

"Dang it," he said, "I don't know what to do with you."

She wiggled her butt to let him know she was on to him. "I could think of a couple of things. I mean, if you're really stumped."

His chest rumbled with a low laugh and he tipped her backward, kissing her softly. A gentle brush of his lips before angling his body over hers on the bed. "Your mother is downstairs."

"You said she's on the porch."

"Still disrespectful. Your family has been good to me. Besides, I'm not interested in a quickie. I'd like to take my time with you." He grinned down at her. "Let's get out of here for a while and figure out what you need to do. We'll go to my place."

His place. She'd like that. Very much. She arched her hips, felt the pressure of his erection. Oh, she wanted that bad boy inside her. Too long she'd been alone.

"Micki!" Mom yelled from downstairs.

Gage hopped off the bed like he'd been zapped with a prod.

"Jesus," he said, "I feel like I'm fifteen again."

The two of them laughed and Micki rolled to her feet, smacked him on the butt, and opened her bedroom door. "What is it, Mom?"

"You have a visitor," Mom said from the bottom of the stairs. "Your boss is here!"

CHAPTER THIRTEEN

MICKI LEFT GAGE STANDING IN her bedroom and tore down the steps. She hit the bottom with her heart slamming and her head whirling.

Phil here.

No doubt to bring her back.

She swung around the bannister and spotted her mother returning to the kitchen. Phil's quiet laugh followed.

Sweat poured down her back as she whipped through the hallway into the kitchen. Just ahead, Phil sat at the giant farm table looking totally out of place in his suit and perfectly gelled salt-and-pepper hair, drinking something—probably tea, knowing him—out of one of her mother's delicate cups.

A squeaking floorboard alerted him to her presence and he turned, his lips spreading into a wide, welcoming, aw-I-missed-you smile, but the truth was in his eyes.

Cold eyes the color of a stormy night sky that somehow burned right into her. Quaking limbs slowed her pace, but she kept moving. *Buck up, here. Don't let him control this.*

From behind, a gentle hand landed on her back and she yelped. She spun back, found Gage on her heels.

"Gage," Mom said, "I thought you were gone."

"No, ma'am. I was talking to Micki."

"Well, sit down. Let me make you something to eat."

He held up his hand. "No need. Thank you."

Phil eyed Gage and stood, holding his arms wide for Micki. She pasted on a smile and rather than get into anything in front of Mom, took the coward's way out and stepped into a stiff embrace.

Phil brought his lips to her ear. "Don't fuck with me," he whispered, his voice tinged with that threatening tone reserved for shakedowns. "I know what you're doing. You'll never get in. Trust me."

Obviously, he knew—or assumed—she'd been poking around on his network. Looking for more evidence she could use against him. *Buck up.*

Her territory now. Too bad all the boys weren't present, but Gage was. And from the way he leaned on the kitchen counter, he wasn't going anywhere.

Micki slid out of Phil's hold and smiled brightly. "How was Mexico?"

"Enlightening," he said.

His gaze drifted to Gage, who stepped forward, hand held out. "Gage Barber."

He stood a good four inches taller than Phil and with that rigid military I-own-you posture firmly in place, Micki sensed a power shift.

Or maybe she wanted to believe that.

Phil shook his hand and nodded. "Phil Flynn."

"I know," Gage said.

Oh, boy.

Gage went back to his spot at the counter, folding his arms over his chest.

Sensing the tension, Mom swung her head between them. "Uh, can I get anyone anything?"

"No, Mom. Thank you."

"Your mother," Phil said, "was just telling me how you liked to bake when you were younger. I never knew that."

Because you never asked.

"Yes," Micki said. "She taught me. I've gotten away

from it over the years." She looked back at her mom. "Maybe it's time to start again."

"That would be great. I've always enjoyed home-baked goods. You'd have a most appreciative boss if you were to bring cookies to the office. I was just saying how much we miss you when you're gone."

He angled his head, waiting for the response he'd conditioned her to give. The one that would have her leaping from her chair to accompany him back to Vegas.

Behind her, Gage cleared his throat and they all looked at him. Just the sight of him fired something inside her. She had work to do with him. Trust to earn back. And if she left with Phil, Gage would know she was a liar. A woman who could work for a man like Phil and put innocent people in prison.

No. She wouldn't be that person anymore. Couldn't do it. All of it needed to stop.

"Mom, would you mind giving me a second with Phil?"

"Of course," Mom said. "I have clothes to fold anyway. Y'all let me know if you need anything."

"Thanks."

Mom left the kitchen, marching down the long hallway to her bedroom, where she closed the door behind her, the latch clunking.

Now or never.

Micki took three steps backward and leaned on the counter, next to Gage, propping both hands on the edge.

My territory.

Phil's oily gaze slid to Gage. Clearly he wanted him gone.

She glanced at Captain America and his icy blue gaze. *He's not going anywhere.* Sure as she was clutching the counter, barely hanging on, he wouldn't leave her.

"Gage is staying," she said.

"Huh. You've always been"—Phil waved one hand and stared up at the ceiling, searching for the words—"protective of your privacy."

Well, not anymore.

"I'm not coming back to Vegas. I miss my family. I want to be here."

"That won't work."

"Sure it will."

Her boss went silent. He didn't need to speak. The look in his eyes, that hateful, harsh stare she'd seen leveled on others, bore into her.

Don't give in.

"All right," he said, "here's what we'll do. It's the weekend. I'll give you the rest of the day alone. Let you think long and hard about what you're doing. Perhaps being with your family has clouded your judgment. Understandable."

"I don't need any more time. I'm quitting."

Gage gave up leaning against the counter and stood tall. "Sounds to me like she's decided. I'll show you out."

She'd worked for this man for ten years. Knowing his personality and how he'd react to her attempts to back him off, she also knew that he wouldn't give up so easily. And he certainly wouldn't be ushered out. Not in this lifetime.

Without moving from his seat, he locked his gaze on Micki. "I trust you received my e-mail?"

The one with the video of Jonah. Oh, she'd received it. "I did. I trust *you* received mine?"

He made a sickening *tsk, tsk, tsk* noise, shaking his head the whole while. "I thought better of you, Micki."

God, she needed him out. She turned to Gage. The hero.

If he had questions, he didn't show it. His demeanor, the determined, stiff-spined stance hadn't changed since Mom had walked out. Phil wanted to rattle him and for once, he didn't get what he wanted.

Micki's heart soared, shoring her up for a battle she would never win.

But Gage had stuck with her, offering his silent support. She so didn't deserve him. In any capacity.

"I'm done, Phil. Whatever you've got, bring it on. I'm not eighteen anymore and neither is Jonah."

Just as Gage was about to bust Phil Flynn's ass from the house, the back door blasted open.

"You're batshit crazy," Reid said to a following Jonah, the two of them too caught up in the argument of the day to notice their visitor.

Reid's instincts must have kicked in because he halted. Stopped cold right there, his eyes shooting to Gage, then to Micki. He got to the man sitting at the table, and the tension level in the room shot into the red.

No introductions necessary here.

"What the hell's this?" Reid wanted to know.

"Ah," Phil said, pointing at Jonah. "The rapist is here."

What the——?

All at once the room exploded and Jonah reached for Phil, grabbing his fancy shirt and hauling him to his feet. "Watch your mouth, asshole."

Gage stepped in, inserting himself between Jonah and his target. "Take it easy." He shoved Jonah back, forcing him to let go of Flynn's shirt. "Don't give this prick a reason to slap you with an assault charge. That's what he wants."

But Jonah was gone, his mind still focused on the insult. Gage gripped his T-shirt and held on. "*Don't* give in."

Jonah snapped to attention. Assuming he'd reined in his temper, Gage let go.

"Get out," Micki said, her voice like jagged glass. "Right now."

The man's way of life, his street smarts alone, would dictate he should follow Micki's advice and leave. No matter how good a fighter, he was still faced with three men, all bigger and younger by twenty years and two of them former Green Berets.

If he wanted to, Gage could have the asshole down in less than two seconds.

And Flynn knew it.

"I'll go," he said. "But I'm flying home tomorrow and expecting you to be with me."

Doing his best to control his need to kick the crap out of Phil Flynn, Gage walked him to the door. As long as he went peacefully, Gage didn't see any need to amp this situation up. Besides, Miss Joan wouldn't appreciate spilled blood on her shiny floors.

For now, Gage would control himself.

But God knew, he had enough pent-up aggravation from the past six months to tear Phil Flynn's arms and legs off and shove 'em straight up his ass.

The minute he booted Flynn out the front door, Reid's voice boomed.

"What the *fuck*?"

"Reid Sullivan Steele! Language!"

And, oh crap. Miss Joan rejoined the party.

Gage picked up his pace, hustling back to the kitchen where Micki now sat at the table, her head cradled in her hands, fingers digging into her scalp. Reid stood over her while Jonah pressed his palms into the counter, rotten energy shooting off him and tripling the already caustic tension.

Miss Joan propped her hands on her hips. "What's going on?"

"Nothing," Micki said. "Sorry."

"Don't you lie to me. I won't abide liars in this house." Miss Joan turned to Jonah. "And why on earth is he calling you a *rapist*?"

What the fuck, was right.

Reid glanced at Gage. *Shouldn't be here*. Should he go? Stay? Jesus, this family. He'd sat through many arguments, but none that involved the word *rapist*.

Being a close friend didn't give him the right to be a voyeur on this level of family intimacy.

He waggled his thumb at the door. "I'll…"

Micki's head shot up and she locked her eyes on him. "No. Please. Don't."

Her panic—or fear?—rooted him to his spot. She needed something, but damned if he knew what.

Maybe his presence leveled things off, kept emotions from getting too crazy in front of the outsider.

Knowing these people, he doubted it. They tended to blow when they needed to blow, company be damned.

Stepping farther into the room, Gage focused on Micki. "Tell me what you need."

"Just, please, stay. I need...help."

Jonah pushed off the counter, walked to the table, and smacked his hands on it. "Help with what? What the hell was he talking about?"

"I'm so sorry," she said, her eyes shimmery with tears.

Miss Joan marched over and wrapped her arms around Micki, holding on with a grip only mothers could pull off without hurting someone.

"Oh, my girl. You're home now. Everything will be fine."

"No, Mom. It won't."

This is it.

Micki had waited for this moment for years. Dreamed of it, in fact. Sitting in front of her family and opening up, relieving herself of her filthy little secrets.

The lying had to stop. Even her grand plan to chase Phil off had failed. Now she'd have to live with disappointing her family. Live with them knowing how she made her way all these years. And how, in the end, by using his own tactics against him, she'd turned out no better than Phil.

She couldn't do it anymore.

She wanted a life lived on her terms.

And Jonah deserved to know the truth.

Everyone did.

She just hadn't expected to tell them this way. She'd wanted to get Jonah alone. That very morning, but...Too late now.

Maybe, if she admitted everything, they might understand. They might not think of her as someone who'd willingly gone to work for a scumbag.

Still in her mother's arms, she sat back, stared straight ahead at Reid, his big body still hovering, crowding her, and her chest got tight. The walls, combined with Reid's looming, squeezed in. Her breath caught and the slow burn of panic curled inside.

Run.

That's what she needed to do. Just get out. Break free of all of it. Even Mom's attempt at comfort made her feel trapped.

She pulled free of her mother and shifted sideways, bumping Jonah's arm and—stuck.

Shoving her chair back, she gripped the edge of the table, her gaze snapping from Jonah to Reid to Mom, and that panic blew apart.

Run.

Rock-solid, steady Gage, all perfect wide shoulders and lean muscle, appeared in the space beside Reid, bringing a sense of calm. A sense of *safety*.

He'd help her. As confused as he had to be, about her, about Phil, about everything, he hadn't turned that damning file over to Reid.

She closed her eyes, forced out a slow breath. *I can do this.*

"Mikayla," Reid barked, "start talking."

She flinched at his tone, opened her eyes and spotted Gage holding his palms up.

"How about we all sit down. You standing over her isn't helping."

Yes. Sitting. Sitting was better. The man was exactly

what she needed now. In control, levelheaded, and commanding. Simply perfect.

No. Not perfect. No one was. But he might be as close as one could get.

All at once, her brothers and mother found a seat. Jonah slid into the chair to her left, Reid and Gage across from her and Mom to her right.

She could do this. Just start at the beginning and lay it all out. She glanced at Jonah, thought back ten years to that one night that had changed everything.

"Jonah, I'm sorry. I didn't want it to happen this way."

"Tell me what the hell is going on."

"It was that stupid party. Senior year. The one at Harrison Shaw's house?"

Her brother's gaze shot to their mother. Yeah, this wasn't ideal.

"What party?" Mom asked.

"I was invited, but didn't want to go to alone. I took Jonah with me."

For moral support. Together, they'd been two nerds treated like outcasts until she'd gotten fed up with Jake Trambly's bullying. Oh, she'd taught him, hadn't she? The star football player found himself with a .075 grade point average. All thanks to her nimble fingers and her ability to hack into the school's admin system.

For the first time, she'd been a hero. Her classmates had loved the prank. And the administrators had no proof it'd been her. Which left her free of punishment.

Three weeks from graduation, she'd become a hero with her classmates and scored an invite to a party at the house of a friend of one of the "cool" kids. A mansion in Asheville no less. That house, with its pool and huge rooms and multiple bathrooms that awed her, should have been paradise.

Should have been.

The pool. She remembered standing next to it and tilting her head back as the warm breeze tickled her

cheeks. Large trees provided a canopy of green against
the backdrop of a starlit sky. Dance music spilled from
hidden speakers as partygoers crowded around her, all of
them loud and giggly and well on their way to being
trashed. She had half a beer, decided she hated the taste,
and tossed it. Besides, she wanted to experience that one
amazing night of being one of the cool kids to its fullest
and not have her senses dulled by alcohol.

Jonah tugged on the back of her shirt. "Micki," he
said, "I need help."

She opened her eyes, found her twin standing behind
her, his hazel eyes wide and wild.

He leaned in, got close to her ear. "Let's go."

"What the hell?"

"Now, Micki. Right now. I need your help. Someone
is in trouble. Inside. She's in one of the bedrooms."

She grabbed his arm and squeezed. "Is she okay?"

"No. Someone drugged her. The guys—" Jonah
sucked in a breath, slapped his hands on top of his head,
and two passing girls laughed at him.

Holy cow. Something had her brother in freak-out
mode.

"Someone," he said, "must have roofied her. She's
wasted and they're..."

Oh, no. "What? They're doing what?"

"Harrison just took me up there. Told me to...have a
turn. He said he'd be back in ten with the next guy.
We've got to get her out."

Rape. These asshole rich kids were raping a girl.
Micki curled her hands into fists, bumping them against
her thighs. "Where is she?"

"Still in there. I've got five more minutes. I can't just
walk her out, though. I need help."

"I'll do it. What's your plan?"

Now, ten years later, it came back to her like it was
an hour ago. Micki bringing Jonah's beat-up truck
around the side of the house. Jonah smuggling a barely
standing girl out the window. Thank God that room had

been on the first floor because it had taken both of them to drag her to the truck. For his efforts, Jonah had earned himself a scratch on the face.

But they'd gotten her out.

For ten years, Micki had kept it to herself, sharing that secret with only Jonah. And now, hearing Micki recite the events of that night, Mom lifted her hand to her mouth and gasped.

"Oh, my God," Mom said, her voice muffled under the weight of her hand. "How did y'all never tell me this?"

Jonah cleared his throat, the misery on his face evident in the harsh, downward curve of his mouth. "We took her home. We were scared, so we left her on the porch. I told Micki to drive the truck to the corner. Then I rang the bell and ran. We made sure her folks got her inside and we left."

"Holy hell," Reid said. "Y'all never told anyone?"

"No. We figured if her folks went to the cops, they'd find us."

"No one ever came," Mom said.

"Someone came," Micki said.

All heads snapped toward her. *This is it.*

"Who?" Jonah asked.

"Phil."

Jonah cocked his head. *"Phil?"*

"After school one day. I was in town. At the café grabbing a shake for the walk home. He came up to me."

"That son of a bitch," Mom said.

"Mama!" Reid said, clearly shocked at her outburst.

For once, she was getting the scolding. Any other time, Micki would have laughed. Now? It all seemed...sad. Heartbreaking even.

"He'd been hired by Harrison Shaw's dad." She looked at her mother. "The party was at their house. A girl had gotten raped, and being the bigshot CEO of North Carolina's biggest bank, he needed to make the mess go away. He knew about us, Jonah. About us taking Tessa home. Harrison must have figured out it was us and told his father. I guess Mr. Shaw wanted to make sure we didn't go to the cops, so he hired Phil. I didn't know it at the time, but Phil had already gone to Tessa's parents and made a deal with them. I don't know what he threatened them with, but it had to be something."

Gage leaned in on his elbows. "Big enough that they didn't seek justice for their daughter's rape."

Jonah pushed his shoulders back, readying himself for the rest of it. "What did he want with you?"

"Harrison told his father about me…" She glanced at her mother and another bout of shame spewed, forcing her to look away and focus on the tabletop. "He told his father I changed Jake's GPA. His father told Phil and Phil offered me a job."

That stupid prank. If only she hadn't done it.

Too late for that.

"He wanted you to hack for him," Jonah said.

"Yes. He needed someone with my skills and I was convenient. I was young, impressionable, and wouldn't ask questions. And he threatened me."

"With what?"

"With you being convicted of rape."

CHAPTER FOURTEEN

JONAH'S JAW DROPPED. LITERALLY.

As difficult as it was, Gage forced himself to sit still. To not do anything that would destroy the momentum of the conversation. Micki had held on to this story for ten years. She'd allowed herself to be thought of as a fuckup and a sellout for ten miserable years.

To protect her brother.

Jonah's head snapped to his mother. "I swear to you, I didn't do it. I got her out of there. Phil Flynn is a scumbag. He threatens people on behalf of his clients."

Micki nodded. "He told me he had a video of Jonah coming out of the room." She turned back to Jonah. "He does. I've seen it."

"That doesn't prove squat," Reid said.

"And DNA."

The room went silent. Yeah, total showstopper, that one.

Jonah's head lopped forward. *"What?"*

Now this was getting crazy. If Jonah hadn't touched that girl, how the hell did Phil have his DNA? That, or Phil had been bluffing.

Micki flicked her nails over her face. "She scratched you on the cheek. Remember?"

"Yeah, but I was trying to *help* her. It's not like I…"

He waved a hand. No need to elaborate on that one.

"Phil said her parents had a rape kit done. That they found DNA under her nails, but couldn't match it to anyone. He said he could get the sheriff to test your DNA and they'd find a match. That you'd go to jail for rape."

Jonah was out of his chair, sending it scraping across the floor as he stormed the length of the kitchen. "Micki! Come on. You know the truth! Why did you let this guy do this?"

She flinched and her shoulders curled in, her head dipping. *Jesus, this poor girl.*

As much as Gage didn't want to get into family business, Micki had asked him to stay and right now, the way she'd recoiled from Jonah yelling at her, she needed an ally. Someone to draw Jonah's fire.

"Hang on," Gage said, angling his body so he could see Jonah. "Let's think about this. You guys were young. I don't care what anyone says, eighteen is still a kid. And Phil Flynn is a master at what he does. It's not a stretch that he could convince a kid that her brother, her *twin,* would get locked up. Particularly when he has the backing of a wealthy and influential banker, a video *and* DNA."

Micki brought her head up, stared at Gage for a few seconds, the look in her eyes something akin to gratitude and relief. Someone believed her. Believed *in* her.

And Gage knew the power of that. Had thrived on it for years.

"He terrified me," Micki said. "I knew Jonah didn't hurt that girl, but he had the video and the DNA. He told me to look up a couple of rape cases. He gave me actual names. So I ran home and researched them. They were cases where guys had been convicted on less evidence." She turned to Jonah, gripped his arm. "I was afraid for you. Then, after being in Vegas awhile, I found out there's no statute of limitations on rape in North Carolina. If Phil decided to, he could make a case *today* and you'd go to prison. Back then, I panicked. I saw a way out for you. For both of us really, because I knew what went on in that bedroom and I didn't report it. I was afraid we'd *both* go to jail. Just for knowing about it. That's what he told me."

"My God," Miss Joan said. "That bastard."

Micki ignored her mother and kept her eyes on Jonah. "I went to Vegas. To keep our secret."

Jonah had stopped his pacing, but his body still moved. Swaying from side to side, then back and forth. Constant motion. He folded his arms, then dropped them again.

He didn't know what the hell to do with himself.

Even Reid was speechless.

And that was saying something.

Finally, Jonah walked to the door, his steps quick and stomping and...pissy. He paused and looked out the window while Micki shifted in her chair to face her brother.

"Jonah—"

His hand flew up. "Just...stop. Let me think."

"Calm down," Reid said. "Everyone take a second here."

Gage nodded. They needed to eliminate the emotion. "He's right. Let's break this down and figure out how to get rid of this so-called evidence. We know Jonah didn't do anything wrong. This girl. The victim? Who is she?"

Jonah shook his head. "Tessa. Jesus *Christ*."

"Jonah!" Miss Joan said.

"I'm sorry, Mom, but this is..." He ran a hand over his face. "I don't know what this is. All these years, Micki has been in Vegas and we could have taken care of it."

"Look, guys. I'm an outsider here."

"You're not an outsider," Reid snapped. "Shut up with that and say what you're thinking."

Gage met his eye. "Thank you, but I'm not family. My perspective is different. I don't have the connection you do. Jonah, I'd suggest getting a lawyer. You didn't do anything wrong, but if Flynn showed up here, he's not playing. He's got an ace in his pocket."

Micki grunted. "He probably bribed a judge."

"Oh, my God," Miss Joan said, her strangled voice barely above a whisper.

Gage touched her arm. This woman had treated him as her own. The least he could do was give her some damned hope that her son wouldn't spend the next twenty years in prison. "It'll be okay. Jonah is innocent and he has the resources to hire attorneys. A good lawyer makes this go away. No fuss, no muss."

"All that time." Miss Joan shook her head. "My girl was gone all that time."

Jonah looked back at his mother, his face a cross between tight anger and pinched torture. "Because of me."

"No," Micki said. "Not because of you. Because I was too terrified to stand up to Phil. This is on me. I just can't do it anymore. I want my life back."

Hours later, Gage sat at the piano in his living room—Miss Joan's living room actually. He was just the renter. Still, the place felt homey and warm and...comfortable. Like Miss Joan. In this house, there was no pressure. Here, he didn't worry about all the things he should be doing for everyone else.

His sole purpose now revolved around tinkering with piano keys until he worked out the song in his head.

His mother had given piano lessons for years and had forced enough of them on him that he'd learned to read music and could actually put a song together. Memories of her yelling at him from the kitchen about wrong notes filled his mind and he couldn't help smiling.

Life had been simpler back then. Before he'd grown into his feet and became the problem solver. The mediator between his sisters, the one who dealt with bullies at school and flat tires and bum tractor engines.

As much as he wanted to blame his father for putting the pressure on him, he couldn't.

Like Micki, he understood the power of the mind. That tricky bastard could make one believe anything.

The doorbell rang and he glanced up. Spotted Micki standing in front of the glass plane.

God help him.

She'd been tearing at his thoughts since he left Tupelo Hill and that crazy family meeting. Hell, since she showed up two days ago. Considering the horny male he was, being alone with her in his house—in the house she grew up in—wouldn't evolve into anything honorable.

Except, there she stood, peering through the glass, and he couldn't leave her there. Not after what she'd been through today. Something brought her to his door and he might as well find out what.

He wanted this girl. Friendship with Reid be damned.

He met her gaze as he walked and something sparked in her hazel eyes. The rest of her features remained neutral. No smile, no tilt of her head, no expression at all.

Micki, Micki, Micki.

Without a doubt, she'd always keep him guessing.

He swung the door open and a blast of forty-five-degree air sent the hairs on his arms to full attention.

"Hi," she said, her eyes raking over his T-shirt, gym shorts and bare feet.

He stepped back and waved her in. "Hi, yourself. Get out of the cold."

Obviously once again unprepared for the weather, she wore a black jean jacket, a plaid scarf, black leggings, and a white gauzy shirt. The edge of the scarf hung across her chest landing—you guessed it—right above her tits and extremely protruding nipples.

When exactly had he gotten laid last?

Crap. Not a break to be had with this Steele bunch.

She stepped across his threshold, bringing the scent of fresh air and powder with her, and he reminded himself to keep his mitts to himself.

"Sorry to interrupt," she said.

"No prob. You need a heavier jacket, though."

"I realized that on the ride over."

"You rode here?"

"I stole Jonah's bike again."

Gage laughed. "I hope you at least told him this time."

"I did. I texted him after I left. Otherwise, they'd all argue over who was driving me because God forbid I should ride a bike five miles."

"They're trying to keep you safe."

"I know. But I've been alone a long time. Sometimes it feels like…smothering."

"I get that," he said. "Believe me." He grabbed a pile of clean clothes off the couch and set them on the chair in the corner. "Wasn't expecting company. Have a seat."

She took in the room, probably recognizing her mother's furniture. "You're actually pretty clean for a guy."

"Thanks. I think."

"Is it weird living here?"

"Not at all. I was just thinking how homey it is. Your mom has that way about her. Whatever she touches."

"My father doesn't want to sell the house. Kind of crazy since he lives at the cabin now." She shrugged. "I never could figure those two out."

"Maybe you're not meant to. Besides, I hit pay dirt with renting the place."

She gestured at the piano. "I heard you playing that old beast. That would make my mom happy. Evie started taking lessons, but I think she quit."

"She dabbles," Gage said.

When he'd first moved in, he and Evie had talked about the piano and how it needed to be tuned. Which he'd arranged his first week here.

The corner of Micki's mouth lifted. "You know more about my family than I do."

"I doubt that."

"What song were you working on?"

This was a question he shouldn't answer. If he were smart, which he used to be, he'd make something up. Grab some random title from the sky. Chances were she hadn't recognized his piss-poor version of a song she proclaimed to love.

Barely three feet from her, he met her gaze, found himself getting sucked into the green flecks and mystery behind them and he knew, as sure as shit, he couldn't fight himself on this one. End of story.

"'Bring It On Home,'" he said.

Her eyebrows hitched up. A millimeter. Maybe half a millimeter, but he caught it. *Micki, Micki, Micki.* Such a puzzle.

"Play it for me," she said.

"It's not ready for an audience."

"I don't care."

She moved to the piano, her gaze still on his. She slid the scarf from her throat, her long fingers curling into it as it glided over the silky skin of her neck.

"Please," she said. "I love that song."

"I know. That's what scares the hell out of me."

It didn't stop him from reclaiming his spot on the piano bench, testing the keys while his mind tripped and whirled and formulated an escape plan he didn't necessarily want.

She stood next to the piano, resting both elbows on it, and the neckline of her blouse dipped, giving him a view of a pale bra and cleavage. Micki wasn't stacked. Not by a long shot, but everything about her worked. Small breasts, long, lean legs, narrow hips.

Twiggy, Reid had called her. The name fit and Gage imagined her in his bed, under him, on top, wherever. Didn't matter as long as her legs were locked around him.

"So." He ran his fingers over the keys and the cascading sound filled the room. "Why did you ride Jonah's bike into town? Aside from needing space."

"I wanted to thank you."

"You could have called."

"I could have. Should I go?"

He stopped playing. "Not if I can help it."

Her face flushed and—yeah—another first from the stoic Micki. The girl was loosening up. Good for her.

"I couldn't have handled that meeting alone," she said.

"Yeah, you could." She needed to get it through that stubborn head of hers. "You don't give yourself enough credit. What you've been living with for ten years? Not a lot of people would do that."

"Most would have the nerve to get away. Don't you think?"

"Some maybe, but Phil groomed you, Micki. You were young and scared and he knew exactly how to bend you to his will. That makes him a predator."

"I swear you're straight out of a romance novel."

That made him laugh. "Nah. I'm trained to understand human nature."

"Oh, then I don't want to know what you think of me."

"Sure you do. Because I think you're exceptional. All you needed today was support. I came in handy since I was the unemotional one in the room."

She moved around the side of the piano, stood beside the bench, her body close enough that he breathed in her powdery scent. Whatever that was, he'd buy her a gallon of it.

He turned sideways, straddling the bench, his growing erection not shy about letting her know what he wanted.

Particularly when she eased onto the bench in front of him, their knees touching, eyes locked. She ran her hands over his face, and the mental war, every logical argument, vanished.

"Is this wise?" he asked.

What kind of idiot asked that question when he knew the answer?

"I doubt it," she said. "But there are perks to being the family screwup. No one expects anything from me. And I've been living according to everyone else's rules a long time. Now I want what I want."

He hooked his hands under her thighs, brought them on top of his and slid an arm around her, boosting her up to straddle him. "You're not a screwup."

His erection pressed into her and she tipped her head back, let out a low moan, and he was gone. Gone, gone, gone.

"I want to feel good," she said. "Being around you makes me feel good. Especially when you tell me I'm exceptional." He nibbled the delicate skin on her neck. "And when you do *that*."

Backing away, he kissed her, let the softness of her lips drive him further and closer to the insanity of sex with Reid's sister.

She ground herself into him and, holy shit, if she kept that up, they'd have problems.

He grabbed her cheeks, cradled her face in his rough hands. Another reminder that he had no right to her.

"Honey," he said, "if you don't knock that off, I won't last too long."

"In that case, maybe you should ditch your shorts."

Gage smiled at her, a quick flashing grin that made something inside her go warm. This man. So hot.

And so not her type.

But she couldn't think about that now. He wanted to be with her. At least temporarily. Whether it was all part of his hero complex—the big bad Special Forces guy helping the screwup or something more, she wouldn't think about. Analyzing the whys of it all wouldn't help her.

All she knew was that Gage Barber, somehow, seemed to know what she needed. Always.

She wrapped her arms around his neck and held on. The lifeline in turbulent waters.

What am I doing?

This world. The sanctuary. The *normal.* It wasn't hers. After all the things she'd done, she didn't deserve it.

No.

Not thinking about it.

Tonight, for once, she'd forget about Phil and secrets and denial. Tonight she'd allow herself freedom.

She squeezed her eyes closed and tightened her grip on him. *Just hang on.* If she could hold on to Gage, Mr. All-American-apple-pie-farm-boy, she'd be okay.

Gage patted the upper part of her butt. "Hey. You okay?"

When he made a move to back away, she held on, gripping so tight she might snap his neck.

God, she couldn't let him see this. This desperation and weakness. Not when all she wanted was to fall into bed—with him—and start her life over.

His hand wandered higher on her back. "You'll be all right."

He knew. A burst of air exploded in her chest, and all that pent-up stress and anger and…emotion…sucked her under, stealing her breath. *Dammit.* How did her life get to be such a fucking mess?

She gripped harder, fighting the urge to run. To disappear and leave Phil and Vegas and the whole cluster behind. *Just hang on.* "He'll never let me go. He won't. And I can't do this anymore. I can't pretend I don't know what he does. And I help him! What kind of person does that?"

He brought his hands up, latching on to her wrists, tugging at her, then tugging harder when she stayed locked on. "Honey, if you don't let me look at you, I'll make you do it."

"I don't want you to look at me."

"Well, too bad, because I love looking at you. I look at you constantly. And I like what I see. Very much. I don't know what this is between us. And I know you're all twisted up. I get that. Believe me. Everyone expects us to be a certain way. Sometimes we need help. So, dump it on me. I'll help you."

He knew her. For a man she'd just met, he knew exactly what she needed.

Gage ran his thumbs over her cheeks and she got lost in those crystal blue eyes.

What he wanted for his future, she didn't know, but he was a picket fence guy. He'd need a blonde, curvy wife, a herd of kids, and a minivan.

Total opposite of her.

"Micki," he said, "stop."

"What?"

"Thinking. Whatever it is, it isn't good."

He'd nailed that one. "I've been alone for ten years. All I do is think."

"You're not alone anymore."

Then he kissed her. His lips so soft on hers, part of her cement shell broke free. She leaned in, the two of them barely touching, but the connection so electric she needed to be closer. And closer.

"You're amazing," she said.

"Nah. I'm just a guy who has a thing for a screwy Steele girl."

Gage, somehow, made her laugh. Maybe she wasn't a dead loss after all. "I'm ready to start over. I feel safe here. In this house. With you. It's…" She cradled his face in her hands and pressed. "It's home. Finally. I'm home. Thank you."

She didn't want his response. Not now. Not when this spell was so potent and beautiful. She threw herself at him, wrapping her arms around his neck again, angling into his body and kissing him with every little desperate piece of herself she had.

Total slut kiss.

And she liked it.

Tongues battled, lips slammed and—oh—it was so good.

He scooped her up. *Bam.* Lifted her right off the bench. Strong man.

But she knew that already.

"That," she said, "was totally hot."

He snorted and with her lips still on his, she giggled and the moment was so light, so ridiculously silly, that she took it all in, locking it away so she'd remember. Always.

Happiness.

For that alone, she'd adore him forever.

"You know, it's too bad the piano is an upright." He waggled his eyebrows. "Always wanted to have sex on a piano. I might have to upgrade to a baby grand."

"I'll help you pay for it."

He stopped walking. Right in the middle of the living room and pressed her against the wall.

"Jesus, that got me going. I have a picture of you bare-assed naked, spread across that thing. Waiting for me."

Oh, the thought. "I'd love that," she said.

He kissed her again, grinding his erection against her, and she combusted. Everything inside imploding. Balanced against the wall, she nudged him away and lifted her shirt over her head. His hands moved over her bare skin, the heat intense and perfect as he locked his gaze on her.

Then he went to work on her bra, sliding the straps off and maneuvering her so he could unclip it. And she wouldn't think about how effortlessly he'd done that. About his experience with this sort of thing. Unlike her.

None of it mattered now.

"Put me down," she said.

He set her down and dragged his mouth over her shoulder and his hands, those rough-skinned palms over her nipples, and the friction blew her mind.

She shoved her leggings down, but they got caught on her boots and... "Dammit!"

"How much do you like these pants?"

"Why?"

"Because if I don't get inside you in the next ten seconds, I won't make it."

"Tear them off."

"Excellent." He gripped the waistband of the leggings and...ripped.

"Oh. My. Goodness! So hot."

He cracked up. "I know. It's crazy. I've never done that before. I'll buy you new ones. Maybe a whole bunch because that was wicked fun."

Her underwear went next. She'd just bought those from Brynne's shop and they weren't cheap, but oh well. Sacrifices needed to be made.

Gage kicked out of his shorts, reaching for the drawer of the side table as Micki stood in her childhood living room, naked as a jay and wearing boots.

She lifted one foot. "The boots are sexy, no?"

He dug through the drawer, found his wallet and plucked out a condom. "Found it!"

"You're such a Boy Scout."

"Actually, I was never a Boy Scout. I play outside the lines too much."

"Really?"

"Yep."

He got the condom on, stripped his shirt off, and—oh, oh, oh—his chest was perfection. Even more so than she'd imagined. Hidden underneath his loose shirts hid cut, rock-solid muscle, and she ran her hands over his pecs, into the smattering of golden hairs. She'd never get tired of touching him. Never.

He looked down at her hands moving over him. "Right here?"

"Yep."

"Against the wall?"

"Absolutely."

He picked her up again and she wrapped her legs around him, felt the press of his erection on the inside of her thigh and let out a gasp. A man. A real man. No casual acquaintance she'd gone out with a time or two in a mad attempt for affection.

In just a few days, Gage Barber knew and understood her. As scary as that was.

"Thank you."

"Sweetheart, I haven't done anything yet."

"Yes, you have."

Then he was inside her, pushing into her, and she gasped again.

"Sorry."

He started to pull out and she gripped his shoulders. "No. It's perfect. You're perfect."

"Damn, Micki, you feel good."

She arched her back and squeezed her thighs and he pushed deeper, rocking his hips as she found his rhythm and...so good. So, so good.

They moved together, figuring it out, experimenting with touches and thrusts, *exploring* with hands and tongues, finding the hot buttons while her belly coiled into a tight, fierce ball. She swung her head back and forth and got lightheaded for her efforts. "If you stop, I'll kill you."

He pumped harder, holding her against that wall, damned near splitting her in two, but she wanted more of it. More of the closeness, the few minutes of feeling that emotional connection she'd been missing.

He drew back, met her gaze while a playful smile lit up his face and...*that's it*...too much. Her body, every inch of her splintered. She cried out as flashes of color, a rainbow bursting, filled her vision.

Captain America kept up his pace. She hung on, rocking her hips harder, giving as good as she got until he thrust one last time, his body tensing as the orgasm tore into him.

He collapsed against her, his chest heaving, but he held her against the wall as her body went limp. He drew long, exhausted breaths and she wrapped him in her arms, kissing his shoulder. All that hard work they'd done.

Together.

Gage braced Micki against the wall, hoping to hell his knees didn't give out, but with the way he was panting, they might wind up in a face-plant. Oooh—eee the girl had given him a workout.

Damn, that was fun.

"Tell me," she whispered in his ear, "we just did that."

"Oh, yeah. We did it."

She pinched his arm.

"Ow! What was that for?"

"Sorry. I had to make sure it wasn't, like, the best dream I've ever had."

"Typically, people pinch themselves. Not others."

But what did he care who she pinched? As long as he got to do this with her again, he had no complaints. Not a one.

Still holding her, and being careful not to move too quickly and give himself a head rush, he straightened. The fact that he hadn't fallen over in the middle of that very active screwing was a damned miracle.

Things were definitely looking up.

Regretfully, he slid out of her, but couldn't help kissing her. Then doing it again as he dragged one hand down her thigh, her skin so soft under his fingers. "You're good for my mood."

"Ditto, but you can put me down, you know."

"Maybe I like holding you."

"Yes, but eventually, you'll have to let me go."

He hoped to hell not. "Maybe you have a point."

Three seconds later, her feet were on the floor and Gage made quick work of dealing with the condom while Micki headed upstairs to the bathroom.

Miss Joan's big grandfather clock chimed, the cascading bells echoing throughout the house. Eight o'clock already. After getting home and squatting at the piano, he'd lost time.

Micki swung around the bannister and stood at the base of the stairs, her hair back in that sexy, messy-on-purpose look. "I can't believe that old clock still works."

"Yep. For some reason, it only goes off every twelve hours. Not that I'm complaining. I get headaches and the chimes would make me nuts. Speaking of which, I'm starving and my head hurts. Have you eaten?"

"Nope. I figured I'd stop in at the B and grab something after I talked to you."

She hit him with a smug grin. *I did that.* Or, at least he'd helped put that grin there.

"Good. How about I buy you dinner? I'll take you home after that. We'll throw the bike in my truck."

"Um." She gestured to the scraps of her clothing on the floor. "We should have thought twice about shredding my pants and underwear."

Shit. What the hell had he been thinking? She had no damned clothes now. And as thin as she was, his stuff wouldn't fit her. Totally irresponsible on his part.

He held up his hands. "Let's not panic."

She slid on her bra and put her hands on her hips. "Easy for you to say. I'm the one standing here in a bra and boots."

Okay. Now that was funny. The two of them, at the exact same time, burst out laughing. What a pair.

"Jeez, Micki, I'm sorry. Should I run up to the house and grab you some clothes or something?"

"No! Are you kidding? What if Jonah sees you rummaging through my stuff?"

He hadn't thought about that. And on a Sunday night, all the shops in town were closed.

"Evie." Micki grabbed her phone from the wallet/purse thing she'd dumped next to the couch. "I'll get her to bring me replacements."

A ball of panic unfurled, stabbing him behind the eyes. Not that he was ashamed of whatever this was with Micki, but really? She wanted to clue her family in before they even knew if it was going anywhere?

He touched her arm. "Uh, you sure about that?"

"Not in this lifetime, but if I go walking into my mother's house wearing a pair of men's sweats, I think it'll stir some controversy." She waved him off. "We can trust Evie. I'll just have her bring me something and we'll buy her dinner. How's that?"

Risky. That's how it was. For a lot of reasons. When Reid found out about Gage and Micki, Gage wanted to be the one to tell him. To let him know that this wasn't a quick lay. A fast meaningless hookup. What exactly he'd describe it as was lost on him, but at least on his part, it wasn't any of those things.

"Unless," Micki said, "you don't want…"

And the way she looked at him, her eyes a little wary and distant and…shutting him down. Snapping back to her guarded habits.

"No," he said. "*I'm* great. I don't want your family hearing about us from the town criers. You know how this place is. They won't talk about me. They'll talk about you. It has to come from me. Or you. If you're comfortable with calling Evie, so am I."

"I trust her. There's girl code and then there's sister code. If I know her at all, she'll love this." She poked at her phone and held it to her ear. "Evie! It's me…Micki."

As if her sister wouldn't know her?

"Can I ask a huge favor?"

CHAPTER FIFTEEN

TWENTY MINUTES LATER, EVIE STROLLED to the front door carrying a La Belle Style bag from Brynne's shop.

Of course, because Gage's luck was shit on toast lately, Evie had already been down at the B, having dinner with—you guessed it—Reid and Brynne. Rather than race home, she'd had Brynne take her down to the shop and bought Micki a pair of jeans.

And underwear.

Jesus. What a clusterfuck.

All under the guise that Micki had "fallen" off Jonah's bike and tore her pants.

And underwear.

Clusterfuck.

Who the hell would believe that?

Not Reid. That was for sure. But they'd deal with that later.

Gage opened the door and Evie grinned up at him, all classic Steele smart-ass, and his face got hot.

This family. When was the last time someone had actually made him blush?

"Don't say it," he said.

Cruising by him, she offered up a little finger wave. "My lips are zipped. But, holy jumpin' Jesus! If Reid finds out about this he'll go crazy!"

"Will you tell him?"

"Not me."

"Brynne?"

"Pfft. She knows my brother is on the brink of insane. This would kick him right over the edge."

"Any day now!" Micki called from the bathroom.

La Belle Style bag in hand, Evie strode down the short hallway and banged on the door. "I've got the goods."

Gage squeezed his eyes shut and let out a grunt. What a crew. The whole lot of them.

Micki cracked open the bathroom door and stuck her hand out. "Evie, you're awesome. Thank you."

The bathroom door closed again. "You're welcome." She held a fist in the air. "Sisters unite! I made sure to get underwear that was still in the stockroom. In the packaging. If you know what I mean."

"Oh, man," Gage muttered. "I don't need to hear this."

Really, thinking about Micki sliding into underwear someone had tried on—because of his inability to control himself—gave him a good dose of guilt.

"You good?" Evie asked. "I have to get back to the B before Reid starts asking too many questions. If I'm there, it'll take the heat off Brynne."

Micki emerged from the bathroom encased in a pair of skin-tight jeans that made her legs look twelve miles long, and Gage started to rethink dinner out.

"Ooh," Evie said, "perfect fit. I knew it."

"I owe you one."

"Nah. It was fun. And now I have a secret about you two. Total blackmail material."

Blackmail. Micki's face fell. Everything literally drooping.

That one word—*blackmail*—had changed her. The whole of her adult life spent under its threat.

Sensing trouble, Evie locked her fingers around Micki's arms. "You know I'm kidding, right? I didn't mean it. I swear, I'd never..." Still hanging on to Micki, she swung back to Gage. "Guys, seriously, I was *kidding.*"

Fix this. Someone had to because Micki was knocked mute and poor Evie's skin had turned five shades whiter. Gage approached them, his eyes on Micki, silently reassuring her that no, her baby sister wasn't threatening her.

He dropped one hand on each of their shoulders. "It's fine. We're in this together, right?"

"Right," Evie said.

Micki held his gaze and nodded.

"We'll take care of each other, right?"

"Right," Evie repeated.

Something in that statement, the ferocity behind it, prompted Micki from her fog. She finally looked at her sister, wrenched one arm free and threw it around Evie. "I love you," she said. "I know you'd never hurt me."

Well, damn, if that didn't beat all. Tough Micki Steele letting her guard down twice in one night.

"Ladies," Gage said, "I'd love to stand around and watch this big family moment, but I'm starved. What do you say I buy you both dinner? We'll face Reid together."

"I'm in!" Evie said.

Micki didn't release her sister, but backed up enough to face Gage, holding his stare for a long minute. "Me too," she said. "I'm in."

First thing Monday morning, Micki made the call.

The one to Phil. Originally, her plan had been to tell him over the phone that she wouldn't be on that plane with him today, but when she heard his voice, the nonthreatening Phil voice, a bit of her resolve disintegrated. After all, she'd spent the past ten Christmases with the Flynn family. He hadn't needed to do that. He could have left her and Tomas to themselves, sitting alone in their apartments. Instead, he'd welcomed them into his home.

For that, she'd always be grateful. The dichotomy of Phil. Good Phil versus evil Phil.

Good Phil kept her comfortable, mostly, and bad Phil? Well, he kept her pinned down. Cornered. Fearful of life outside the bubble he'd created for her.

All of it played in her mind, confusing her, twisting her thoughts. After everything, how could she care about this man?

Easy. He'd been her family when she needed one. The deciding factor when he requested she meet with him. To talk.

And she caved.

She spent the bike ride into town rationalizing it. *Closure.* That's what she needed when it came to Phil. To be done once and for all.

Phil had wanted to meet alone. Of course he did. Alone, he could do his black magic and emotionally work her over. Refusing to let that happen, she'd insisted on meeting at the Triple B. At 9:00 a.m., when the morning crowd would still be strong and reinforcements could be found.

She paused at the door, gripped the handle, and held on, allowing the cold metal to center her. Ten minutes. That's all she'd give him. She'd tell him she wasn't going back and that would be that. Simple.

"Good morning."

Dammit.

Life with Phil. Always uncharted. She glanced back, found him behind her in one of his five-thousand-dollar suits. An intimidation tactic. He'd admitted as much to her years ago. People found it hard to say no to a man who was smart enough to afford Brioni suits.

"Good morning." She opened the door.

"You really want to do this inside?"

I sure do.

"Yes. It won't take long."

"I don't like the sound of that, Mikayla."

Well, it's about to get worse.

Micki stepped into the B where the thick morning crowd huddled at the end of the counter and an aroma of baking blueberry scones and cinnamon mingled with fresh brewed coffee. She'd never been a fan of coffee, but right now, standing in this spot, where life as a normal person lay just within her reach, she might have to try one of Randi's lattes.

"Hey, Micki," Randi called from behind the espresso machine.

"Hi, Randi."

"Get you something?"

"Not yet. Thanks. Do you mind if we sit for a few minutes?"

Randi eyed Phil in a way that made Micki think Britt must have filled her in. *Perfect.* Another who now knew her secrets.

She couldn't worry about what Randi thought of her. Not now, anyway. This meeting required her full attention.

Ten minutes and I'm free.

Free of Phil and Vegas. Free to start a new life. And if a hunky former Green Beret were involved, even better.

"Hello, Mikayla."

Mr. Greene, King of the Gossips, tossed a wave her way and, cane in hand, shuffled into the adjoining bar, where the overflow from the coffee shop spread.

Assuming the bar area would be less noisy and not as crowded, she led the way, commandeering the table in the back corner. The one she'd sat at with her family on Friday night. That alone would bolster her confidence. Silly? Maybe. But at this point, inspiration came in different forms.

"I'm having breakfast," Phil said.

The man never ate breakfast. Never. Today? Breakfast. Again, she should have prepared for it. The master manipulator wanted to rattle her, throw her off her game. He knew she wanted to get this over with, so he'd draw it out by holding his finger on the button that brought Micki to heel.

"I can't stay long," she said.

"We'll see."

Phil went back to the coffee shop for his food while Mr. Greene and Mrs. Royce—who had to be 120 by now—argued over a new ordinance Grif wanted the town council to vote on. As in most small towns, change didn't come easily. From what Micki overheard, the locals enjoyed the new wave of tourism and the economic boost, but they didn't so much love the rules that came with it.

Progress. Always a bitch.

Phil returned, setting a muffin and a steaming mug of coffee on the table. Taking his time, he slid his jacket off and gingerly hung it on the back of the vacant chair beside him, adjusting the shoulders as he did so. One thing about Phil, he took great pride in his appearance. The minute his butt hit his seat, Micki leaned forward. *Now or never.*

"I didn't want to do this over the phone," she said.

"I'm glad for that. Surely, after all I've done for you, I deserve more than a phone call."

This man had hijacked her life. Robbed her of her family and the love that came with it, and he had the nerve, the absolute balls, to sit here and lecture her?

Of course he did. A week ago, before she'd spent time with her family and Gage and experienced what true affection was, she'd have fallen for Phil's machinations.

No more.

She worked up a vision of Gage, so good and honest, imagined him standing behind her, shoring her up.

"If we're being fair," she said, "I've done everything you asked. You also made a lot of money because of me. I'd say we're about even."

"Is that what this is about? You want a raise?"

A raise. If only.

"No raise. I'm done. I can't do this anymore. I miss my family."

"I'm sure." He glanced around and his lips dipped into a disgusted frown. "Why don't we reach a compromise? You come here, to this little Podunk town every few months. I'll give you a week off each time. Come back for holidays. My girls would miss you, but if it'll make you happy, they'll adjust."

Now he brought his daughters into it? How had she never seen it before? The evil.

"No," she said. "It's over, Phil. Obviously, if you leave me alone, our work together will remain confidential."

"Don't be stupid."

"Pardon?"

Gently, he set his coffee and plate aside and leaned toward her, his face just inches away, all that cool confidence morphing into focused rage. His dark eyes stabbed at her, and her pulse hammered so hard it stole her breath.

Calm. Stay calm. Whatever threats he'd make, her family had assured her they'd help. She steadied herself, lifted her chin, and met Phil's gaze.

"You stupid bitch," he said. "Do you really think I'd let you go? No one leaves me. Especially not you. I'll bury you, your family, and that Green Beret you're fucking."

Her head snapped back and he made a *pfffting* noise. "I knew something lured you back here. Hell, if I'd known it was a cock, I'd have gotten you one of those long ago."

The foul words hit her and her tight spine nearly snapped.

This is what Phil did. *Finger on the button.*

"You crazy old bat!" Mr. Greene yelled at Mrs. Royce. "You don't know what the hell you're saying."

Phil scoffed, as if the locals only proved the point about this Podunk town. *My town.* Podunk or not, he was on her turf and she didn't have to listen to him. Not anymore.

She set her hands on the table and pushed out of her seat. "Thank you for whatever kindness you've shown me, but it's over, Phil. I'm not coming back to Vegas."

He snagged her wrist, gave it a hard squeeze while a greasy smile lifted his lips. "You want your brother in jail?"

"Get your hand off her."

Micki whipped her head sideways, found Gage standing two feet from them, his feet planted, hands loose at his sides and his face molded into hard cement. Gone was Mr. All-American, her apple-cheeked lover.

"Great," Phil said. "A hero."

That wouldn't sit well. Exactly what Phil wanted.

"Yeah. A hero," Gage said. "I'll tell you one more time. Get your hands off of her or your suit will get bloody."

The ten or so patrons in the room all swung their way, curious gazes locked on. Mr. Greene used his cane to lever up from his chair, then smacked it on the table leg. Reinforcements by way of the geriatric ward.

Phil let out a small huff. "Hicks. I've always hated dealing with you people."

Micki slid her gaze to his hand still on her. No more. She locked eyes with him. "Threatening to put my brother in jail won't work anymore. I told him everything. The video, the DNA, all of it. He's ready for war. And, with all that I've seen, so am I."

Gage took a step closer and Phil, apparently realizing the *hicks* would come to her aid, let go.

Down deep, a small part of her broke off. Backward as it was, she'd cared about him. Cared about Tommy— Tomas. Now?

Over.

She moved away, heading for the door with Gage.

"Mikayla," he called, "you've known me a long time."

Before he said anything that would get the gossips

going, she turned back to him and he stood, getting right into her personal space.

He leaned in, keeping his eyes on hers. "Do you really think you can blackmail *me*?"

Gage led Micki out of the Triple B into the bright morning sunshine and checked over his shoulder. No one following. Phil Flynn being the master strategist that he was, Gage assumed the fixer's henchman lurked somewhere, but Tomas hadn't appeared yet.

Having no idea how Micki had even gotten into town, he hooked a left out of the B, the two of them hustling down Main Street. Micki kept quiet beside him. That alone pissed him off.

What in hell was she doing meeting with this guy? At least she'd had the good sense to do it in public, but—Christ—this guy was an animal. An animal with some sort of twisted hold on her.

"You're crazy for meeting him."

She halted in the middle of the sidewalk, her eyes narrowing so hard it looked painful. Disregarding the stroller moms power-walking toward them, she shrugged free of his grip and smacked his hand away.

"Watch it. You don't get to talk to me like that. I'm done with controlling men."

Oh, nice. Now he was controlling. Wasn't this always the way. Everyone wanted his help, and then when he helped, they got pissy. Classic. Double-edged sword that one. And a woman like Micki, with issues that needed tending, dragons to be slayed, and all that bullcrap, for him? Catnip. High-quality.

The moms cruised by, both of them staring him down, obviously ready to come to her aid. One of the women curled her lip and Micki held her hand up. "I'm fine. Thanks for your concern, though."

Pissed as she might be, she'd covered his ass on that one because the women kept moving.

"I'm not controlling you. Hell, it's probably the other way around because I was going about my normal business when your brother called and told me to haul my ass to the B."

"Which brother?"

"Britt. Randi called him. He's working a job on the mountain. He took a chance that I was still in town. Which, luckily, I was."

Micki sighed. "I'd have been fine. Just because I'm back doesn't mean you boys get to order me around. I know Phil as well as he knows me. Something he's not used to. He's *used to* dealing with strangers and it's throwing him. I just have to figure out how to get rid of him."

"Easy. You threaten him. Turn his shit back on him. And then hold on to your ass. You do that with the help of the people who care about you."

She flapped her arms. "Oh, here we go. But guess what, Captain America? I did that. And it backfired royally. I've been trying to hack into Phil's system for three days to compile as much evidence as I can. I thought I could use his own tactics against him. As you can see, he's not afraid of me. Whatever I have, whatever I dig up, he will always respond and he can still put my brother in jail. Period."

The rattle of an engine sounded and Mrs. Cunningham pulled into a parking space. Her son was career military, a Marine, God save him, and each time she ran into Gage, she shared all the latest news from overseas. Knowing the stress of having a loved one in a war-torn country, Gage always took the time to talk with her. Sometimes for an hour. Least he could do. No matter how much it screwed up his schedule. Today? He didn't have it in him.

She worked her way out of her car and wandered to the curb. "Hello, you two. Don't you look fierce on such a fine morning."

"Ma'am," Gage said.

"Hi, Mrs. Cunningham."

"Hello, Mikayla. Nice to see you. Gage, I have an update from Mark."

Damn. He couldn't do this now. As much as he wanted to be respectful, chitchat wouldn't work. Not with his mind overloading. Still, he looked her straight in the eye. "Is he okay?"

"Oh, yes. He's just fine."

Phew. Now that he'd determined all was well, he'd have to put her off. For the first time. "Ma'am, I'd like to hear about it and I hate to be rude, but we're in the middle of something. Can I find you later today when I have extra time?"

"He's over in Pakistan—wait." She paused, snapped her head back, and blinked.

The woman had gotten so used to him always being available, no matter what time of day, she almost looked…offended. Something that simultaneously irritated and amused him. At that moment, Mrs. Cunningham represented everything he needed to change. The constant need for him to disregard his own agenda so he could please someone else. Right now, he was pissed enough about this Micki situation that he couldn't, wouldn't make someone else happy. For once, he came first.

Mrs. Cunningham took pity on him and patted his arm. "Certainly. I'm sorry to interrupt."

"That's no problem, ma'am. You couldn't have known."

The woman walked off, leaving him with Micki.

"Did you have to be nasty to her?"

What? "You are just spoiling for a fight today. Why? So you can run again?"

"Shut up."

"No. If you want to run, do it, but you're not blaming me for it. No way, sweetheart. And I *wasn't* nasty. We're busy here."

"Actually, we're not. I'm sorry Britt bothered you. I thought I should handle it alone."

Gage made a buzzing noise. "Sorry, babe. Not happening."

"What?"

"You can't take this guy on yourself." He held up his hands. "Before you get pissy and wax on about how you've been on your own and taking care of yourself, *no* one should deal with this maniac solo. His reach is too long. We need to pool resources."

When his statement was met with blessed silence, he took that as agreement. Might as well call it a win because he wasn't exactly getting many of those this morning.

"How'd you get into town? Tell me you stole Jonah's bike again."

"I'm getting my exercise."

"Where is it?"

"I locked it behind Brynne's shop. Why?"

"Because we're throwing it in my truck and I'm taking you home. Where we'll tackle Reid and Jonah and figure out how to turn the tables on Phil Flynn."

Gage, Micki, and Reid marched into Jonah's command center and found the billionaire with his nose in his computer screen. What else was new?

Jonah had knocked out the dividing wall between what had been two bedrooms and created a combination office/bedroom suite. Which explained the dust collecting in his designated spot in the training center. The Baby Billionaire, as he was affectionately known, preferred staying in his own space, fiddling with his computers and gaming software.

Gage also suspected Jonah didn't want him assuming the boss was watching. Something he appreciated, considering the healing time he'd needed.

Jonah dragged his attention from the giant monitor in front of him, looked at Micki first, then Reid, then Gage.

"I can only imagine," he said.

"Listen up." Reid jerked a thumb in Micki's direction. "She just dropkicked Phil Flynn."

Jonah swiveled his chair to fully face them. "What now?"

"I told him I wasn't going back."

"And how did that go over?"

Micki swerved her lips one way, then the other. "Could have been worse. Captain America here showed up and got into a pissing match with him."

Good one. Gage held up a finger. "At the request of Britt, who called me because Randi had called *him* to say Micki was in the B with Flynn."

"Enter Captain America," Reid gave him a winning smile. "I like that name."

"Fuck off."

Micki flopped onto the love seat on the other side of Jonah's desk. "Now, now, children."

Gage shook his head. These people. Sometimes it was damned hard to keep them all focused. "If we're all done screwing around, maybe we can get on with it? I have work to do. I mean, it's not like we don't have a training center opening soon."

"Right," Jonah said. "Is Flynn leaving?"

Micki stayed quiet, so Gage took that one. "Not without your sister."

"He'll go," Micki said. "Eventually. His business is in Vegas and the thing Phil loves most is money."

Jonah sat forward and rested his elbows on his knees. "I want him gone. Him being here isn't good for any of us. We have enough distractions."

"Okay, Baby Billionaire, what do you suggest?"

"Well, *lunkhead*, I have calls in to a couple of criminal attorneys from Asheville. If this asshole thinks he'll blackmail us with my own fucking DNA and that video, I want to know my options. I've got money to burn, so Phil Flynn can shove *that* up his ass."

CHAPTER SIXTEEN

MICKI APPRECIATED JONAH'S TOUGH talk, but he didn't understand Phil's temperament. In his world, nothing was too extreme. Plus, this went beyond business. This was personal. If Phil couldn't control his own people, how could he be expected to control others?

"Guys," Micki said, "this isn't about me or Jonah. This is about Phil's ability to control a situation."

"Okay," Gage said. "Then what do *you* suggest? You know him. What'll back him off?"

"Me going back to Vegas."

Gage sliced a hand across his throat. "Not an option."

Both Jonah and Reid swung their heads in his direction, staring at him with their own brand of curiosity and wonder. By now, after the pants issue last night and Gage and Micki showing up at the B nearly at the same time, Reid clearly suspected something. And he'd already warned her it wouldn't work between them.

None of his business.

Jonah waved a hand. "He's right. If here is where you want to be, then that's it. I'll call the lawyers again. We'll go into Asheville and talk to them. See what's what."

"In the meantime," Gage said, "I'd like to keep a

better eye on Flynn. I want to know where he is at all times."

Reid nodded. "He's staying at Mrs. Tasky's B and B. I'll poke around, see what he's driving."

"We've got those GPS units TechPro sent us to beta test. If we slip one on Flynn's rental, we can monitor his location."

"Good idea. I'm on that." Reid took two steps and the lights went out.

What the heck?

A crack of sunlight streamed from the bottom of the window blinds and mixed with the glow of Jonah's laptop screen, but otherwise darkness devoured the room. Even Jonah's giant computer monitors had gone black.

Closest to the door, Gage checked the hallway. "Lights are out there, too."

"Hang on," Reid said. "Mom sometimes blows a breaker. Let me check the fuse box."

Reid left and Micki's brain looped. Could it be a coincidence that she'd just defied Phil and suddenly the power went out? Considering part of her duties included hacking into phone service providers and utility companies?

Just a breaker. Unlikely.

Gage stood in the doorway, half his body shadowed in darkness, but still looking over at her.

"Guys," she said, "Phil has a system."

"Don't we all," Jonah cracked.

"Yes, but Phil's includes crashing into people's personal lives and disrupting things."

"Like the power?"

"Yes. He's had me hack into power companies before." She shot out of her chair. "Jonah, give me that laptop. Do we still have Wi-Fi?"

Jonah swiveled to his laptop and checked the screen. "Uh, yeah. Why?"

"He'll have everything shut down. Cable, Wi-Fi,

electric. All of it. And call your bank. Before he cleans out your accounts."

While Reid called the power company, Gage hauled ass to the training center only to find the building dark and the furnace silenced. Cursing Flynn, he stood in the middle of the reception area taking in the eerie, inherent silence that came with power outages. From the time he was a kid, blackouts and the weird tension that came with them gave him the creeps. Flynn—the son of a bitch—worked fast. Assuming this wasn't some fluke coincidence and the power on the property, on a sunny day lacking a whisper of wind, had randomly crapped out on them.

His phone rang and he ripped it from his back pocket. Reid. He punched the screen hoping his buddy had good news.

"What's up?"

"You got lights down there?"

"Nope. What'd the power company say?"

"They're stumped."

Translation: We have no fucking idea when this will be fixed. Excellent.

"And what? We're supposed to sit around with our thumbs up our asses while they figure it out?"

The front door swished open and he turned to see Micki storming into the building, laptop in hand.

"Reid, I'll call you back. Two minutes." He disconnected just as Micki strode past him. "What's up?"

He followed as she hustled down the hall, her boots clunking against the tile. "Phil thinks this power failure will scare me. *He* knows that *I* know this is a warning shot. The precursor to something bigger."

"Safe to assume, yes."

"He's expecting me to fall in line and come back to

him. His threats have always kept me from defying him."
She jabbed her thumb in the air. "I've been under his
thumb too long. Let's change things up. Shall we?"

"How?"

"By turning the power back on."

Once in his office, she set the laptop on his desk and
hauled his guest chair closer. "I'm going to screw with
him."

Oh, this girl, so complicated.

He moved around the desk. "Well, all right then."

Her fingers pounded the keyboard, moving like
lightning. He'd seen Jonah do magic at the computer, but
the way she typed, the myriad of code flying across her
screen, was something different. Something instinctive
and on a whole other level.

"Shit on a shingle," he said. "You're fast."

"Years of practice. Unfortunately."

Half in awe and determined not to distract her, he
stood behind her, keeping his mouth shut while she did
her thing.

The seconds ticked by, stretching to a minute while
she made a variety of grunting noises, occasionally
clucking her tongue in some sort of Micki hacking
language.

Finally, she held up her hand to high-five him. "I'm
in."

"Seriously?"

"Yep." She went back to the keyboard. "Hang on,
handsome."

The lights in his office flicked on. Three minutes.
That's how long it had taken her to hack into the power
company's server. His time in the Army had hardened
him to a lot of things. The Internet—and what occurred
on it—wasn't one of them. The whole damn thing
terrified him.

He scanned the laptop screen. What he saw wasn't
one of the three languages he spoke. Code, he'd never
understand.

"Oh," she said, "would you just look at that?"

"What is it?"

"Whoever Phil had do this is still in there." She tapped the screen. "This code right here is him. Or her."

The lights went off.

"You little bastard." Micki pounded the keyboard, a small smirk lifting the corners of her lips. "Let me get rid of them."

She went to work again, humming the entire time. Humming. Later, he'd have to think about how it felt to watch her break any number of laws. Something she didn't seem to mind all that much.

But, hell, all she was doing at the moment was righting a wrong. Or was that him justifying it because he had a thing for this girl? Not to mention a business to protect.

This was how it must have felt to her over the years, to inch across that legal versus illegal wire, finding ways to make sense of her decisions as she went.

A minute later, the lights in the office flashed on, the clunk of the furnace sounded through the vent, and Gage forgot all about his ethics dilemma.

"Well, holy shit."

"Ha!" Micki shook her fist at the screen. "Take that!"

Gage's phone rang again—Reid. He tapped the speaker button. "You got power up there?"

"Yeah. You?"

"Yeah. Micki just kicked the crap out of someone inside the power company's server."

"Shit."

Gage held the phone out. "Tell your brother it's fine."

"It's fine. I've been doing this for ten years, they won't catch me."

One could hope.

"Jonah called the bank. So far, no activity on his accounts. They have their IT people on it."

"Good," Micki said, still pounding away on the keyboard. "If this idiot is any good, he'll figure out how to get around me, so it could be a long night of the power going on and off."

The lights went out again.

"Jesus," Gage said. "This is nuts."

Micki continued on, seemingly unfazed. "The good news is, Phil will realize this game is dangerous. If he or his hacker is caught, he has way more to lose than I do, so he'll eventually give up."

Eventually. But how the hell long would it take? And would Micki wind up in handcuffs before it was over?

"Keep at it," Reid said. "Suds and I are gonna plant a GPS unit. You ready, boss?"

"You know I am."

Phil gave up. It took an hour, but he'd realized she'd win that particular battle. With power fully restored and Jonah throwing his billionaire weight around, Micki followed him into the law office of Richards and Calibee.

The slick marble, polished wood, and white leather chairs made her twitchy. Somehow, her faded skinny jeans, black button-down, and battered boots didn't fit the decor.

Too much light to her darkness. There seemed to be a run on that lately.

Even the receptionist—an absolute stunner with her expertly applied makeup, form-fitting light gray dress, and blond hair pulled back so tightly it looked painful— could have jumped off the cover of *Vogue*.

Headset in place, she gave them a wide, toothy smile as they approached the giant rectangular desk.

"Richards and Calibee. Please hold." She clicked another line. "Richards and Calibee. Please hold." A third line. "Richards and Calibee. Please hold."

From the looks of the place and the fury with which

this woman worked the phones, Jonah had picked the right lawyer.

The receptionist went back to the first call, dealt with it, and then got rid of the other two. All the while, her smile in place. Ice could form on this woman's ass. Total pro.

She removed her headset and folded her hands on top of the desk. "I'm so sorry for the wait. How can I help you?"

Her brother turned his hazel eyes on the woman and ripped off one of the patented Steele grins. "I'm Jonah Steele. This is my sister Micki. We have an appointment with Owen Richards."

"Ah, yes." She quickly rose and gestured to the hallway. "Mr. Steele, Ms. Steele, welcome. He's expecting you."

She led them down a long, curving hallway painted the same muted beige as the reception area. She stopped at a set of glass doors and waved them into a conference room that sat ten. "Please have a seat. Can I get you something to drink?"

"I'm fine, thanks."

Jonah offered up another smile. "I think we're good. Thank you."

"Excellent. I'll let Owen know you're here."

Ms. Vogue returned the smile, adding a little extended eye contact, and Micki nearly gagged.

Forgoing the chair at the head of the table, Micki took the second one on the left and Jonah grabbed the one beside her. She slid into the supple white leather—who was crazy enough to do white in an office?—appreciating the softness of the obviously pricey chairs yet still feeling as if she soiled the place.

"Jonah, I feel like a homeless person in here."

"Don't worry about it. That's what's awesome about being rich. Nobody gives me shit about how I dress anymore."

She laughed. "A perk to be sure."

The glass doors swung open and a guy no older than forty with bright red hair and freckles strode in. He wore a black suit with a white shirt and a red tie with—hold on, was that Snoopy? This was Jonah's shark? A guy wearing a Snoopy tie?

"Hi. I'm Owen Richards."

He held his hand to Micki—ladies first—and then Jonah. Already she liked this guy.

Jonah stood and shook hands with his new lawyer, then returned to his seat. Owen ditched his suit jacket, hanging it on the back of the chair at the head of the table and then shocked the heck out of Micki by taking the seat across from her rather than the I'm-in-charge one he'd just set his jacket on.

She glanced at Jonah. "Seriously, I like him already."

Flipping open his portfolio, Owen snorted. "Thank you. So, what's up? What can I help you with?"

Where to begin? Jonah looked over at her, clearly sensed her hesitation, and sat forward. "I'll start. You can fill in what I miss. That work?"

"Sure."

Not that she wanted to share the entire sordid story, but moving on from Phil, and the life she left in Vegas, required it. She faced Owen again, took in his kind face and freckles and the Snoopy tie.

It all registered.

Like Gage, the apple-cheeked look worked for him. For a defense attorney, who probably spent his days carving up witnesses, it was a brilliant disguise. Prosecutors, and guys like Phil, would take one gander at Owen and assume they'd trample him.

Micki grabbed Jonah's arm. "Wait. I need to say something first." He nodded and she went back to Owen. "I want you to know that we were young, really young, when all this started. I've made bad decisions along the way."

"Hey," Jonah said, "you don't—"

"No. It's true. I meant well, but I screwed this whole thing up. Jonah has never done anything wrong."

Owen dropped his pen and held out his hand. "Give me a dollar."

Angling his hip up, Jonah slid his wallet from his back pocket. "All I have is hundreds."

Micki laughed. "You are *such* a billionaire."

"First off," Owen said, "whose lawyer am I?"

Jonah waggled his thumb. "Hers." He handed her a crisp bill. "Give that to your lawyer."

"I'll pay you back," Micki said as she handed over the cash.

"No. You won't. After what you've done all these years, I owe you at least this much."

Owen pocketed the money. "That's your first installment on my $15,000 retainer. Everything you tell me is protected by attorney-client privilege."

Fifteen *thousand*. This time, Micki gagged. She might have even done it out loud because both Owen and Jonah shot her a look.

"Look," Owen said, "I'm your lawyer now. You'll pay me a ton of money to help you get out of whatever jam you're in. I'll go to war for you. The only thing I ask is that you don't lie to me. If you do, I'm cutting you loose. Got it?"

"Yes, sir," Micki said.

"Got it," Jonah added.

"Good. Now tell me everything. And don't call me sir."

Ninety minutes and no less than a dozen pages of notes later, Owen set his pen down and sat back.

"What do you think?" Jonah asked.

"First, Jonah, I'm going to recommend you to someone I trust to represent you. It would be a conflict of interest for me to take on both of you."

Jonah nodded. "No problem. I figured that."

"Then I think Phil Flynn needs to be brought down, but one thing at a time." He held one finger up. "The video. You said he sent you only part of it. Can you get the rest?"

If her attempts to hack into his server hadn't been a bust, maybe. Micki shook her head. "Doubtful."

"The DNA could be a problem. Will the victim—"

"Tessa," Jonah said.

"Will Tessa give a statement exonerating you?"

"I could ask."

Micki cocked her head. "You know how to find her?"

Jonah shrugged. "At Steele Trap. I brought her on as a consultant before I sold it."

At that, Micki simply gawked. "You gave her a job? Really? I didn't know that."

"What's your point?"

Huh. Now who was the secretive one?

"We have to be careful with this," Owen said. "We don't want it looking like you gave her the job to keep her quiet."

"Hell, no."

"And the assault happened in Buncombe County?"

"Yes," Micki said. "In Asheville. Why?"

"The DA and I started out in the public defender's office together. Five years into it he jumped the aisle."

He knew the DA. All around it seemed Jonah picked the right guy.

"That's handy," Jonah said.

Owen tapped his notepad and ran his hand over his chin.

While he mulled things over, Micki leaned forward. "If Tessa agrees to tell the DA that Jonah didn't do anything, can we get him out of this?"

"He'll have to talk to his lawyer, but if you're asking my opinion, it's possible. Once he's cleared, if Tessa decides she wants to press charges, she's free to do so. I'll tell you though, the DA can press charges on his own if he wants."

Jonah groaned. "We'll need to tell her that. She's been through a lot."

"Jonah, she's our chance to clear you."

"I know, Mick, but she's built a life and I'm not

tearing that away from her. It has to be her decision. Just…let me deal with that."

Whatever Jonah's relationship with Tessa was, clearly he felt comfortable enough—as comfortable as one could anyway—to at least approach her on the subject. Micki nodded. "You take care of Tessa and I'll handle Phil." She faced her new lawyer. "How do I get rid of him?"

"I have an idea. You probably won't like it."

Chapter Seventeen

AFTER A HECK OF A long day, Gage sat at his kitchen table, opening the only outstanding e-mail. Thanks to his newly created organizing method, the growing number of daily e-mails he received had been downgraded from hateful to barely hateful. Prioritizing came in the form of color-coding. Red equaled hot and to be handled ASAP. In between were three other colors leading to blue. Blue he eventually got to, but not all that quickly. Only so many hours in the day, kids.

This particular message he'd marked red. Flaming red.

The cement company Britt hired to build the walls separating the firing ranges was running behind and instead of showing up first thing tomorrow morning, they were looking at Thursday. Terrific. Two days late.

Adding this to the Steele family drama would send Reid into a psychotic break. For that alone, Gage should get a bonus. Call it the keeping-psychos-controlled incentive. However, if he delivered this information to Reid before anyone else, he'd control the message.

And minimize the shit-fit.

"I picked the wrong damned day to stop sniffing glue," Gage muttered, mimicking one of his favorite movie lines.

"Me too."

Startled by Micki's voice, he snapped his head up and immediately regretted it when the room flipped. He closed his eyes, drew a long breath, and let his swaying vision settle.

"Sorry," she said. "I knocked. I wouldn't have come in, but..."

"No," he said, "it's fine. I was working. Didn't hear you."

She turned back, gestured to the front door. "I can go if you're busy."

Go? That was the last thing he wanted from her.

He stood and walked to the archway separating the kitchen and the foyer. "You're not going anywhere." He dropped a kiss on her lips. Nothing too crazy, just a casual hello.

Pulling back from the kiss, she tugged on his T-shirt. "Everything okay? You looked frustrated when I walked in."

"I am frustrated."

Huh. How about that? Before his injury, he'd never have admitted that. He'd have just dealt with the problem and made it go away. Back then, he'd have felt like a pussy if he complained. Now? Complaining to—or maybe confiding in—someone wasn't so bad.

"Oh, yay, Captain America. You *are* human. Tell me about it. Please."

"It's nothing. Contractor running behind."

"I'd say that's something when you're opening soon. And then there's dealing with Reid—and of course, Britt—because they are sure to be at war over something like that. So, yes, you're entitled."

He grabbed her hand and curled his fingers around hers. "How about we forget it and I buy you dinner. We can go into Asheville if you want. Get out of here for a while."

"Actually, I just came from Asheville. The attorney Jonah hired is there."

"He got the appointment that fast?"

"I don't know if he got it or forced it. Being a billionaire has its perks."

"Good meeting?"

She shrugged. "I guess."

"Do you want to talk about it?"

Damn, he hoped she did. Micki, with her secrets, made him nuts. As much as he didn't want to be in the middle of everyone's problems, she was the exception. Which, intellectually speaking, sucked because he'd handed over his own carefully held secret to a woman he barely knew. A woman who'd spent her adult life throwing open the proverbial closets on people.

She met his gaze. "That's why I'm here. To talk. I couldn't decide if I should just deal with it on my own or ask your advice." She smiled up at him. "It's new to me. All this asking for help."

Good for her. "I know. But I'm glad you did. What'd the lawyer say?"

She blew out a breath. "He said I can be Queen for a Day."

Gage waved her to the living room, waited for her to sit on the sofa, then dropped beside her, angling his body to face her. "What does Queen for a Day mean?"

"My lawyer, the one *Jonah* is paying for—"

"Don't worry about that. He doesn't care."

"How do you know?"

Gage shrugged. "I know enough about your brother to know he'd do anything for his family. And he doesn't stress about money. At least when it comes to the training center. Most of the time. He leaves that up to Reid. Reid watches every penny."

How did he know so much? About *her* family. That whole thing about Jonah not stressing over money? She had no idea. Her twin brother and she hadn't a clue how he felt about his finances.

Now that she'd be staying, she'd get to know her twin again.

"I won't be a freeloader."

"So pay him back. What's Queen for a Day?"

"The lawyer—Owen—wants to call the US Attorney."

"Oh, boy. That's federal."

She nodded. "Yep. I did a little research on our way home. With all the work I've done for Phil, I could go to prison for thirty years."

"Don't get rattled by what you find on the Internet. Federal sentences are all over the board and judges have discretion. Hell, if a judge wants to, he could give you probation."

"That's what Owen is hoping. He said a Queen for a Day agreement is for people who cooperate in a criminal case. What Phil does easily qualifies as criminal. Between racketeering, witness tampering, computer fraud, and, let's not forget, destruction of evidence, I can stick a fork in him."

"Why do I feel like there's a but coming?"

Was there? She honestly didn't know. The entire ride home with Jonah had been filled with silence. She'd been too busy asking herself endless questions—did she have the guts to do it? To be a rat?

To separate a man from his family?

Just as he'd done to her.

After all Phil had done to tear her from Steele Ridge, how could she not be sure?

She scooted closer and rested her head on Gage's shoulder. Allowing herself, for just a few seconds, to be still and not think. To enjoy snuggling with a man she hoped to see a whole lot more of in the future.

He kissed the top of her head. "You're okay. Just talk to me. This Queen for a Day. What does it entail?"

The truly fun part... "I'd go into the US Attorney's

office and admit everything about Phil and his business. For that one day, no matter what I tell them, they won't prosecute me. After that, if they think they can make a case against Phil—which, believe me, they will—I enter into a cooperation agreement. It's called a proffer agreement."

A *hmm* noise came from his throat and she brought her fingers up, running the backs of them against his neck. "What are you thinking? Say it. Please. That's why I came here."

"Would you have to plead guilty to something?"

"Owen said it's an information case, rather than an indictment. If I plead guilty, the case doesn't have to go before a grand jury. No trial."

"How do you feel about that?"

Did he have six months? Even then she wasn't sure she'd truly understand her own feelings. "I'm…conflicted. Not about pleading guilty. That's a weird relief. To just be done with it. But I'm hung up on being a squealer. Phil calls them rats."

"Uh, Phil is an asshole."

"I know. But he's been my asshole for ten years." She waved it off. "As much as I hate the idea of cooperating, I love it, too. For the first time, I can see a way out. A chance to live my life the way I choose." She finally sat up and met his gaze. "I want that."

I want you. She couldn't say it. Not yet. One thing at a time, because if she went to jail, she didn't anticipate Captain America waiting around for his convict girlfriend.

He ran one finger down the side of her face and over her jaw. "For what it's worth, not a lot of eighteen-year-olds would have made the sacrifice you did. I'd say you deserve to live your life the way you want."

"I wanted to save my brother."

"And you did. It's time to let it go. If that means cooperating with the feds, you do it. Your family will support you."

"What about you? Will you support me?"

"I'm sitting here, aren't I?"

Yes. He was. Gage Barber. Honorable, heroic. The light to her darkness.

Crazy.

She leaned in, kissed him gently, let her lips linger. "Thank you. You're...amazing."

"Honey, you've spent too many years around scumbags. But thank you." He kissed her again, then sat back, his mind clearly working on something.

"Gage, what's bugging you?"

"Thinking is all. What happens after you plead guilty? I mean, you're cooperating, but plenty of cooperating witnesses serve jail time. What's the prosecutor recommending as far as sentencing?"

That was the second half. The gamble. "Owen said after the proffer agreement, if I've fully cooperated, the US Attorney will write a recommendation letter to the judge. It's called a Five K letter and it outlines everything I've done to assist the government. At that point, the judge decides my sentence. He can give me probation or..." She dipped her head. "Or send me to prison."

"What does the lawyer think?"

"He thinks I could get probation."

"Phil would be locked up and you'd be free. Sounds like a win-win."

Of course it did. Only, Micki hadn't experienced a lot of win-wins and when it came to Phil, she wouldn't count on anything. "Phil has a far reach. Prison won't keep him contained."

"He won't get to you. I can promise that. With the resources you have behind you, you'll be safe."

When Gage said it, she believed it. But was that all starry-eyed want? The fairy tale she'd never gotten. Prince Charming and all that bullshit.

For her.

Why not?

"You think I should do it?"

"I do. Unless you can come up with another way to get rid of Phil, if you want your life back, it's the only option. Running is off the table, right?"

Staring at this man, listening to him talk about keeping her safe, running was most definitely off the table. "Yes. That idea came from desperation. He'd either find me or I'd be on the move constantly."

Fucking Phil. Once again backing her against a wall.

She couldn't—wouldn't—do it anymore. She'd given him way too much of herself. It had to stop. All the hiding and secrecy. If she took the deal, though, she'd be forced to admit her guilt and make amends.

It'll gut me.

Was it such a bad thing? To be rid of all the pent-up shame and rebuild herself? Maybe, if she got really lucky, Gage Barber could be part of the renovation.

She studied the wall straight ahead where the seams from a bad patch job—one of Britt's early attempts— made her smile.

"See that wall? Grif put Reid's head through it one night and Britt tried to patch it before Mom got home. Poor Britt, always fixing everyone's problems." She swung back to Gage. "Kinda like you." She patted his leg, leaned over, and pecked his cheek.

"What was that for?"

"For helping me. For being my sounding board. I'll do it."

"Yeah?"

"I need a fresh start and this will get it for me." She lifted her chin and smiled up at him. "It's no fairy tale, but hey, I'll get to be a Queen for a Day."

Gage watched Micki put on her show. Her I-can-do-this show. This girl—woman—had lived one hell of a life so far. "You know," he said, running his hand over the side of her head, "you told me *I* was amazing. Really, I think you're the amazing one. Look at what you've done. What you're about to do. That takes a spine. You could be on the floor wailing about the injustice of it all, but not you. You own it. I love that about you."

Love. That sneaky little word didn't enter his vocabulary too often. By his way of thinking, all kinds of love existed. Sibling love, parental love, romantic love. That last one had eluded him most of his thirty-one years. He never minded. If it happened, it happened. Now, though, looking at Micki Steele, he might have lost his mind because romantic love didn't seem like such a bad idea.

His mother would lose it. *Hey, Mom, meet my hacker girlfriend who's spent the past ten years breaking a multitude of federal laws.*

Jesus.

In front of him, though, Micki's lips spread into a flashing smile that was apparently cemented into Steele family DNA. They all had that spark. And it was killer.

He reached his fingers up, dragged them under her chin, along the silky skin there, heating up the space between them. He loved touching her. When he touched her, something changed. The hard edges smoothed out and the hyper-standoffish Micki softened, yielding just enough to let him believe that he made a difference in her life. *Micki, Micki, Micki.*

"Gage?"

He stopped his exploration and flattened his hand, curving his fingers over her neck and stroking her hammering pulse with his thumb. But his eyes were on her lips, and his brain? Well, that horny bastard was busy coming up with all the things he wanted to do with those lips.

"Gage?"

He snapped his gaze to hers.

"What?"

"Is it crazy for me to want you inside me?"

"Is it crazy for me to want to *be* inside you?"

That earned him another small grin, but he'd gotten to know her cues, that little tell in the way she drew her eyebrows together, that something was up with her.

"I don't want to drag you into my mess," she said.

He dipped his head, ran his lips over hers, dotting kisses along her jawline to her neck, his tongue flicking over the delicate spot behind her ear. "Honey, it's a little late for that now." She tilted her head sideways, giving him more access. "Atta girl," he said.

Her arms came around him, pulling him closer—breasts, legs, all of her flush up against him—and his erection said hello in the most obvious way possible.

"Mmm," she said. "You feel good. Everything about you. I don't deserve you. I'll never deserve you."

Before he could argue, she kissed him. Absolutely fucking mauled him. With her tongue, her hands, that crazy lean body that was all legs and made him constantly imagine her wrapped around him.

Levering off the couch, he scooped her up, tucked her legs around him and carried her to the stairs, tripping on the first step but catching them both before she clocked her head. Gently, he lowered her to her back. Right on the goddamned stairs.

She went to work on his shirt, lifting the hem as the tips of her fingers connected with his stomach.

"Keep that up and we won't make it to the bed. Again."

"I don't care."

She bucked her hips, sending him into another crazy wave of lust. As much as he wanted to pound himself inside her, he wouldn't do that. The first time he'd nailed her against a wall. This time, they'd get to his bed.

Even if it killed him.

"No," he said. "You're about to have a long night. I want you comfortable."

CHAPTER EIGHTEEN

COMFORTABLE? THE MAN HAD TO be joking. One thing she could honestly say, with the steam roasting her from inside out, she was far from comfortable.

He picked her up again, effortlessly carrying her gangly body upstairs, and as nice as a bed sounded, she was about to burst. Just come right out of her skin. She reached down, cupped his crotch where his monster erection waited for her.

All mine.

He halted mid-step, grabbed onto the handrail and tipped his head back, moaning as she stroked him through his jeans.

"Jesus, Micki. Are you trying to kill us?"

"If it gets you inside me, yes."

He let out a little moan and his face melded into a strained look of concentration. She rocked her hips, loving the feel of all that hardness, imagined him sliding into her, making her feel what she'd felt the other night.

The connection. The acceptance. He knew her secrets. A lot of them anyway, and he still wanted her.

"If you're going to be stubborn," she said, "get moving. Otherwise, I want you to screw me right on these steps."

He met her gaze, those blue eyes scalding hot as he trudged up the last few stairs. "Not on the steps. But I'll touch you everywhere, find every spot that makes you come apart. You know that, right?"

Every spot? Even she didn't know all of them. There'd never been a man around long enough, who cared enough, to take the time to discover them.

"Captain America," she said, "I would welcome that."

He kicked the bedroom door open, took four steps and tossed her on the bed. "By the time I'm done, you'll be begging me to stop."

He ditched his shoes then pulled his shirt off, exposing all the yumminess underneath. The coiled muscle of his arms, the cut of his abs and chest. The blond hair that ran in a line down the center and dipped below his waistband. Micki licked her lips and he watched the motion, the slow slide of her tongue.

"Dream on. I will never beg you to stop. Never."

She sat up, kicking off her shoes while unzipping his jeans and sliding them and his boxers down, down, down. *Hello*. His erection, every giant, fabulous inch of it, sprang free and her breasts tingled, anticipating that moment when he'd be inside her.

While he stepped out of his pants, he yanked on her zipper. The two of them wiggled her free and all of a sudden, in a frenzy of activity, she was peeling off her shirt as he dug through his nightstand. Hopefully for a condom. Or many condoms.

He lifted a box out—yay—and set it on the table.

"Let me," she said.

"Seriously?"

"It's a fantasy. Some people want to swing from chandeliers. Me…" She shrugged, half embarrassed by the admission.

He handed over the condom. "Have at it. It'll be a first for both of us."

At that, she smiled, plucked the foil packet from him and tore it open. The second her fingers touched him, he sucked in a breath, but she continued on, drawing the rubber over him, taking care not to rip it.

"Jeez, Micki. Way too slow."

Not bothering to hide her silly grin, she looked up at him. "I'm so crazy about you. Around you, I'm…special."

Condom on him, she let go and lay back on the bed, drawing one leg up and holding her arms out, opening herself to him as he lowered on top of her. He propped himself on his elbows and kissed her, a gentle brush of his lips as she wrapped herself around him, pulling him closer.

"Open your eyes."

She looked up at him, met his gaze and held it, took in his smile and the lightness she saw in his eyes. Then he did it, just slid into her with one hard thrust, and she cried out, loving the feel of him pushed so far inside her. She opened her legs wider, rocking her hips and guiding him deeper.

Please.

She'd never get enough. Never.

He pulled out and she locked her legs around him, waiting for him to enter her again. And again, and again.

I want him.

Always. She clamped her hands on his ass, held him in place and ground her hips, giving as good as she got.

"You are wicked," he said.

"I want you to lose control. I want to see it."

"Keep that up and it won't be a problem."

She let out a laugh, enjoying the playful, unfiltered moment, and he pushed deeper inside her and—oh, wow. Wow, wow, wow.

She reached behind her head, gripped the pillow as she rocked her hips, and her body morphed into a coiling rope of tension. He picked up the pace, perfectly reading her signals.

"Here it comes," she said. "Please. Oh, please."

She wanted this. Wanted to feel that rush, that insane

moment when she let her world blow apart like she never had before.

Finally, she closed her eyes, let the light show take hold as the tension built. Higher and higher she went, and Gage thrust and pulled back and thrust again and she cried out, a low guttural sound as the orgasm ripped her apart. The release came fast. A massive rush—too damned fast—that left her skin buzzing.

She slowed her breathing, forcing her body to relax and extend the euphoria.

Not done yet.

She reared up, rolling him to his back, intent on giving him the same insanity he'd treated her to.

He gripped her hips, guiding her along, showing her the pace he wanted. He flattened his hands against her breasts, then squeezed her hyper-sensitive nipples and she knew, before this was over, she'd come again.

She leaned forward, still using the motion he wanted, and kissed him, sliding her tongue into his mouth. His fingers locked onto her hips, digging into her flesh as he moaned.

He tore his lips away, lifted his hands to her face, his eyes on her as his own release hit him. He bucked under her, driving, driving, driving, one last time, howling her name before he collapsed under her.

"Is it cliché to say I'm starved?"

Micki grinned up at Gage, burrowed further into his side, and eased her leg over his. If she could stay like this, happy and content over a simple thing like spending time with a man, she'd do it. Just stay in bed, with Gage, forever.

When she didn't answer, he lifted his head. "Micki? Everything okay down there?"

"Everything is great." She snuggled closer. "Sorry. I was daydreaming. I'm hungry, too."

"Eat out? Or in?"

"In." She looked up at him, ran her hand over his chest, twirling her fingers in the fine blond hairs. "Could we watch a movie? For ten years I've watched movies alone. Now I'd like to try doing it with you."

Another new experience she'd enjoy with Gage.

He kissed the top of her head and rolled sideways. "Good plan. I have menus downstairs. We'll order and see what's what on cable."

Cable.

A memory of last Christmas at Phil's house popped into her mind. His kids had been teasing him about his tendency to call Netflix *cable.* For whatever reason, he couldn't grasp the concept of Netflix. Silly memories. The good ones she'd hopefully remember by the time this was all over.

Cable.

Naked as a newborn, she sat up.

Cable. The e-mail from Phil. *Whoa.* She tossed the sheet back, jumped out of bed.

Gage kept his eyes on her as she whipped her clothes off the floor, gathering up her underwear, searching for her bra, then giving up and just shoving her arms into the first shirt she grabbed. Gage's.

He followed her out the door as she ran for the stairs. "What's up?"

"I need my laptop."

"Okay. *That,* I've never heard from a woman after sex."

"The e-mail Phil sent me the other day, the one with the video, it came from his personal account."

"And?"

"His personal account is through his cable company. The *number one* cable company in Nevada."

"Alrighty. I have no idea why that should be so exciting."

Her brain racing, she reached the stairs and inhaled, forcing herself to settle down. The fresh scent of her mother's detergent registered. "Tell me my mother does your laundry."

"Hell no. I just like the smell of her soap so I use it."

"Oh, thank God."

He laughed. "Would that be a deal breaker?"

"I don't know." She flapped her arms and hopped off the last step. "I've never been interested in a man my mother does laundry for."

"Micki, what's up with this e-mail from Phil?"

"It's not the e-mail itself, but the cable company. There's a lot of information that can be garnered about people. Particularly if that company handles the phone lines."

"You hacked the cable company?"

"I'm not proud of it, but think about it. Porn rentals, online activity, phone calls to mistresses. It's a gold mine for a guy like Phil."

She snagged her backpack from the floor. "Phil likes to e-mail himself files. He hates dealing with thumb drives. If I know him at all, I'd bet he had someone e-mail him a zip file with the video of Jonah leaving the room the night of the rape. He probably edited it down so he could send it to me in clumps."

"You think you can retrieve the full video?"

"Hoping so. Combine that with Tessa telling the DA or the US Attorney or whoever the hell would handle the rape case that Jonah helped her, and we can clear him."

"It'll destroy Flynn's leverage."

Micki dug her laptop from her backpack, set it on her mother's old coffee table, and parked her butt on the couch. "Yep."

"It'll also piss him off. You ready for that?"

No one could ever be ready for that. "Do I have a choice?"

Assuming it to be a rhetorical question, Gage let it

linger, but sat down beside her. After dealing with a pesky password issue, she logged into the cable company's server and went to work. Within minutes, she brought up Phil's e-mail account. First things first. She clicked on the tiny gear at the upper right.

"What are you doing?"

"Changing his password."

"Why?"

"Because I want to. And he'll know it was me. For once, he'll know I had the upper hand. It might be silly, but there you go."

"It's not. I get that. He's a big bear to poke, though, when you could be in and out without being detected."

No more hiding. No more secrets. She was done with all that, and him knowing she'd been in his account, that she was no longer afraid to defy him, would solidify it. She stopped typing and looked over at Gage. "Tomorrow morning I'm calling my lawyer to tell him I want to be Queen for a Day. I'd say the bear will get poked anyway. Will you go with me? To the US Attorney? They probably won't let you sit in, but—"

"Absolutely. I can wait outside."

He's so good. And he wanted to support her. Despite everything he knew, he saw the real Micki, the good Micki, buried beneath the rubble. *I could really get used to him.* "Thank you."

After changing the password, she clicked back to the inbox where Phil's e-mails flashed in order of the date received. She scrolled, skimming the ones from the past week. His sister with an invitation to his niece's birthday in a couple of weeks.

If things went Micki's way, Phil would be sitting in a cell by then. Ugh. She couldn't think about that. About the shock his family would suffer. The loss of him. *Not going there.* He'd never cared when Micki had suffered that same loss. Back then, he'd seen it as a victory. A conquest. One that separated an eighteen-year-old girl from *her* loved ones.

Back to business here.

She kept scrolling, skipping the e-mails lacking attachments. She needed that video.

Who knew Phil received so many e-mails in a day? To avoid distraction, she locked her gaze on the right side of the screen stopping at each e-mail with a paper clip icon.

Gage nudged her shoulder. "No luck yet?"

"Not yet."

Wait. An e-mail from Tomas. With a paper clip. She clicked on the e-mail, found a zipped file. *Oh, Tommy.* Half sick over her so-called friend's possible betrayal, she clicked again and the folder downloaded. Another click revealed an MP4 file and her head damn near exploded. A week ago, these men had been her central focus. On some level, she'd trusted them.

Given the things they'd accomplished together, this business of destroying lives, she couldn't fathom why they even deserved her trust.

So much for loyalty.

The man next to her, though? He was the one deserving of trust. She bumped his shoulder. "I think I found it."

"Seriously?"

She clicked the file and a black-and-white video of a long hallway with—one, two, three—doors lining it filled the screen. The night of Tessa's attack, Micki hadn't gone into that part of the house. She'd mostly stayed in the yard, only venturing into the kitchen once for a refill of her soda. The house had been huge, though. At least ten thousand square feet. At the time, she'd marveled at the wealth.

One of the doors off the hallway opened and a man— a kid really—with short blond hair stepped out, tucking his shirt in, and Micki's empty stomach rolled.

Behind that door, Tessa was stoned and being violated in the worst way a woman could.

Time stamp: 12:08 AM.

Any minute now, Jonah would be led to that room. The events of that night—the one that obliterated her life—were a constant loop in her brain, each element committed to memory.

Time stamp: 12:10.

As the empty hallway loomed in front of her, the video played and she slouched back, hugging her arms around her torso.

Time stamp: 12:11. And there was Jonah, innocent laughing Jonah, being led around the curve of the hallway by Harrison Shaw. Heartbreak and rage spewed, an instant burst of hatred and horror and agony. That pig. That fucking degenerate, lowlife. That *monster*. He'd stolen all of their lives. Tessa, Jonah, and Micki. Gone. She wanted to pound on him. Just take her fist and smash it into his skull. Beat him until he bled.

And then she'd line up his friends, every one of them, and pound on them, too. Over and over and over. Let them experience being a victim. Being violated.

For Tessa. For every woman who'd been victimized.

"Sons of bitches."

Needing to move, to get rid of the energy devouring her, Micki hopped off the couch, pointed at the images.

"This is it." She jabbed her finger. "Jonah is going to walk into that room. When Harrison—he's the kid that lives there—leaves, Jonah will come out. To find me. I haven't seen this part of the video, but Jonah told me what happened. He took Tessa out of that room and brought her to one at the end of the hall. It faced the side of the house where we smuggled her out. I can still see him opening that window. He literally shoved her through and she toppled to the ground. She could barely walk."

Gage's gaze stayed fixed on the screen as she paced around him, sometimes moving in circles simply to burn off energy. All the while, sneaking peeks at the screen.

That damned night. Everything changed after that. And behind that door, Tessa was…God…what they were doing to her. What they *would* have done to her had Jonah not been invited to join in.

She stopped pacing, put her hands over her eyes. "Those animals!" she cried, her voice jagged and rough. "They destroyed us all. That girl had to live with what they did to her!"

Heart slamming, absolutely banging against her chest wall, Micki dug the heels of her hands into her eyes. *Block it out.*

"I hate them for what they did."

Gage's warm hand landed on her shoulder and she flinched. He snatched his hand away, taking the heat with him.

"I'm sorry," he said. "I know better than to put hands on someone without them seeing it coming."

She dropped her hands and stepped toward him, her body craving his and the comfort she found there. "It's not you. I'm just…not used to people touching me."

He folded her in his arms and she rested her forehead against his chest. Exhausted and strung out, she concentrated on leveling her emotions off.

"Are you sure you can watch the rest?"

"I have to see it. Compare it to what I've imagined all this time. Those boys should be castrated."

"Yeah, they should."

Gage rolled the SUV to a stop in front of Miss Joan's porch and the outside lamp threw enough light to illuminate the interior of the SUV.

"So," Micki said, "I'm thinking I won't kiss you good night, right here."

"I think that's probably a good plan. For now. Your brothers aren't known for their tact, and I'm not sure either one of us is up for an interrogation about what's going on with us."

"Reid and Jonah know something's up. And Evie promised to keep it to herself. I think she likes having sisterly secrets." Britt and Grif she wasn't sure about.

"I think if Britt suspected, he'd come to me."

Micki smiled. "Oh, yeah. He'd give you the what-are-your-intentions speech."

"And won't that be fun?"

Micki yanked on the door handle and slid out of the SUV, dragging her backpack over her shoulder. "Thank you for tonight."

Across the seat, he met her gaze. "I didn't exactly suffer through it."

"Not that! Cripes, men are pigs. I meant talking me through the whole Queen for a Day thing. I needed a level head." She nudged her chin toward the house. "I'll tell Jonah I'm cooperating. He said it was my decision, but I'm not sure he liked the idea."

"He's probably worried about you."

She nodded. "I know, but I can't live with the constant threat of Phil. It's time to end this."

So she could get on with her life, settle into her hometown, and connect with her family again. Make some friends and hopefully, if she caught a lucky break, get to know the man in front of her.

At the moment, she didn't necessarily deserve Gage, but if she could put Vegas behind her, admit her wrongdoing and make amends for it, she might become whole.

Something she hadn't been since she'd left Steele Ridge.

Gage looked beyond her at the front porch where Jonah stood on the threshold.

"Everything okay?" he called.

"Yep," Micki said. "All good. I'm coming in now. I need to talk to you." She turned back to Gage, met his gaze for a long minute. "Goodnight, Mr. All-American. Thank you and I still think you're amazing."

"Ditto. Call me when you're done with Jonah."

Gladly.

She closed the door and marched up the porch steps, ignoring Jonah's curious stare. "Don't ask me about him. I don't know."

"Fair enough. Did you decide anything about Flynn?"

She stepped inside, but turned back to watch Gage's SUV travel down the long drive. Jonah stood, his hand wrapped around the doorframe of her mother's new house. The place Mom had always told her she'd love to live in one day.

Now she did.

This was Mom's sanctuary.

Maybe it could be Micki's, too.

Jonah gently closed the door, then flipped the lock. "Mom's asleep. We can talk in the kitchen if you want."

She led the way, snagging a water bottle from the fridge before she sat. Assuming he'd want to see the video, she set her backpack on the table. Jonah took the spot across from her and tapped his fingers. Nervous. Her mind drifted back to the night of the party. The only times she remembered seeing her laid-back brother agitated revolved around that damned party.

Well, she'd fix that.

"I'm calling Owen in the morning and telling him I want the Queen for a Day deal. Once they hear what I have, they'll want my testimony."

"Are you sure?"

No. When it came to her boss, anything could happen. The variables were endless. "I'm terrified. For sure. As long as I've known Phil, the recent trip to Mexico aside, he's been able to avoid prison. My putting him there will fester. Every day he sits in that cell will get him angrier. I'll have to face that when he gets out."

Jonah shrugged. "He's in his fifties. If we get lucky, he'll die in prison."

"His reach is long, Jonah." She couldn't worry about that, though. She let out a sigh. "Still, cooperating is the right thing to do. It'll get me my life back."

Her brother leaned forward, rested his hands flat on the table. "I'll support you. You know that. We all will. We just want you back."

Pressure built behind her eyes, in her throat, along the backs of her shoulders, and she squeezed her eyes closed. If she started spewing, just unleashed the years of pent-up frustration, it might take all night to get rid of it, and she still had a lot to say to Jonah.

She opened her eyes again. "I want to be back. I've always wanted that. I should have come to you sooner. I was scared and then, as time went on, I don't know, I was so immersed in Phil's world, I'd lost control of my own life. I gave it all to him. It took all of you to make me see that."

"Which is exactly why he isolated you. He's the classic abuser."

"You're right. But starting tonight, I'm fighting back. *We're* fighting back."

Together, they'd do this. She dragged her laptop from her backpack, fired it up, and turned it toward Jonah. "This is the entire video of you leaving that room with Tessa."

His features hardened, his jaw literally popping from the pressure of locking his teeth together.

"How'd you get it?"

"I took a chance that Phil had it, all of it, in his e-mail."

"You hacked into his e-mail?"

"Yes. And I got what we needed. You weren't in that room long enough to attack her. Now you can take this and hopefully Tessa's statement to your lawyer. It should prove you're innocent."

Jonah sat back, ran his hands through his hair, and scrunched his face. "Damn. How did one fucking party create such a mess?"

"Because people are evil. We can make it right, though." She pointed at the laptop. "Do you even want to see it?"

He paused for a moment, then shook his head. "I don't need to. But thank you. You shouldn't have hacked his e-mails. That could come back on you."

"If I admit to it while I'm Queen for a Day, it won't."

Jonah snorted. "Queen for a Day. Unbelievable."

Micki reached across the table and held her hands out until her brother, her twin, grabbed hold. "We've got this," she said. "You and me. Like always."

The next morning, Gage rolled out of bed, hopped in the shower, and decided it was a great day to go to work. Even the normal morning headache had given him a reprieve and that fact alone, aside from getting laid in spectacular fashion the night before, sent his energy soaring.

Sex did things—really good things—for his overall existence.

He opened the front door and a burst of sunlight streamed in. The weather guy said to expect unusually high temps today, which worked for him because he needed to jump on one of the four-wheelers and check the progress on various areas of the training center.

On his way up to Tupelo Hill he'd call Micki, see if she wanted to ride along. Maybe pack a picnic lunch. Him, the guy who'd never put much stock into romance, doing a picnic lunch. Go figure.

Plus, he couldn't picture Micki doing it either, so between the two of them, it could be a stumble into hilarity.

He locked the house up, flipped his key ring on his finger, and headed across the small patch of lawn to the driveway. One day he'd make room for his car in the garage, but for now he was stuck parking outside.

Five yards from the truck, he stopped. Froze in his

spot, his gaze fixed on something—an animal—on his hood.

Squirrel? He glanced up at the tree where the branches hooked over the driveway. In the months he'd been here, he'd never had a squirrel fall out of that tree. And the way this one was lying there, it couldn't be alive.

He moved closer, noticed the long wiry tail, and his head started to pound.

Three strides around the front of the vehicle gave him a clearer view.

Rat.

Son of a bitch.

Ignoring the throb, he scanned the area, searching for anything out of place. The neighbors' garbage cans weren't in their same order—recyclables, garbage, smaller garbage—but that could have been their son doing his normal half-assed job of stowing them. Half the time the kid left them tipped on their sides.

Gage went back to the rat and stepped closer, studying it. The head and tail were intact, but the lower half was crushed. If, by some chance, the animal had gotten onto his hood on its own, there was no way it could have done it with its body damned near flattened.

Timing being what it was, with Micki talking to a lawyer yesterday and then spending time with him last night, it wasn't a stretch to figure out how a dead fucking rat wound up on his hood.

Someone—and he knew who—had put it there.

Fucker. Hot, primal anger flashed inside him. If they didn't deal with Phil Flynn, he'd never leave Micki alone.

Was she safe? He'd watched her go into the house last night. With Jonah. If something had happened, he'd know by now. Wouldn't he?

Heading back to the house—no sense standing in the driveway making a nice bull's-eye for someone—he slid his phone from his pocket and propped it between his ear and shoulder as he unlocked the door and slipped back inside.

"Good morning, Captain America. How's the stud today?"

She's safe. A surge of relief broke up the tension in his neck. "Hey. Good morning. You okay?"

"I'm great. Actually waiting for my mom. We're doing some baking this morning. And then maybe a walk around the property. She says I need to get out more and get some sun on my pasty skin. And to think I've missed her terribly."

They were going walking? Alone? "Is Reid there? Or Jonah? Not sure it's a good idea for you two to be out walking alone."

Micki snorted. "Lord, not you, too. We're fine. We won't leave the property."

Gage glanced at the dead rat. He'd need a couple pics of it in case they could use it as evidence. "Don't forget about Phil. Can't get too comfortable."

"He won't try anything on the property. He knows my family is here. And he definitely knows you and Reid were Special Forces."

The pounding behind his eyes kicked again, and he shoved the thumb and middle finger of his free hand into his eye sockets. "Still. I think you should wait on the walk. If Reid and Jonah aren't around, I'll be there shortly. Just...wait. Please."

He glanced at the rat again. He should tell her. For no other reason than to make sure she stayed put. "I—"

"Hey, Mom," Micki said.

He heard Miss Joan's voice in the background and then Jonah's, and the pounding in his skull backed off, gave him a second to get his thoughts together.

"Let me talk to Jonah," he said.

"Um, sure. You're acting strange. Are *you* okay?"

Great. Now she thought the brain-damaged guy was going off the rails. Nothing like total emasculation for a Green Beret.

"I'm good. I have a few errands to run and then I'll be up there. I'll stop and see you."

And tell you about the dead rat.

"I will look forward to that. Here's Jonah."

The line went quiet for a second while she handed it off.

"What's up?" Jonah said.

"Are you going anywhere this morning?"

"No. I'm locking myself in to go over that budget you left me. Seriously, do we really need that much gunpowder?"

Yes, they did, but he didn't have time to discuss it now. "Good. Keep an eye on Micki."

"Why?"

"I just found a dead rat on my truck."

CHAPTER NINETEEN

GAGE RECITED THE CONDENSED VERSION of his plan to Jonah, disconnected, and shot off a text to Reid. If he'd stayed with Brynne last night, he might still be in town before heading to the office. Gage would give him a few minutes to respond, then, Reid or no Reid, he'd pay a visit to Flynn.

While waiting, Gage grabbed a trash bag from the kitchen and headed back outside to deal with the rat.

Well, this wouldn't be the only rat he'd deal with today. Not if he had his way.

His phone buzzed. Reid. Excellent. Three texts later, a couple of pictures snapped and one rat packaged for transport, Gage found the big man in front of LaBelle Style gabbing with one of the locals.

No questions asked—had to love a Green Beret—Reid broke away from his conversation and hopped in the car.

He pointed at the garbage bag at his feet.

"What's that?"

"That would be the dead rodent I found on my hood this morning."

"Say again?"

Gage hit the gas. "You heard. I walked outside and found a mutilated rat on the hood."

"What the—?"

"And, by the way, your sister was at my place last night. She wanted to bend my ear about taking this deal from the US Attorney."

Among other things.

"Shit."

"Flynn probably thinks she stayed over."

If they were trying to keep whatever it was they had going on a secret, that just ended. In grand fucking fashion.

"Oh, man," Reid said. "Are you screwing my sister? I am *not* putting that vision in my head."

"You don't need to. What I'm doing with your sister isn't your business. Focus on the fact that this asshole either knows Micki and Jonah went to a lawyer yesterday or he's doing an end run to scare her before she does talk to someone."

Gage hooked a left onto Buckner and drove by the sheriff's office where Maggie, Reid's cousin and the top cop in Steele Ridge, stood next to her cruiser reading something on her phone. If he were smart, he'd pull over, show Maggie the rat, and let her deal with Flynn.

Today, he'd pretend to be dumb.

As they cruised by, Reid waved to his cousin. "Where we going?"

"We're going to leave Flynn a present. According to our handy tracking device, his car is parked at the B and B."

"Guess he hasn't figured out we're tailing him."

"That or he doesn't care. Either way, we're giving him his rat back."

Heavy on the drama, Reid clasped his hands in front of him. "Let me do it. Pretty please, can I do it?"

"No. My truck. My rat."

"You suck."

"Blow me."

Reid pulled a face. "*Someone's* cranky today."

Cranky didn't do it justice. He'd say this about Phil Flynn, the guy had balls bigger than the damned mountain in front of them. "We have to get rid of this guy. He'll never leave her alone."

"And what? You wanna *eliminate* him? Bury his body where he won't be found?"

Gage considered that a minute. If they wanted to, between him and Reid, they'd get the job done. No muss, no fuss. Would the world suffer without Flynn?

No.

Would it make Micki's—and by extension, Jonah's— life a whole lot easier?

Yes.

But for every argument he conjured for getting rid of this prick, down deep, despite the lives he'd ended in service of his country, he wasn't a stone-cold killer. When it came to Phil Flynn, he'd leave the man's fate to the justice system.

"Dude!" Reid said, "You're not seriously—"

"No! Of course not." He cocked his head. "For a second, maybe. But that's done now. All we need to do is back him off until the feds can handle him."

"Shit." Reid dragged one of his giant hands down his face. "I can't believe my sister worked for this asshole for *ten* years."

"I can. He uses fear to control people. Total predator. As evidenced by our dead rat."

He swung into the driveway of Steele Ridge's most popular B&B. A giant farmhouse with glossy white paint and green shutters and a porch with twin rocking chairs. Quiet and elegant, the place didn't deserve trash like Flynn sleeping under its roof.

A few cars were parked on the tree-lined street, and sitting at the curb was the black Mercedes Reid had planted the GPS unit on. Only the best for Flynn. So much for low profile in this quiet town.

Gage pointed at the garbage bag at Reid's feet. "Hand me that."

"What are you gonna do?"

"I'm giving him back his rat."

Reid yanked the door handle. "In that case, I'm coming with. No way I'm missing this."

"I'll handle it," Gage said, "I don't need you going off on him. You're the backup in case *I* get pissed and wind up popping him. This prick'll have me arrested. No doubt."

"Huh. Usually *you're* the reasonable one."

True dat. The difference was Gage allowing himself to be emotionally involved. His need to protect Micki, to help her gain control of her life, put him squarely in the middle. Oddly enough, the one place he'd convinced himself he didn't want to be. Enter the harsh realities of Micki Steele. If Gage intended things to move forward with her, Flynn had to go.

Otherwise she'd never be free.

Gage climbed the porch of the B&B and hit the bell. Mrs. Tasky, the owner, a woman in her fifties with a shock of curly blond hair, opened the door.

"Good morning." She eyed him, then Reid. "I know Reid, but don't think we've met. You're Gage, right?"

"Yes, ma'am."

Her gaze dropped to the bag in his hand. "Bringing me your trash?"

In a way, yes.

"No, ma'am. Dropping something off for Mr. Flynn. Do you know if he's here?"

"I believe he is." She stepped back and waved them in. "Let me tell him you're here."

They stood in the neat, white-walled living room where a beige couch was anchored by two leather armchairs. A giant trunk served as a coffee table and a weathered, sliding barn door separated the living room from the dining area.

"I like that door," Reid said. "We should do that in the common room at the hotel. Gives it a homey feel."

"What are you, Martha Stewart now?"

"I'm just saying."

And I'm the one with the brain injury?

Creaking wood drew their attention as Phil Flynn descended the stairs in one of his slick suits and a bright red tie. He made eye contact with Gage first, then Reid, holding the stare for a minute longer than necessary. Gage fought the urge to mouth off or waggle his hands in mock fear.

Mrs. Tasky, being the typically nosy townie, dropped behind the small reception desk in the corner.

Flynn shot her a look and she blessed him with a perfect I'm-not-leaving smile.

Witnesses. Not ideal, but he'd roll with it. One thing about the people in this town, they protected their own.

Gage held the bag to Flynn. "I believe this is yours."

His eyes cut to the bag and no doubt figured out what it was. "It's not mine."

"How do you know? You haven't looked yet."

"Whatever it is, it's not mine."

"I think you're lying. I think you left this on my truck for me—or Micki—to find. You must be slipping, Flynn."

A brief smile appeared. "I doubt that."

"If you were on your game, you'd know she wasn't with me." Gage pointed at the bag. "This whole dramafest you set up was a wasted effort."

"Huh," Reid said, "I don't know that it was wasted. I mean, he did manage to piss you off. That's gotta be worth something."

"Is everything all right?" Mrs. Tasky asked.

Gage flashed his best choirboy smile. "Yes, ma'am. Thank you for asking."

When Flynn didn't take the bag, Gage dropped it on top of his three-thousand-dollar shoe.

Behind him, Reid snorted.

"Come near Micki again," Gage said, "and I'll be so far up your ass, I'll pop out your ear. Understand?"

The only sign of a reaction from Flynn was the slight widening of his eyes. Gage had to give him credit for a poker face, but his dark gaze was like a black hole that led nowhere. Soulless individual right here.

Mrs. Tasky cleared her throat.

"We're good, Mrs. T.," Reid said. "The message is delivered and we'll head out now."

But Gage didn't move. "Do you understand?"

Was he pushing it? Absolutely. Did he care? No. He wanted this asshole to acknowledge the threat. To experience himself what he'd built a career on.

Gunning for people.

Flynn gripped the garbage bag, wrapping his fist around the loose plastic and swung it so it bounced off his leg. This was one twisted fucker.

"I think we understand each other," he said. "Thank you for stopping by. Always a pleasure. Now, if you'll excuse me, I have work to do."

Mom lifted the baking sheet from the oven just as Gage and Reid tore through the kitchen door, destroying the calm, cookie-creating euphoria.

"What on earth?" Mom dropped the cookie sheet on top of the stove. "Y'all scared the daylights out of me."

"Sorry, Mom," Reid said.

When she turned to inspect the cookies, Gage pointed at Micki, then jerked his thumb toward the door. "Talk," he mouthed. "Outside."

First the weird call that morning and now this. In the span of time since he'd dropped her off last night, something had rattled him. She grabbed her jacket from the hook by the door and slid it on over her apron. Her favorite apron. The one with tiny skulls and crossbones all over it. Mom had found it at a craft show twelve years ago and given it to Micki for Christmas. All this time, her mother had saved it for her. As if she'd known, someday, her girl would return home.

"Mom, I'll be right back."

Mom spun back, spatula in hand. "Where are you going? We're not nearly done."

"Just outside. I won't be long."

Unsatisfied with that answer, she eyed Gage, then Reid, and then Micki. "What's wrong?"

One thing Micki would have to get used to about being home was her family constantly up in her business. Which meant she would have to become quick on her feet. Usually not an issue. "It's business. Jonah and I talked about me doing cyber warfare classes for the training center. I want to talk to Gage about it." She shifted her gaze to Reid. "In private."

Given that Reid and Gage had walked in together, she made the assumption that whatever was so important that Gage needed to talk to her about it, Reid was in on.

Or maybe Captain America wanted to set up a nookie date. Which would be a whole lot nicer than anything else she could think of.

"Oh," Mom said. "That's wonderful. All my children *finally* working together."

Reid rolled his eyes and Micki couldn't help the smile tugging at her lips. She'd missed this. The guilt trips.

The love.

Gage held the door open and waved her out.

On the porch, she inhaled, filling her lungs with the cool morning mist. Vegas didn't have this. It got chilly there during the winter, but not this moist, lung-clearing air.

She leaned against the rail and folded her arms, anticipating, readying herself, but Gage kept moving, his body almost catlike as he hopped down the steps into the yard.

"Where are we going?"

"Away from the house. They can still hear us from the kitchen."

"Really?"

"Really."

Wow. The things she needed to learn about her mother's new house. The first being how thin the walls were.

She followed Gage into the yard, where the expanse of property rolled as far as she could see. Bright sunlight washed across her cheeks, promising a mild afternoon.

On a morning like this, on this property, she believed in God again. Believed that some higher power had created nature's beauty to sustain people during hard times. Once Phil was out of her life, she'd walk every morning. She and Mom. They'd make up for lost time and get to know each other again while starting the day off surrounded by nature.

They reached the middle of the yard and Gage turned to her. "First off, good morning."

"Good morning to you."

"How was your night?"

She grinned. "Slept like a baby. Thanks to you."

He smiled. "Ditto."

"Why don't I think you called me out here to check on how I slept?"

He stepped closer, tucking his thumbs into the pockets of his jeans. "Is there any chance Flynn knows you talked to an attorney?"

Uh-oh. "Why?"

His hesitation was enough to create a dull pounding in her ears. A gust of wind brought the chill back and she folded her arms. "What did he do?"

Gage slid his jacket off, swung it around her, and draped it over her shoulders. "I had a message waiting for me on my truck this morning."

"What message?"

Please, no. She'd heard rumblings over the years. Snippets of conversations between Phil and Tomas. For her own sanity, she'd chosen the path of denial. Hear no evil, see no evil…

Lame? Of course. What choice did she have? If she

couldn't get away, creating an alternate reality—one firmly planted in denial—seemed the best option.

Gage shook his head. "It doesn't matter. I think he knows you saw a lawyer. Did you tell anyone outside the family or me?"

The dull throb moved from her ears into her jaw. She breathed in, held it for a few seconds—*one, two, three*—and exhaled. If Phil knew about her lawyer, he'd…God…What *would* he do?

"I didn't tell anyone," she said. "Are you sure he knows?"

"No. But the message was clear. I went to see him before I came up here."

"Talk about poking a bear. What were you thinking?"

"I was thinking someone needed to put that asshole in his place. I don't bow to bullies."

Ah, yes. "That was dangerous. What if Tomas was with him? They could have hurt you."

"Which is exactly why I brought Reid with me."

Reid and Phil in the same room? Dear God. She slapped her hands on top of her head.

All of this was her fault. She'd dragged her family into it. It hadn't been her intention, but had she been thinking straight before leaving Vegas, she'd have anticipated the problems. Problems she needed to fix. Dammit. Phil showing up at Tupelo Hill should have been her first clue he wouldn't go away.

Not with all she knew.

Wait.

Slowly, Micki angled back toward the house, pictured Phil sitting at her mother's table.

That son of a bitch.

"Micki, you know this guy. Could he be playing a head game with you? Maybe he doesn't know you went to a lawyer, but figures you will. The ra—the *message* he left could be a warning."

"It's a warning all right. But it's no head game. He knows."

"How?"

She faced Gage again, her mind reeling, picturing Phil moving around the kitchen, the possible hiding places—cabinets, table, pictures.

"If I were to make an educated guess, I'd say he bugged my mother's house."

CHAPTER TWENTY

"HE BUGGED THE HOUSE?"

Gage had seen a lot of crap in his life and he could add this to the pile.

"In Phil's world," Micki said, "information is key. Ninety percent of what he does is investigative in nature. He's constantly digging. "His two favorite means of data gathering are wiretaps"—she held up her thumb, then her index finger—"and listening devices."

Wherever he can put them. Cars, houses, offices. It's easy. When he came here, he was alone in the kitchen for a few minutes."

"When?"

"When my mother walked to the stairs and shouted up to me that I had a visitor."

She was right. In the time Miss Joan had left the kitchen, that asshole could have planted a bug. Which meant… "Shit."

In his mind, he replayed the conversation that happened after they'd thrown Flynn out. Micki talking about the party, rescuing the girl, Flynn threatening her. All of it streamed, including the part where Gage suggested getting a lawyer.

Now it made sense. Flynn had listened to the recording and since Gage had been the one to suggest it, he'd multitasked by leaving the rat for him to find. Not only would it send a warning to Micki, it sent one to Gage.

Only Flynn had gotten sloppy. The man was obviously too used to people caving. He expected Gage to back down. Most people would.

Most people, however, didn't serve in Special Forces and experience the hell that came with that. Back down? Not in this lifetime.

He headed for the house, his hiking boots sinking into the dew-drenched grass.

Micki hustled up beside him. "What are you doing?"

"We need to find that bug." He stopped, angled back to Micki. "How do we get Miss Joan out of the kitchen?"

Micki thought about it a second, then slipped her phone from her back pocket. "I'll get Evie to call her and tell her she needs to talk or something. If I know my mother, she'll do that in private."

A minute later, Micki explained to Evie, without giving too much detail, that they needed Miss Joan out of the kitchen. After answering a couple of questions, again keeping it vague, Micki ended the call. "Okay. She'll tell her she left anatomy notes in her room, but she's not sure where. It'll keep Mom busy for a few minutes. We'll need to work fast."

"That's fine. With three of us looking, it shouldn't take that long. And Flynn didn't have much time. It's probably in an accessible place."

The two of them entered the kitchen just as Miss Joan closed the oven door. "Last batch is in. Your brother already ate three and said they were good."

"It wasn't three," Reid huffed.

"You know it was. I saw you take that last one when I poured you a glass of milk."

Miss Joan didn't miss a trick. Which didn't bode well for them on this Evie mission. He did not want to have to tell this woman her house was bugged.

On cue, the phone rang. Miss Joan scooped the cordless from the base and checked the number. "Ooh.

Evie." She poked the button. "Hello, sweet girl…What's wrong?…You did? Well, all right, don't get uppity about it. I'll look."

She put her hand over the receiver. "Evie thinks she left some notes in her room and she has a test today. I need to take a look. Watch those cookies."

Mom left and Gage snapped his fingers at Reid while Micki checked the underside of the table. The big man eyed her and Gage snapped again, drawing his attention.

Not wanting to waste time writing a note, Gage pointed to his lips. "Kitchen," he mouthed. "Bugged."

Reid's jaw flopped open. "Shit," he said.

Amen to that. The three of them spread out, working in silence, running hands along every surface, checking under the lip of the counters, the cabinets, the inside of the pantry door.

Where are you, you little fucker?

Micki dropped to her knees, checking the baseboards and the kickplates on the bottom of the cabinets.

Nothing.

Okay. *Back up here.* Flynn had been sitting on the other side of the table so Gage moved to the spot and sat.

Options.

To get to the counters, he'd have to walk around the table and that would cost him time.

Closer. Wherever he'd hidden that bug had to be closer.

He spun back, scanned the wall and the framed photo of the original Tupelo Hill. He bolted from the chair and lifted the frame to check the back. Nothing. He reset it. Beside that hung a letter organizer with a slot for storing larger envelopes. The slot angled outward at a forty-five degree angle.

There.

Lifting the envelopes out, he ran his fingers along the inside of the slot and…hello.

He waved his free hand at Micki and Reid. Reid lifted the organizer from the wall, studied the inside of it and…nodded.

Bingo.

They'd found it. The son of a bitch had actually bugged the place. Reid made a move to pop the tiny listening device out, but Gage shoved his hand over the top of the slot. If they removed the bug, Flynn would know they'd found it.

He gestured to Reid to hang the organizer, then replaced the envelopes and pointed outside. All three of them filed out, heading to the same spot where he and Micki had talked.

Reid flapped his arms. "What the hell, man? We gotta get that thing out of my mother's house."

"If we remove it, he'll know. And if Micki talks to the feds, I'm not sure we should touch it. I'm no lawyer, but if she tells the feds it's there, let them be the ones to remove it. He's planted an illegal listening device. It's evidence. Now that we know it's there, we're a step ahead of him."

"Meanwhile, my mother's privacy is invaded."

"Not if we tell her."

"Oh, no way," Micki said.

"It's her house. She has a right to know."

Reid wandered in small circles. "He's right, Mikayla. I mean, we could pop that sucker out, but we might be better off letting him think we don't know it's there."

Gage poked a finger. "Exactly. Why give him the heads-up? If we get lucky, the feds'll move quickly, and with what Micki has to say, they'll arrest him. The bug alone will get him jail time."

Micki dragged her phone from her pocket again. "I can't wait any longer. I'm calling Owen. If he can get me a meeting, I'll talk to the US Attorney today. This is my fault. Now I have to fix it."

After leaving an ATV—aka The Gator—hidden

behind the tree line and buckling into the work truck that was normally kept in the barn, Gage drove down a pitted dirt road with enough holes to rattle Micki's teeth as they bounced in and out of them.

Two hours earlier, Reid and Gage had driven the truck to this secluded spot on the property as part of their sneak-Micki-out plan.

"Wow," Micki said. "Didn't even know this was back here."

Gage swung left to avoid a crater-sized hole. "It's new. We wanted multiple access areas for emergency vehicles. Obviously, we have some repair work to do, but if someone gets hurt, first responders don't have to go all the way around to get on the property. No one knows this is back here yet."

"So if Phil is watching the main entrance, he won't see us leave."

"Correct."

"How did this become my life?"

"Crappy circumstance, that's how. You're dealing with it. Don't get hung up about it."

Micki's phone rang and she checked the screen. Her lawyer. She tapped the speaker button. "Hi, Owen."

"Good afternoon." Owen's all-business lawyer voice filled the cab of the truck. "We're all set to meet with Emily Roberts at three o'clock. She's the lead AUSA—assistant US Attorney—for the Western District of North Carolina. Based on the information we've provided, she will have a couple of AUSAs with her and possibly an FBI agent. I wouldn't be surprised if she pulls the IRS in as well. More than likely, they'll be able to catch Flynn cheating on his taxes."

No doubt about that. The man ran extensive cash transactions and Micki knew for a fact he kept stacks of money hidden in a wall in his attic. For emergencies.

Or for Doomsday, when he'd have to bug out.

Micki shifted to look at Gage, who'd worked his way

down the rutted path and turned onto the mountain road leading into town.

"We're just leaving now," Micki told Owen.

"That's fine. The US Attorney's office is only a few blocks from mine. When you get close, call me. There's a parking garage you can pull into. It'll give you some cover rather than on-street parking. I know I don't have to tell you this, but be careful. If you think you're being followed, let me know and we'll figure something out."

"She'll be fine," Gage said, his voice taking on a flat, almost bored quality.

As if Owen should know Gage was a one-man wrecking machine.

Micki smiled. "Owen, say hello to Gage. He's my own personal Green Beret."

A pause. "Green Beret? Really?"

"Former," Gage said.

"Well, this'll be easy. If it works, I may hire you to handle all my Queen for a Day clients."

At that Gage snorted. "Let's not get crazy."

"We'll talk," Owen said. "See you in a few."

Micki tapped the screen. "How funny would that be? You getting a job out of this deal."

"I already have a job. One that keeps me plenty busy." He cruised to a stop at an intersection a few miles from town and tucked a ball cap over his head. "Do me a favor and slide down in the seat. I'll detour through side streets in town, but let's be cautious in case Flynn is out and about. Between the different truck, the ball cap, and no one in the passenger seat, we should be fine, but..."

"I know." She unbuckled and lifted her backpack from the floor to make room. "Just in case, I'll leave my phone with you when we get to Asheville."

"Why?"

"Because I've made a living hacking into people's phones to track them. By now, Phil probably has another black hat on me."

She folded herself onto the floorboard, maneuvering

to find a somewhat comfortable position for her stilt legs. "Good thing I'm skinny," she cracked.

"Once we get away from Steele Ridge, you can get up. Until then, I won't look at you. Can't risk it in case anyone sees me. And, you're not skinny. You're lean. Big difference."

She smiled up at him, Mr. Sunshine, always finding the upside. "You're funny."

"Why am I funny?"

"You can see the positives in any situation. Me? I'm the glass-half-empty girl. If something bad will happen, it'll happen to me."

"I don't believe that, but even if I did, I'd say we balance each other out."

There, he might have a point. "The way I see it, you're the light to my darkness."

He cocked his head, keeping his gaze on the road and refusing to look down at her. Maybe her light to dark analogy didn't sit well with him.

Snap. Relationships had never been her forte. She'd always been too paranoid to allow herself to open up. To let someone in. A girl with secrets didn't make for great company.

In reality, there hadn't been a lot of guys in her life she'd been gooey over. *Gooey* didn't fit with her lifestyle. What fit was denial and hiding and ignoring the immoral side of her job.

At least until Gage. With him, gooey felt all kinds of perfect.

She propped an elbow on the bench seat and stared up at her Iowa farm boy, the sharp angles of his face, the expanse of his shoulders that were just the right side of muscular, but not beefy. How a man could look so insanely perfect was lost on her. *And* she adored him.

Which meant, in the midst of figuring out how to break free of Phil and the wretched life she'd been living, she'd found a safe harbor in Gage Barber.

"Huh," Gage said. "I don't know that I agree totally.

I'm not Mary Sunshine all the time. Regardless, I think we're good together."

"Well, Captain America, I'm with you on that."

Ninety minutes later, Gage and Owen did their James Bond thing and managed to get Micki safely to the US Attorney's office in Asheville. The office was located in the federal courthouse and Owen had made arrangements for Micki to be brought in the rear entrance of the grand, six-story limestone building.

Everything about the building, the massiveness, the Art Deco carvings etched above the entrances, the terrazzo floors, the marble, did exactly as it should. Inside these walls, Micki, and every other criminal—because yes, that's what she was—became a teeny-tiny bug. Someone to be crushed by the weight of this mighty building.

Except her visit meant making things right. Coming clean. Literally washing away her sins. Once she did that, maybe she'd forgive herself for the past ten years.

Maybe she'd even go to church.

Owen, dressed in a *GQ* suit à la Grif, led her to an elevator bank. Her boot heels clunked and echoed in the cavernous space, setting off a weird pulsing in her stomach.

This sure wasn't church, but she was about to confess her sins. Sins that might land her in jail.

But not today.

Today?

Queen for a Day.

At the elevator bank, Owen hit the up button. "This shouldn't take long. Two hours at the most. If I tell you not to answer a question, don't answer it. Our goal here is to wet their beaks. A nibble, if you will, that will compel them to offer you a plea agreement. Once the agreement is signed, you give them everything. Understood?"

Micki nodded. "Yes, sir."

"Don't call me sir."

He hit her with a wide smile and the full force of his charm. No wonder he'd been dubbed the best criminal defense attorney in the county.

The elevator doors whooshed closed and Micki focused on the seam in the door. "Yes, sir."

"So that's how it's going to be?"

"Yep. Live with it. If you get me out of this, I'll call you sir for the rest of my life."

For her, it was respect born of her Southern breeding, but more than that, he'd taken a chance on her. Sure, her billionaire brother greased the wheels, but Owen didn't need her.

She needed him.

The elevator doors opened. "You'll be fine. It's a conversation. That's all."

"Got it."

Inside the US Attorney's office—a neat, no-frills space—a receptionist's desk kept company with six metal armchairs and a veneer coffee table. The receptionist immediately led them down one of two narrow hallways to a conference room at the back of the suite. Fine with Micki. The fewer people who saw her the better, because Phil was a master at finding weakness. He'd unearth someone—perhaps the nice receptionist who probably only made twenty-five K a year—looking to make fast money in exchange for information.

The receptionist opened a door and waved them into a long, narrow conference room with a tattered table and cloth chairs straight out of the '70s. Stacks of boxes three and four high lined the far wall, where shades had been lowered to block out daylight.

The door closed again and Micki faced her lawyer. "Why do I get the feeling they don't want me seen?"

"They could have another witness in here and they don't want you two passing at the water cooler. It's safer for everyone if they keep witnesses out of sight."

The door opened again and in walked a tall woman of

about forty with sleek red hair that hung over her shoulders. She wore a no-nonsense sea-green dress topped off with a rope of intertwined pearls.

Behind the woman were a shorter, balding man, another dark-haired man with a nose so crooked it had to have been broken a minimum of six times, and a woman about Micki's age. Between her frizzy hair and puffy eyes, she might not have slept in a month.

The gang's all here.

The redhead held out her hand to Micki, meeting her gaze directly. "Good morning, Ms. Steele. I'm Emily Roberts. Thank you for meeting with me today." She turned, gesturing to the balding man behind her. "This is Dave Relind from the IRS and Special Agent Frank Norford. Frank is from the FBI. And this is Donna Tremain another assistant US Attorney."

Introductions were completed while Emily and Owen said their hellos. Clearly, these two had worked together before, because it was all how's the husband and the kids are fine.

Emily took the power spot at the head of the table. Good for her. A woman in charge. Owen dropped into the seat to her left and directed Micki to the open chair on the other side of him. If the United States Attorney's office wanted access to Micki, they'd have to go through Owen. More and more, she understood why Jonah had gravitated to this guy.

First Gage had come into her life and now Owen would help her navigate the legal system. For the first time in a really long time, Micki considered herself a lucky girl.

Emily flipped her portfolio open and slid the pen from the little sleeve. All business, but not rude. Then again, prosecutors, Micki supposed, shouldn't get too chummy.

"Ms. Steele, I want to advise you that anything you say in this meeting, if you're truthful, cannot be used against you. Whatever you share with us, the government has a right to pursue. That applies to any leads we get from this session. Please be completely open and honest and provide any relevant information. Once the meeting adjourns, we will determine whether the government would like to proceed in utilizing you as a cooperating witness. Do you understand?"

"Yes, ma'am. Thank you."

"Of course. Let's get started."

And here we go. Micki held her breath against the stale, closed-in air, eyeing each person at the table. Could she do this? Out Phil?

Panic crawled inside her and she gripped the arms of her chair until her knuckles stretched her skin. She glanced at the closed door, the ugly white walls and the old cloth chairs, and suddenly she needed oxygen. *Outside.*

Beside her, Owen set his hand over hers and leaned in, getting right next to her ear. "I'm here for you. You're fine. Queen for a Day."

Yes. Queen for a Day. No harm in just talking.

Particularly if it meant reclaiming her life.

She pictured her mother, in one of her Adirondacks, sipping lemonade. That's what she wanted. Time with her mother to just sit and enjoy the view. *Time to do this.* Micki nodded and Owen sat back. Go time.

It took thirty minutes for Micki and Owen to give the group the summation of Micki's life. The nerdy girl with a gift for hacking, the loner, the invitation to a party, the attack on Tessa, Phil recruiting her, all of it dished out like a bad television drama. When she'd been asked who hosted the party, Owen slammed the brakes, obviously saving that potential carrot until after a deal had been made.

"All right." Emily jotted a note. "Let's talk about the wiretaps. Mr. Flynn regularly uses them?"

"Yes, ma'am."

"And you've been involved?"

Micki met Owen's eye and he nodded. "Only to the extent that I've heard them. Last week, one of my coworkers listened to a call between a judge and his assistant."

"Why?"

"One of Phil's clients is going before the judge next month. Phil was hoping to catch the judge doing something potentially embarrassing."

"And did he?"

"It was the start of something, yes, ma'am."

"Can you elaborate?"

Oh, boy. This was quite the experience. Sitting around a table with a bunch of federal employees, about to summarize an episode of phone sex between a filthy old judge and his extremely young assistant.

The whole thing sickened her. Which, in reality, was a relief. At least she felt *something.* A week ago? The judge's disgusting behavior had been commonplace. Nothing to get uppity about. Micki had been dead inside, literally empty from years of witnessing depravity at every level.

Reclaim your life.

Micki cleared her throat and sat up a little. "He was having phone sex with his assistant. And, uh"—she scrunched her nose, fought the wave of humiliation— "masturbating."

But, hey, old Emily was a pro. She rolled right through it, jotting more notes. "I see. You mentioned payoffs. Tell me about that."

Okay. That worked. If she could talk about the masturbating thing, the rest should be easy.

"I'm often asked to hack into investment accounts, bank records, that sort of thing, to see if we can find any evidence of impropriety. If so, Phil threatens the person with disclosure. Particularly if it's a public figure or someone, such as yourself, who is held in high public regard."

On and on it went, the volley of questions and answers, Owen interrupting occasionally to stop her. *Wet the beak.* That's all he wanted.

At an hour and forty-five minutes, Micki's energy plummeted. Fatigue from her post-adrenaline rush had set in, not to mention the oily coat of her transgressions suffocating her. Dammit, she needed to be done. To finish this nasty exercise and get home, where she'd soak in a hot shower and then curl up next to one extremely hot Green Beret.

After perusing her last page of notes, Emily made eye contact with the FBI agent and Mr. IRS.

"Gentlemen, any other questions?"

Both men shook their heads. Merciful God, this ordeal was coming to an end.

"All right." Emily faced Micki again. "Thank you for coming in today. We'll need to look into this. If necessary, I'll call Owen to set a follow-up meeting where we can discuss a plea agreement. You'd be willing to appear, in court, as a witness against Mr. Flynn?"

The big question. In truth, the thing they'd come here for. Could she testify? Live with Phil's brewing hatred when she understood, better than most, what he was capable of?

A picture of Gage popped into her mind. Next to her mother, he might be the most honorable person she knew. Now they were both here for her, Mom and Gage.

Micki met Emily's gaze and held it. "Yes, ma'am. To make this right, I'll do it."

Gage met Micki around the corner from her lawyer's office, where they once again used a parking garage for cover.

The whole James Bond-ish scenario seemed to unnerve her, but she'd have to suck it up. Staying safe was the goal. Still, after being alone for so long, it had to be...a lot.

Gage waited for her to drag the seat belt over and,

needing something to do, grabbed it from her to buckle it up.

"Thank you," she said. "But I'm pretty sure I can buckle my own seat belt."

"I know you can. I'm antsy. How'd it go?"

"You're antsy and I'm dog tired and feel like crap. I suppose it went great."

This poor girl. She'd been through the wringer these past few days. He tickled her cheek with the tip of his index finger and took it as a good sign when she didn't pull away. A few days ago, she'd flinched when he got within a foot. "I'm sorry," he said. "That had to be rough."

She avoided eye contact by staring out the window. "Talking about it was easier than I thought. The hard part was knowing I helped him. As much as I wanted to believe I didn't get directly involved with the shakedowns and threats, sitting through that meeting was like floating outside myself, watching and listening to it all, yet somehow not believing it." She finally looked back at him. "Admitting it helped me realize how manipulative Phil is. He's a pro at it, really. With the family I have, I shouldn't have been so weak-kneed, and yet he still got to me. As much as testifying sucks and terrifies me, I think it'll help me move on."

Not wanting to sit idle too long and attract attention, he backed out of the parking space and hit the gas. "You're doing the right thing. Absolutely."

"I know. You're a big part of it. Thank you."

He shrugged. "You're welcome. It helps that I'm crazy about you and I'm hoping you'll hang around a while."

"Assuming I don't go to prison, I think that's exactly my plan."

"Good. So, where to? Home?"

The day had been long and the dull headache wouldn't quit, but he wasn't ready to let loose of Micki yet. Still, dealing with the Steele family, at this point, might get complicated. He loved them, but when they got dug in, the whole lot of them, they weren't easy to handle.

"How about…"

"What?"

"Dinner? Will you go on a dinner date with me?"

He came to a stop at the garage exit, checked right and left, glancing at her along the way and grinning like an idiot. "Easiest decision I've had all day. I think we should go to the B."

Time to let the people of this town know he and Micki were…what?

Eh, who cared what it was, he didn't like sneaking around.

"The B? After everyone seeing us at the tree lighting, that'll get the tongues wagging. Are you ready for that?"

"I wouldn't have suggested it if I wasn't."

"Well, be prepared, because the busybodies will be planning our wedding."

That thought, no matter how preposterous after only a few days, didn't seem so awful. Plenty of time for that, though.

He hooked a left, heading for Highway 64, a winding two-lane road with no stops. He liked the simplicity of it, the calming energy found in the trees and random roadside foliage. He'd pass on the clouds rolling in, but as long as the damned rain stayed at bay, he'd live with it.

"Sit and relax," he said. "You've had a long day."

"I don't want to be rotten company."

"You're never rotten company. Close your eyes, give yourself time to rebound. You'll feel better." He grinned over at her. "I promise."

With that, he flipped on the radio and hummed along to an old Brooks and Dunn song. For the next ninety minutes, if all went well, they could pretend they were simply out for a drive.

And not about to clash with a seriously bad guy.

CHAPTER TWENTY-ONE

RATHER THAN SWING INTO ONE of the open spots in front of the Triple B, Gage drove around and parked in the alley near the back door. Precaution never hurt. Plus, ugly black storm clouds threatened and they'd at least have a quick run back to the truck if the sky opened up.

On a Tuesday night, the place was quiet, leaving half the tables open. A few regulars sat at the bar watching CNN, clearly engrossed in the latest political wranglings.

Randi stood at the register, poking at the screen, but raised her free hand in greeting. "Hey, you two. I'm expecting Britt any time now. He'll be happy to see you. Sit where you like."

"Thanks, Randi," Micki said.

Gage grabbed his favorite table and slid into the seat against the wall so he could watch the doors.

One of Randi's servers cruised by, dropped two menus, and took their drink orders. Gage opted for one of the craft beer specials and Micki went with a sweet tea. Did she even drink alcohol? As yet he hadn't witnessed it, but there hadn't been many opportunities.

In addition to her many secrets, there was a lot he needed to learn. Simple stuff. What kind of food she liked, her favorite sweets, assuming she ate sweets as well as baked them.

The front door opened and in walked Britt, still dressed in jeans, an untucked work shirt, and steel-toed boots. His usual workwear. He beelined for Randi, but she pointed toward the back table at Micki and Gage, so he detoured.

"Hey." He pushed a hand through his shaggy blond hair, shoving it out of his eyes. "Didn't know you were coming in tonight."

Micki smiled up at her older brother, and suddenly all the tension she'd had on lockdown vanished. Her face softened, stealing the hard angles of stress, and Gage couldn't move. Taking his eyes from her, the way he felt right now, would be a tragedy of the worst kind. This side of her, the relaxed, unfiltered side, made his chest hurt. A good hurt. The kind that made a man want to stay put awhile.

Britt leaned in and kissed the top of her head. "Jonah told me where you went today. I'm sorry you have to go through this."

"It's all right," she said. "It could have been worse. We should set up another family meeting."

Gage glanced around, making sure the town gossips were out of earshot. "Britt, no offense, but we probably shouldn't do this here. We'll need to fill you in on some stuff."

Dude, don't ask me to explain.

Not here anyway.

Fully understanding the nonverbal signals, Britt held up a hand. "I'll call you later." He angled back, checking on Randi, and Micki touched his arm. "Do you want to join us?"

"Nah. I'm just picking up Randi. Looks like she's about ready. I'll take a rain check, though."

"You'd better take a rain check," Micki said. "I'll hold you to it."

"Mikayla, I'd welcome that." In true older brother

fashion, he cuffed her on the shoulder and made his way to the end of the bar, where he settled on a stool to wait for Randi.

The waitress dropped off their drinks and Micki sipped at her tea, taking in the room and fiddling with her straw, smacking it against the inside edge of the glass and stabbing at the ice. "Sitting here with you and talking to my brother is nice. I don't feel...desperate."

"Desperate?"

"Two weeks ago, I couldn't imagine sitting in a bar, just talking. Now I can't believe I did without it for so long."

"Don't think too hard about it. Just enjoy it."

"Oh, I will, Captain America. Don't you worry."

Something popped in his chest. *Day-am.* He set his mug down and fought the urge to lean in, to touch her, to satisfy his craving to put his mouth on hers.

At least until someone dropped into the chair next to him. *What the hell?* He sat back, whipped his head to the dark-haired man.

Tomas.

Son of a bitch. Right in front of him, the guy had slipped in. Gage had been too busy fantasizing about Micki to even see it.

Dumbass.

Slowly, Micki shifted and all the softness, the relaxed easiness disappeared as fast as it had arrived.

Not now.

Gage pushed his chair back, facing Tomas and letting his hands dangle at his sides in case he needed them. "You're not welcome here. Leave."

Micki plowed right over that. "How'd you know we were here? I thought you went back to Vegas."

Tomas ignored Gage, instead giving his full attention to Micki. "Look, we can still fix this."

She let out a frustrated laugh. "Can we? Really?" She sat forward and jabbed her finger into the tabletop. "I'd lay odds you paid someone in this place to spy on me, and you think we can *fix* this?"

"Micki," Gage said, "don't talk to him."

"No. It's okay."

It's okay? What? She'd just spent two hours confessing her misdeeds—misdeeds that the guy across from her took part in—to a United States prosecutor, and somehow it was *okay*?

Not.

Ixnay.

Bullshit.

Tomas finally looked at Gage, a satisfied smirk in place. Smug son of a bitch.

He went back to Micki, holding one hand out. "I shouldn't even be here. Before this gets nuts, tell him you'll come back to Vegas. Come back and we'll all talk it out."

"Micki—"

She swung her head to Gage and held his stare for a long minute. "Please. *I* need to handle this."

After everything they'd talked about, the conversations they'd had, ones she'd initiated by asking for help, suddenly she didn't need him. Perfect.

But—all right. He'd see how this rolled. Not get twisted about it. Letting her take a stab at dealing with this asshole would probably help her. Allow her to, as she'd put it, move forward.

He sat back, still keeping his hands ready. His skull pounded. Damned headaches. Total hassle.

"Tomas," Micki said. "*Tommy*, I'm not going back. I can't do this anymore."

"We've been doing this together for years. This is me, the guy who sat with you when your appendix blew up."

"Come on, man," Gage said.

Tomas turned, gave him a hard look. "Not. Talking. To you."

"Stop," Micki said, her voice carrying an edge sharp enough to slice metal. "Both of you."

She might have been speaking to him, but she

wouldn't look at him. That alone sent his oh-shit radar into the red. "Look at me," he said, forcing the issue.

Immediately, her shoulders flew back and the hardness he'd seen that first day, when he'd met her on her mother's porch, roared back into her eyes. Everything about Micki, right now, had literally turned to stone. Jesus. Complicated woman.

But at least she'd finally looked at him.

"Don't let him inside your head. You know how this works."

"I'm fine," she said.

Tomas jerked his chin at her. "I can't be here long. Phil thinks I'm in Georgia."

"You shouldn't have come," she said.

Wasn't that the world's largest understatement? And Gage had to sit here, like a good little boy, and listen to this bullshit when all he wanted to do was rip this guy's throat out. One good yank and—boom—done.

The Vegas contingent needed to leave her be. Whatever Tomas's—*Tommy's*—motives were, hell, he might be sincere in wanting to help Micki, but convincing her to go back to Vegas was the dead last thing she needed.

And who was Gage to be involved in this? The dead last thing *he* needed was to be in the middle of Micki Steele's problems. This was the reason he hadn't gone home to Iowa. The whole being everyone's go-to guy. How the fuck did he wind up right where he'd fought so hard not to be?

Fuck me.

Suddenly, the meditation he'd done in the truck while waiting on Micki in Asheville wasn't cutting it and his eyeballs throbbed. Damned fatigue.

"Micki," Tomas said, "Phil is losing his mind. Totally unhinged. He's got your mother's house bugged, for Christ's sake." He poked his finger at her. "You know he'd skin me if he knew I told you that. But I'm doing you a large on that one because you and me, we're a team. Always have been. And I'm telling you, he won't stop."

Micki glanced at a fuming Gage. He didn't like this. Not one bit. She had a news flash for him, because he couldn't fix everything. She created this mess and *she'd* be the one to fix it. Certain things were her responsibility. Including making Tomas realize she couldn't go back.

Really, neither should he. Once she signed the proffer agreement, Tomas would go to prison right along with Phil. Depending on the deal Owen negotiated, *she* might even have to do time.

All the years together, the camaraderie, as dysfunctional as it was, streamed in her head. Tomas had been more than a coworker. In him, she had had an ally. The one person who understood her life.

Now, he'd just admitted Mom's house was bugged. He'd broken Phil's most valued rule and defied him. For her. Finally, the Tomas she knew—*Tommy*—was back.

"Thank you for telling me that."

"Of course," he said. "What'd you expect?"

"I don't know. This is all crazy. I want my family back. Why do I have to choose?"

"Come on. You know better. I'm telling you, he's losing his grip. Tell him you'll come back and we'll work something out that lets you visit every couple of months. Be smart about this."

"Hey." Britt walked up to the table and stood between Tomas and Gage, his huge looming presence stirring the already tense air.

She straightened up. "Hi."

"Who's this?"

"That's her coworker," Gage said. "From Vegas. He's trying to talk her into going back."

The glare Britt sent Tomas's way should have blown him to China. "She's staying here."

Micki circled a finger. "Britt, just so you know, your girlfriend has a spy in here. Probably a waitress or a busboy looking to make fast cash."

Tomas rose from the table. "I'd love to sit around and talk this shit through with *y'all,* but I'm busy."

He pushed his chair in, then put his hand out to Micki. Working on habit, she smacked it and they fist-bumped.

After watching the exchange with his jaw locked and his mouth zipped, Gage hopped to his feet. "You said you were leaving. Go."

"Whoa, there." Britt set one of his big hands on Gage's chest. "Relax."

Tommy rolled his eyes, clearly baiting Gage. And with his head injury, a brawl in the middle of the Triple B could land him in the hospital.

"Thank you, Tomas," Micki said. "You should go now."

"I'm going. Trust me on this, he won't give up."

He headed to the door and her mind tripped back to her last day in Vegas, when he'd left the office and that same sadness, the weighty pull of loss and disappointment, pressed down on her. He'd been her friend, she thought. Now, she didn't know what to think.

God, this was awful.

This, this…moving on. Rebuilding. Starting over.

"You've got to be kidding me?"

The harsh growl in Gage's voice snapped her from her thoughts. "I know you're mad at me."

"*Mad* at you? I'd love it to be that easy. I get over being mad pretty goddamn fast. This goes beyond mad. I don't know what the hell you're doing."

"Settle down." Britt clasped Micki's arm, lifting her from her seat, then shoved Gage to the back door. "Outside. We don't need the B talking."

Gage jabbed a finger at the door. "That guy doesn't give a *shit* about you."

Micki flinched at his uncharacteristic yelling just as a couple at the next table made a show of looking at them.

He pulled his wallet out, tossed a twenty on the table. "Forget it. I'm not doing this. I'm tired and my head hurts."

Now he wanted to leave? To be a jerk. All because she'd had a conversation with a man she'd spent years working side by side with.

Men were dicks. Just total assholes.

"You know," she said, "a little understanding right now wouldn't kill you. You're pissy because I wouldn't let you save the day. Sorry, Captain America, some things aren't yours to handle."

"Knock it off with the Captain America crap."

"Why? You love it. You know you do. What is it, Gage? A fix you need? And here I am, the poor damsel in distress."

He gawked. Just stood there with his mouth hanging open, and shame washed over her. Finally a decent man comes into her life and she lashes out at him. *Way to go, girlfriend.*

"I'm sorry," she said. "That was mean."

He shook his head. "Forget it. It's all bullshit anyway."

"Of course it is," she said, heavy on the sarcasm.

The blast of his half-insulted-half-enraged deadly stare set her back a step. *Dammit.*

Britt gave them another shove toward the door, but Gage wasn't ready to give up the fight.

"Since you showed up, I've done everything you needed. Plus some!"

"Guys," Britt said, "shut up."

She followed Gage, ignoring the curious looks from patrons. "Britt, we're adults. Adults fight. If the gossips want to run with it, let them. I don't care."

"Well, I do. Now shut up."

Gage pushed through the door, his pissy attitude going with him. Outside, in the blackness of the alley, a clap of angry thunder greeted them, and Gage whipped his head up. He swayed on his feet and set his hand on the hood of the truck to steady himself. He stood for a minute, looking down at the ground, eyes closed, his chest rising and falling. She'd pushed him too far and now he looked...sick. Ready to pass out.

What she didn't want was this argument setting him back on his recovery. The stress couldn't be good for a brain injury.

She moved closer. "Are you okay?"

The first fat drop of rain plunked on her head, then another on her nose. Gage finally looked up.

At Britt. *Oh, no.*

"Britt," he said, "give us a second. I need to talk to your sister alone. Then I'd appreciate it if you could give her a lift home."

Britt set his big hand on Gage's shoulder. Her brother, always the protector. "No problem. Are you all right? Do we need to get you to a doctor?"

"No. I'm good. Headache. I'll go home and close my eyes and I'll be all set."

"Fine. Call me if you need something, though. Got it?"

Gage nodded and Britt left them in the alley to finish their battle. Micki let the restaurant door close before she spoke.

"Please let me explain."

"Explain what? How you just spent the past four days confiding in me, asking for help, *fucking* me, and now you want me to sit around and watch this guy play you? These people are animals, Micki. I'd like to know where he was when I found a dead rat on my car this morning. That's what that prick wants to send you back to."

"What rat?"

"Exactly! I didn't tell you about it. I was afraid this might happen. That you'd get spooked and rethink the whole goddamned thing. That you'd decide it would be easier to go back. You will never be free of this guy if you go back."

"I'm not going back. I told you that."

"Yeah, you did. But somehow, sitting at the table, watching you talk to him, after what you've been through, I'm not sure I believe that."

"Well, you should. I'm happy here."

"Then why didn't you kick that asshole out?"

That stunned her for a second. Tomas was her friend, he'd been her default family for years. Down deep, she loved him. They shared some weird version of a bond and maybe, even after the past few days, she couldn't quite break free of it. Loyalty, no matter how misplaced, was fluky that way.

She held up her hands, opened her mouth and— stopped. What could she say? For years, denial had been her constant companion. Denial meant surviving, and as much as she didn't want to go there again, the day had been stressful, had tested her in ways she hadn't known existed. And now Gage wanted to interrogate her and yell at her and make her feel…what? Confused? Angry? Guilty?

No thanks.

She'd take being a loner in denial over that any day.

"Never mind," Gage said. "When you figure out what you want, let me know. I'm not doing this back-and-forth thing. I can't. You know these people are evil. You *know* it. And I'm not having that."

Of course he wasn't. He was, after all, Captain America.

Steaming mad, Gage fired the truck engine just as Micki strode back into the B. Goddamn drama. He didn't need it. Or want it.

Maybe this was his fucking lot in life. Wherever he went, drama, drama, drama. He locked his fingers around the steering wheel and squeezed. Then squeezed harder. These last days had sent his nice, controlled life into a whipping frenzy. And he didn't like it.

Liar.

With Micki he'd hit the Lotto, the big jackpot, the mother of all wins because he'd gotten the killer combo of great sex and a needy girl. Yep, that was him. Mr. Fix-It. The guy who thrived on strapping on his cape. And she'd just fucking called him out on it. Micki Steele had head-shrinked him.

And nailed it.

He couldn't even argue. Hell, that strapping-on-his cape feeling had pretty much been his undoing because the more he felt it, the more he wanted it.

Son of a bitch.

Damned old habits were easy to fall back on.

Dumbass. He'd never learn.

He let out a grunt, smacked the windshield wipers on, and shifted the truck into gear. He was getting out of here just in time for a mother of a storm to blow in.

Rather than make a right at the end of the alley toward Main Street, he went left. This time of day, Main Street would be activity central and he wasn't in the mood to run into anyone. Particularly one of the Steeles. He'd shortcut it home, sit on his couch, and close his eyes. Get this motherfucking headache tearing him up under control.

Damned Micki. He didn't know what the hell to do with her. And now he was in it. Knee-deep. Not only his relationship with her, but with her family. All of it wrapped around a job he'd taken so he didn't have to return to Iowa and face his own family. He ran one hand down his face. *Idiot.* His entire life revolved around the Steeles.

"You did it this time, buddy," he muttered.

At the corner of Belvue and Vine, the quiet streets

were devoid of traffic and the only noise came from steady rain against the windshield and the smack of the wipers. Tucked way back here, the number of houses dwindled to single digits, leaving only the few residents traveling these roads. Still, given his distraction, the rain and crippling headache, he checked the intersection twice and lifted his foot off the brake.

The engine quit.

Oh, come on. Total suckfest of a day.

Gas. Couldn't be. He'd filled up in Asheville. He scanned the dashboard. Nope. All good. Lack of fuel wasn't the problem. "What the hell, man?"

He shifted to park and tried the ignition. Nothing. Dead battery? God only knew when Reid or Jonah had swapped it out of the old beast.

He glanced up at an inky-black sky and a crack of thunder loud enough to shake the truck let fly. Engine had to quit *now?* Shit. He dug his cell phone from his pocket, scrolled his contacts for Reid's number. Just as he was about to poke the screen, the doors on both sides of the truck flew open, the burst of activity startling him, sending adrenaline pouring from his brain. He swung his head left, found a wet Phil Flynn—in duplicate—reaching in. Gage's mind was screwing with him again. He blinked, tried to clear his vision. No good. And Flynn had his hands on him.

Not happening.

He whipped his elbow up, aiming for the spot between the two noses. One of them didn't exist, but maybe he'd get lucky and hit the one that did.

The blow skidded off Flynn's damp forehead, knocking him back half a step.

"Phil!" Tomas said.

The truck rocked and Gage shifted right. Tomas already on the seat—dammit—doing a fast spin on his ass and bringing his legs up, about to blast Gage. *Whap!* Flynn clocked him. A solid hammerfist to the side of the head that made his vision swim again. *Not the head.* His body tipped forward and he grabbed the steering wheel, hanging on. *Don't pass out.* Later, there'd be time for that. Now he needed to fight at least one of these assholes off so he could get out of the truck and have room to maneuver. On his feet, he'd take them both. No problem.

Of the two of them, Tomas was the bigger threat. Younger. In shape. Faster reflexes. But Flynn was closer.

Thunder roared again and Gage cocked his arm. Something slammed into his back, a kick from Tomas, sending a shot of pain clear up his neck, snapping his head forward. Momentum propelled him into the open doorway, his torso hanging over, the now pounding rain pelting him. Flynn grabbed him by the shirt, dragging him to the pavement.

On your feet, soldier.

Head still reeling from the blow, Gage hopped up, spotted three of Flynn and busted off the start of a Hail Mary. For this, he'd need all the help he could get.

He planted his feet, focused on the middle Flynn's arm moving. Something in his hand. *Gun.* Gage stepped in to grab the barrel and twist the weapon away.

Zzzzppp. Searing shocks ripped into his thigh, the pain so intense his body stiffened—legs, arms, back— everything a solid wall. *Stun gun.*

The zaps continued and Gage let out a howl that shredded his windpipe. His brain stayed active, but his motor skills were gone and he fell forward, stumbling as he went over. He twisted sideways, taking the brunt of the landing on his hip rather than doing a face-plant.

The volts stopped. *It's over.* That fast. Still, the pain, that absolute fucking agony, pounded him. He let out another roar. "Fuck!"

Goddammit, that hurt. Finally, his body relaxed and he curled his knees in. No time. *Move.* He rolled, ready to push himself up, felt a counterweight and looked down. Tomas held his legs.

And then the stick came. A quick pinch on his upper

arm. Needle. He jerked his arm, but even as he did it, his head looped and everything went foggy. The men's voices melded together, garbling into a *whum, whum, whum.*

Whatever drug Flynn had given him did the trick. His vision blurred, the edges increasingly fuzzy. He blinked, blinked again and then everything went dark.

A repetitive tapping sound and splintering pain behind his eyes drew Gage to consciousness.

Pain.

In his shoulders. Not the jabbing kind. This was different. Dull.

Shoulders? *Huh.*

Slowly, consciousness crept in and he battled the heaviness of his eyelids. Jesus, his head hurt. For a few seconds, the banging against his eyeballs paralyzed him, brought him back to that first day after his injury. The hospital.

Was he in the hospital again? That would well and truly suck.

The tapping continued above him, pelting his eardrums. Rain hitting the roof.

Where the hell was he?

He needed to open his eyes. Get his bearings. Figure out what happened. His eyelids might as well have been sandbags. Too damned heavy to lift. He'd wait another minute. Let his mind adjust. Then he'd make a plan.

Observe, analyze, act. The mantra from his Special Forces days came back, bringing his thoughts to order.

His stupor slowly subsided and a series of images cycled in his mind. The truck. Doors opening. Flynn and…Tomas.

Needle. They'd drugged him. Which explained the mush in his head. But he didn't remember a beating and right now he had pain everywhere. Head, shoulders, ankles. *Suck it up, buttercup.* Flat on his back, eyes still closed, he moved his feet and...whoa. Something held them. What. *The fuck?*

Panic, sharp and cutting, sliced through the brain fog and his pulse went frickin' haywire.

Take a breath.

He took three even exhalations to force his heart rate down. *Focus.* Finally, he popped his eyes open. Dark room. He let his eyes adjust to the blackness and swiveled his head around taking stock. Hard floor under him. That explained the ache in his back and shoulders. He'd always hated sleeping on a hard surface.

He lifted his head, the heaviness almost too much until he let it drop back. Staring straight up, he lifted his right hand and...wait...his left went with it. Shit.

The sons of bitches tied his hands.

And his ankles.

Trussed up like an animal. Terrific.

He wiggled his hands and moved his feet, checking the tightness of the rope. Snug, but not enough to restrict blood flow.

Here we are, kids.

How long had he been out? A lack of windows in the room made it impossible to know the time, so he could have been unconscious for hours. Or minutes. Fighting to control his nerves, he inhaled, sucking in the dank smell of the room.

Observe, analyze, act.

The rope. What kind? Scratchy. Not too thick. Hemp. Maybe half-inch. If he had to choose rope to be bound with, hemp wasn't a horrible option. With enough time, he could chew it enough to shred it.

A door came open and threw a shock of light that blinded him. He closed his eyes, turned his head sideways and slowly opened them again.

"Seems our guest is awake."

Ignoring Flynn, Gage checked his bindings, his mind

already ticking ahead to an escape plan. Wrists tied with a shorter piece and then a longer rope looped in the center. What the hell?

The lengthier rope had been slung over a crossbeam above his head, the end now hanging loose.

Not good.

Gage levered up to a sitting position and faced Flynn in his fancy suit and shoes. "When I get free, you're dead."

"Who says you're getting free?"

I say.

Gage kept his mouth shut. Most negotiations failed due to diarrhea of the mouth. Even with Gage's legs tied, all he needed was for Flynn to get a little closer and he'd wallop him. A good kick to the knee and he'd go down. Or…

"I need to piss."

"Do it in your pants. You think I'm stupid? I'm not untying your feet."

We'll see about that.

Plan B. Feigning an itch, Gage rubbed his chin against the inside of his arm while he used the newly acquired light to scan a room no bigger than a small bedroom. With the exception of a metal-framed chair, a stepladder and an old workbench with a vise on it, the room was empty.

A vise.

Great.

But there was a second door. Along the back wall. Exterior door? Hopefully, he'd find out.

Flynn grabbed the chair and, keeping his distance, set it just out of reach of Gage's legs.

He sat, crossed one leg over the other, and brushed lint off his pants. "This should have been so easy," he said. "She's been with me a long time. I trusted her."

"No you didn't. If you had, you wouldn't have isolated her."

Flynn let out a dramatic sigh. "You could never

understand." He waved it off. "None of it matters. The time for working it out is gone. The deal, as they say, is off the table."

"She's not going back."

"We'll see." He worked his hand over his pant leg again. "I know her. She's easy. Always has been. Which is why, whatever she's done, whatever she's told that lawyer of hers, she'll recant."

"It won't work, Flynn. Jonah Steele is a big boy now. He's got money to burn. Money that'll buy him a lawyer and freedom. You're done."

"Oh, this isn't about Jonah. I knew my time was limited there. But you'll tell her to recant."

Gage snorted. "Not likely."

Phil stood and calmly set the chair back in the corner. "Then I'll kill her. And her family. And I'll let you watch. How does that sound?"

"Peachy."

He stuck his head out the open door. "Tomas, let's get this production started."

Tomas entered and met Gage's eye as he walked to the length of rope hanging from the crossbeam.

Refusing to give these pricks any body language, Gage sat still, his gaze shifting to Flynn who reached behind his back and pulled a weapon. Logic dictated that if they were going to shoot him, they'd have done it already. Whatever this production was, Flynn needed Gage awake for it. Otherwise, they'd have gotten rid of him lickety-split.

"Stay still," Flynn said, the weapon trained on Gage.

Tomas stepped closer and Gage swiveled on his ass, trying to get his feet around and—whap—got cracked on the back of the head hard enough that his vision flashed white. Still hungover from the drug, he swayed sideways and Tomas made use of the time and…hoisted.

Gage's arms flew up, the rope bringing his wrists over his head. Shit. Not only was he trussed up, he'd soon be hanging.

No way.

Leverage. If he could get some leverage, he'd yank the rope down from the crossbeam. And buy time.

He wrapped his fingers around the rope, made a move to tug and came face-to-face with the business end of a .45.

"One more time," Flynn said, "stay still."

Another yank from Tomas brought Gage's arms up again.

Gage waited. Options: get shot or get hung.

They both sucked.

And getting shot would seriously hinder an escape. He glanced around the room again, spotted the workbench and the vise and a plan started to form. Better to have no holes in him while he attempted to get his ass out of this mess.

Tomas yanked again, this time harder. Joint shredding pain ripped at Gage's shoulders. Son of a *bitch*. He hung there, arms overhead, gritting his teeth while Flynn set up the ladder and Tomas tied off the end of the rope around Gage's wrist.

A wave of panic sent Gage's mind spinning. *Focus.* But, damn, everything hurt.

"Okay," Flynn said to Tomas. "Get your phone out. Time to have some fun."

The e-mail from Tomas popped up just after 9:00. Micki dropped her head into her hands. The day, it seemed, and the drama that went with it, didn't want to end.

After the grilling from Britt about what was going on with Gage, and her refusal to talk, Micki grabbed some cold chicken from the fridge, a giant glass of Mom's lemonade, and retreated to her room. Where she'd sat mourning her ruined dinner date while messing with her software program and battling the urge to call Gage. Who was mad at her.

Well, she was mad at him, too. Sort of.

But not really.

Now that she'd calmed down, not to mention replaying the incident with Tomas in her mind a few thousand times, she could see where Gage might have misinterpreted her intentions.

Distance always gave clarity. No matter how many times she told Tomas her life in Vegas was over, from Gage's viewpoint, her inability to send her old friend packing reinforced the idea that she could be talked into going back.

Which she couldn't—wouldn't—do. Steele Ridge was where she wanted to be.

Now to convince Gage of that. Which meant opening Tomas's e-mail and telling him to never contact her again. Period. No exceptions.

She'd miss the fun parts of her relationship with Tomas, but the remaining ninety percent? That grew from Phil's threats and scheming. Never a healthy concept.

Unwilling to sacrifice her computer to a potential virus, she picked up her phone—the one she'd only had a couple of days—and tapped on the e-mail, her thoughts already forming the good-bye message. She needed to end this. To move on. Give living her own life a chance. A life that hopefully included Gage, the guy who'd managed to somehow understand her.

And not hate her for it.

The e-mail popped up. No message. Only a video attachment. Oh, boy. *Here we go again.* How many times had he asked her to grab a piece of footage for him? Hundreds? Thousands, even. She'd never sent the videos out, but denial only took a girl so far. Down deep she knew he used the clips as leverage.

Now she sat on the other side of it, anticipating what she'd see, her body stiffening as she prepared herself for the emotional hell about to kick in. Outside, a loud crack of thunder drew her gaze to the French doors. She'd raised the shades and was now met with blackness similar to her mood.

She clicked the file and a dark image appeared. She tapped the arrow to roll the video. A few seconds in, a flash of light shined on a door opening. Whoever was holding the device shooting the video moved left, angling the camera away from the light, pointing it down to a pair of hiking boots.

"Oh, no."

She froze the image. Gage's boots?

Please no. She clicked, letting the video roll so she could get a better look. The camera operator moved back, bringing more of the boots into view. Laces, hem of jeans. Rope.

She kept watching, willing her mind to be still. This was a highly organized production with Phil in the director's chair. He expected panic. She wouldn't give it to him. Not this time.

On the screen, the man's legs moved. Just an inch or two, but he definitely moved and her shoulders drooped a smidge.

The camera inched up, to his waist, and his shirt. Gage's shirt.

It's him. From the second she'd hit play, down deep she'd known, but had hoped...

Wait. All she saw was his chest. No arms. Images of Gage's arms being severed flashed and Micki sucked in a hard breath. The resolve to stay calm crumbled and she grabbed a fistful of her comforter, squeezing so hard the skin over her knuckles stretched. What did Phil do? A groan shredded her throat.

He wants this.

Breaking her down was the plan.

The camera panned up, revealing Gage's shoulders, his jaw, his *arms.*

Relief brought a surge of energy plowing into her and

she let go of the comforter, hopped off the bed and shook out her legs.

Finally, the person holding the camera, panned wide enough for her to get the full image. The money shot.

Gage, trussed up like an animal and hanging from the ceiling.

The scream Micki let fly brought Jonah bursting into the room. Already working with frayed nerves, the thwack of the door against the wall sent her reeling.

"Jonah!" She shoved the phone at him.

He snagged the phone, punched at the screen and watched, a horrified look transforming his features. "Holy God, this guy is insane."

"We have to do something."

"Oh, we'll do something." Jonah tapped at the screen. "You got Reid's number in here? Never mind, got it." He tapped a few more times and seconds later, the sound of Reid's phone ringing echoed in the room via speakerphone.

"Hey, bro."

"Are you at Brynne's?"

"No. She's out with her friend. I'm at the bunkhouse. Why do you sound spooked?"

Jonah whirled and headed for the steps, motioning for her to follow. She grabbed her laptop and hurried behind him.

"Micki and I are coming down. We've got a huge fucking problem."

CHAPTER TWENTY-TWO

"YOU JUST GOT THIS?" REID asked, his gaze still glued to the video on the third time through.

"Yes. They e-mailed it to me a few minutes ago."

"They?"

"Tomas found Gage and me in the B earlier. I assume he and Phil are working together."

And oh, what a bitter pill after her good friend Tomas had assured her he'd help.

Conniving liar. She'd get them. Both of them. After this, she'd rip herself open for the government. She'd give them every ounce of blood.

"Any idea where this was shot?" Jonah asked.

"No." She opened her laptop. "I'll find out, though."

Reid handed Jonah the phone and hustled to his own laptop. "While you're doing that, I'm gonna check something."

"What?"

"I slapped that GPS unit on Flynn's car. I can locate the car."

Jonah stepped behind Micki, watching over her shoulder as she typed. "Do you see what I'm doing here?"

He hesitated a minute, then bumped her shoulder. "Oh, yeah."

"If I know them," she said, "they're waiting for me to respond."

"And when Tomas opens your e-mail they'll get a nice surprise by way of malware."

Yep, yep, yep. She had, after all, learned from the master. "The malware attacks the signaling system. Once it's downloaded, I'll be able to track their location."

She CC'd Phil, hit send, and sat back. "Come on, boys. Open that sucker up."

Micki minimized the screen, then opened another one. "I developed an application to work with the malware. As soon as they open the attachment, a map will pop up and show us where they are."

"Damn, I forgot how good you were at this."

Not something to be proud of, at the moment, but if her nefarious creations saved Gage, she'd live with it.

Three seconds later, said map popped up with a blinking red dot in the center.

"I'm in," Reid called from behind his own computer.

"Me too. I've got an address on Barkley."

"Bingo. That's what I've got."

Jonah waggled a finger at her screen. "Zoom in a little. I think that's the vacant strip mall on the edge of town."

Reid headed for the door. "Let's load up and roll."

Minutes later, Micki sat in the passenger seat of Reid's truck bolting down the slick, pitch-black mountain road. The rain had let up, but in the distance another round of thunder rolled, moving out to the east.

The only illumination as far as Micki could see were the truck's headlights shredding the blackness and the glow of her laptop while she made use of her hotspot and that bit of malware she'd planted on Tomas's phone.

Jonah popped his head between the bucket seats and raked his hands over his scruffy face. How many times had he done that since watching the video of Gage?

"We should call Mags," he said. "You know how she gets when we butt into police business."

Reid shrugged. "So call her."

Micki glanced up. How would they explain this

nightmare? "Does she have the personnel to handle a hostage situation?"

"She'll call in SWAT."

Jonah grunted. "They're all county."

Micki gave up on her keyboard. "What does that mean?"

"It means Steele Ridge isn't big enough for our own SWAT team. Around here, that unit is comprised of guys from all over the county. Mobilizing takes time."

Micki went back to her laptop, scanned a few more files and...there. *Yes!*

"But," Reid mused, "that timing might work. We'll get a head start on them and have Suds busted out by the time they show up. Then they can handle Flynn and his pain in the ass sidekick. Yeah, Jonah. Call Mags."

If the load of weapons Reid had thrown in the truck bed was any indication, he was about to launch a small war in their little town.

Out of the corner of her eye, Micki saw Reid glance at her, but she kept pounding on her keyboard. Another few keystrokes and she'd be in.

"What are you doing there?"

"I CC'd Phil on my response to Tomas. I have control of both of their phones. I'm poking around. Like most people, Phil has weaknesses. His biggest, most soul-sucking one is money. Particularly his. He's constantly moving cash between accounts. It's our good fortune he's a fan of online banking."

Jonah, still trying to reach Mags, snorted. "His passwords are on his phone."

"You are correct, my brilliant twin. Talk about the emperor wearing no clothes."

"Damn. I got voicemail." He left their cousin a message and disconnected.

Reid took a turn a wee bit too fast, and the truck swerved. She held the laptop with one hand and grabbed the door handle with the other, but big brother, completely at ease behind the wheel, maneuvered the S-turn like a pro. Between him and Evie, their driving was insane.

"Mikayla," he said, "tell me you're not cleaning out his bank account."

"I'm not cleaning out his bank account."

"Thank God."

"I'm cleaning out his investment account."

At that, Jonah hooted and Reid sighed. Interesting reactions from her brothers. "Relax, Reid. All I did was move it. His broker will realize there's a problem and find it. I just need to scare him."

"Remind me not to piss you off."

Satisfied with her work and her personal safety, she released her death grip on the door handle and shut the laptop. Time to check in with Phil.

She shifted in her seat so she could see both her brothers. The argument with Gage had taught her an important lesson and she wasn't about to blow it again. "Both of you, listen up. I'm about to call Phil." Before either of them could argue, she held up her hands. "Let me finish. I know him. He needs my attention right now. It has nothing to do with me. It's about the win. That's what he loves and I want him to think he's won."

Jonah shoved his head between the seats again. "How?"

"By telling him I'm going back to Vegas."

"No."

"The two of you, just…shut up. I'm not really going back. I'm just *telling* him that. When you hear me say it, don't freak. Okay? I promise you, I'm not going back. Whatever happens, I'm not."

And, God, she hoped they got to Gage before Phil did something really stupid. Well, more insanely stupid than what he'd already done. She'd fix this. For what he'd done to Gage, she'd make sure he went to prison for a good long time.

This time, she had control.

She snagged her phone from the cup holder, punched

up his number, and hit the speaker button so the boys could listen in.

It only took two rings.

"I'm surprised it took you this long," Phil said by way of greeting.

"Let him go."

"Sorry. Can't do that."

Micki let out a long, desperate sigh. "You win, Phil. Is that what you want? I'll go back to Vegas. Just please, please, let Gage go."

Begging couldn't hurt.

Phil made his usual, demeaning *tsk-tsk-tsk* sound. "We are way beyond that. You betrayed me. Now you'll pay."

"Please, tell me what you want. I'll do it. Anything."

"You'll recant. Whatever you told the State's Attorney—"

"I didn't—"

"Don't lie to me!"

Jonah's head appeared through the seats again and his gritted teeth let her know her twin was at the end of his patience. Before he spoke, she sliced her hand across her throat.

What her brothers didn't know was that Phil didn't lose control often. He wouldn't allow it. People, he said, made mistakes when out of control.

Right now? Phil was out of control.

"Please," Micki said. "Gage has nothing to do with this. Let him go and I'll give you whatever you want."

Except admitting she'd spoken to the SA. Knowing Phil, he might not have confirmation of that and could be bluffing her.

He hesitated. "In one hour, meet me by the fountain in town."

"Why?"

"One hour!"

The line went dead and, just in case, she tapped the end button. She set the phone into the cup holder feeling...calm. A week ago, that argument with Phil would have terrified her. Now? Being home, surrounded by people who loved her—her real family—somehow she'd found the spine to stand up to him.

Operation reclaim-my-life in full swing.

"I just bought us time," she said. "He thinks I'll see him in an hour."

Reid nodded. "Good work. When we walk in on him, he'll be surprised."

They cruised into town, where all the shops had closed for the night. In contrast to the dreary gray-black sky, a rainbow of festive holiday lights formed a canopy over the buildings, reflecting off shop windows and bringing an odd comfort. Christmas with her family this year.

Only the B was open at this time of night and a smattering of cars sat parked in front of the building. In Vegas, things would just be amping up about now. Grif and Britt stood in front of the old Murchison building where Grif kept an office. Even at this hour, he wore his slick Hollywood clothes. Not exactly proper attire for this mission, but since they'd caught him on his way home from a board meeting, he didn't have time to change.

Reid hit the window button. "Hop in."

The two of them piled into the back, squeezing Jonah into the middle.

Once inside, having driven with Reid enough to know the potential threat, Britt reached for the seat belt. "What the hell's going on?"

"Phil's got Suds."

All sound ceased and Micki swung back to see the rare sight of Britt stunned into silence. "No way," he said. "When? We were just in the Triple B a couple of hours ago."

Micki pulled the video up on her phone and handed it back. "I was e-mailed this."

"God Almighty," Grif said.

The breathy edge in his voice said it all.

"I bet," Micki said, "they used a starter interrupter to disable the truck's engine."

She turned and met Britt's gaze. "I can't believe I didn't see this coming. When Tomas came into the B, he probably called Phil and told him we were in there. Phil went looking for the truck and found it behind the B."

"You were in the work truck. How'd they know?"

"I told you. Randi has a spy. That person probably tipped them off that we were in the B. They know Gage, they know he comes in the back door a lot. Phil probably saw the truck, knew we were inside and ran the plates. It wasn't a stretch that we'd be in a vehicle owned by the Steeles. Simple logic."

The emperor wearing no clothes.

How many times had she overheard Tomas on the phone, talking about starter interrupters. He had a contact that kept him in a steady supply of them.

They drove out of town, cutting through a heavily wooded street with ancient, towering trees and thick brush that she suddenly realized she'd missed, living in Vegas. Nature in all its glory.

Purity.

Clean living. One without secrets and denial and fear.

Here, she found freedom. Freedom with a man who was now hanging from a ceiling. She couldn't have that. No, sir. Gage Barber had given her hope, something she'd been without for ten years and now that she'd had a little taste, a sampling of what normal life could be, she craved it. All of it.

With him.

"Here's the plan," she said.

Reid let out a laugh. Yes, she'd shocked him. The woman surrounded by alpha males was taking control. Reid might be the warrior, but she knew their enemy. Understood him on a level her brothers couldn't. Plus, she had the stomach for getting into sewers with Phil.

"When we get there," she continued. "I'm going in."

"Ha!" Jonah said. "You think you're gonna walk right in the front door?"

"That's exactly what I think." She held up the laptop. "I just removed five million dollars from his investment account. Whatever he's doing to Gage, he'll stop if it means getting his money back."

"Jesus, Mikayla," Britt said, heavy on the judgment.

If she'd offended him, or perhaps enlightened him regarding a side of his sister he didn't like, too bad. When it came to rules of engagement, Phil Flynn didn't have any.

Neither would they.

"That's nuts," Grif added. "You're not going in there alone. I'll go with you. I'll talk him down."

"If someone goes with me, he'll get nervous. Guys, believe me. When I walk in there and tell him I have his money, he won't hurt me. I know this man."

Reid made a humming noise. "As much as I hate it, she's right. If we send *her* in the front, we can bust in the back. With the right timing, it'll be over in seconds. Even if his sidekick is watching the back, there are four of us. What's he gonna do?"

"I'm not having it," Britt said. "One of us stays with her. End of it."

Oh, these men were infuriating. One thing she hadn't missed while in Vegas was the pushy side of her brothers.

Jonah let out a sigh. "Don't bother arguing with him. It won't work and it'll wind up a bloodbath. I'll go in with Micki. Flynn's been using me to manipulate her for ten years. If he sees a united front, it'll set him back some. And I haven't had a chance to tell you this, but my lawyer called earlier. Tessa agreed to speak with the State's Attorney and the Asheville District Attorney— we're covering all bases here. She'll clear me. Phil's got nothing on us. We're free."

Micki whirled around and with only the light from

the dashboard met Jonah's gaze. A sudden fury of mixed emotions rolled inside her. All these years of being alone, of responding to Phil's every whim and at the same time harboring self-judgment that, if she'd thought too long about it, would have leveled her. Or sent her to a psychotic break.

And it could have been fixed with a phone call? So much for Gage's theory about her being heroic.

A phone call.

"Jonah," she said, her voice barreling through a chokehold. "That's great."

He nodded. "It is. Before your wheels start spinning, stop. Every decision you made, I'd have made the same one. You were scared and we were broke. It's easy to fix problems when you're rich. And we sure as hell haven't been rich that long."

We. Not *I.*

She reached back, extending her hand and Jonah grabbed hold, squeezing hard. "We've got this. We're here for you."

"Jesus Hotel Christ," Reid said. "Can we deal with this foo-foo emotional crap later? I mean, I'm not built for this shit."

Harsh words, for sure, but when Micki looked at him, her idiot brother's lips quirked.

"He's a dumbass," Grif said.

Micki smacked Reid's arm. "We love him anyway." She faced front and nodded. "Jonah can go in with me, but I'm doing the talking. No matter what he says, I'm talking. And *that's* the end of it."

A vicious stab sliced through Gage's shoulders as Tomas hoisted him up to the crossbeam for the third time. Jesus. His arms might come right out of the sockets.

This was their game. Hang him, let him down long enough to get the feeling back in his hands and arms—and keep him from passing out—and then reel him back up again. Whatever their plan for Micki was, they obviously wanted Gage at least somewhat coherent. And hanging a man by his wrists for more than twenty minutes wouldn't give them that.

In the world of a good mind fuck, these guys weren't amateurs.

Lucky for him, neither was he. Exactly why he'd let them haul him to that crossbeam, while he raised enough of a protest to make it legit, yet not get shot for his efforts.

Even with the short breaks, his body was breaking down, his arms and fingers becoming too fatigued to be of much use.

And the pain. He could deal with it, but the longer he waited to make a move, the more he'd have to endure and eventually he'd wind up with nerve damage or some other godforsaken injury.

Go time. Had to be.

Tomas finished his task and left, closing the door behind him. Gage let his head dip back. Above him, the end of the rope had been tied off around his wrist, leaving him roughly twenty inches of space between his hands and the beam. If he could get some slack...

Fifteen minutes. That's how much time he had. Gage knew this because he'd been counting the seconds between each check, and the last three had been between fifteen and twenty minutes.

Not a lot of time, but enough. Already, his fingers were tingling and a bead of sweat trickled down his face. *Get to work.*

The only light spilling into the room came from the crack under the door, but he'd worked in worse conditions. This beat a sweltering cave or rat-infested underground tunnel any day.

Three feet away, the workbench held that vise. If he

could get there, he might have a shot. He arched his back, snapped his legs forward and started a swinging motion. Not nearly high enough. Momentum was his friend, and he needed enough force to create slack on his wrists when he reached the highest point of his swing.

Goddammit.

Try again. The strain on his arms, that feeling that another inch of movement would rip them right from the sockets, couldn't be denied. Staying like this though? Not an option.

He gripped the rope, visualized what he needed to do and—*here we go*—propelled his legs forward, picking up much-needed height to move the slackened rope, little by little, down the beam. Seven, maybe eight more swings and he'd be close enough to stand on the corner of the workbench.

Swing. Swing. Swing. Fatigue burned like a hot poker in his shoulders, and more sweat dripped from his forehead, stinging his eyes. *Ignore it.* The post-drugging fog continued to dissipate and his mind ticked through his next steps. Next steps? Hell, if he didn't get to that bench quick it wouldn't matter. Tomas would walk in and bust his ass.

Swing. Swing. Swing. He kept at it, gradually moving closer and closer. Sweat poured off him now, and he rubbed the side of his face against his upper sleeve.

Slowly, he gained a rhythm, the small success powering him through the agony in his shoulders. *Scoot, swing, scoot, swing, scoot.*

The workbench was right there. *Focus.* His arms shook, the muscles angry and overused from hanging so long, but the bench. *Right there.* If it wouldn't blow the whole thing, he'd let out a fortifying yell, get himself pumped up for one last attempt to get this shit done.

Swing, swing, swing.

Observe, analyze, act. He pictured his feet, solid on that table, then mentally worked backward, analyzing each tiny detail of what had to happen to achieve his goal. More force. That's what he needed.

One, two, three. He swung back, snapped his legs hard, and his body sailed. A burst of adrenaline drowned the pain in his shoulders and he jerked his arms, sliding the rope directly overhead, his body swinging just above the workbench. The sudden tension release in his upper body sent a burst of air exploding from his lungs. Tomorrow, his arms would be toast.

Today? Halfway there.

He set his feet flat on the workbench and took a break. A small minute to get his head straight. He glanced down at his feet and the vise beside them. Rust lined the edges and part of the handle had broken off and now sat on the table. If Flynn had intended to put that vise to use, it wouldn't do much good. Gage tilted his head up at the crossbeam.

Too high.

Little more. More, more, more. He gripped the rope, slid it a few inches until directly overhead. He held his breath, tightened his core and—*now*—pulled, drawing his legs up and toeing the vise, checking its stability. When it didn't crumble, he set one foot on it, his ankle wobbling slightly as he boosted himself up, closer to the overhead beam.

He stayed there for a second, his ankles still bound and his mouth level with the rope at his wrists. He let out a quiet laugh. When he saw Reid again, he'd thank him for all the miserable workouts he'd put him through. Without them, he'd have been cooked.

His body trembled. His core sending a warning that the break was over. Time to get this done. Sweat beads dripped into his eyes, and he swiped his head against his shirtsleeve. *Pain is weakness leaving the body.*

His energy roared back. How much time did he have? He'd lost count. Too much going on. He bit down on the rope, chewing and tearing at it like an enraged animal. Seven, maybe eight minutes, barring any interruptions, he'd gnaw through the rope, untie his ankles, and kick some ass.

Micki ran her teeth over her bottom lip while Reid cruised along the back of the strip mall. Headlights off, they used the swath of dripping wet trees between the road and building as cover. Not that it mattered. The spotlights on the building were either off or burned out and darkness shrouded the southern portion of the parking area.

The streetlamp from the main road threw light on two vehicles parked behind an end unit on the north side of the building.

"That's Flynn's rental," Reid said. "I put the GPS on that one."

Micki poked her finger against the windshield. "Park down there. Around the side so they can't see the truck. Phil is paranoid. He's probably checking both entrances every ten minutes."

Reid drove to the south entrance and parked parallel to the building, leaving the truck hidden from anyone standing in front or behind the mall.

"I'll leave the truck here. Britt, Grif, and I will hit the back entrance. You and Jonah take the front. Keep them occupied until we bust Suds out. Then get the fuck out of there. Mags can deal with the rest."

Jonah made a buzzing noise. "Mags is mobilizing SWAT. She said to stand down."

Micki met Reid's eye. If she knew her older brother at all, he wouldn't like that idea any more than she did.

"No," she said. "Tomas said Phil is unhinged and I agree. At this point, I have no idea what he'll do and I'm not risking it. I'd sooner trade places with Gage than have him hurt. Or worse."

"Relax." Grif opened his door. "It's not the first time

we've defied Mags. She'll forgive us. It'll be painful and might include the silent treatment for a while, but she loves us."

Reid hopped out of the truck, lowered the tailgate, and started grabbing weapons from the polymer cases that kept them dry in wet weather. "Let's do this, boys. I brought some C-4 in case we need to blow the door."

"C-4?" Britt said. "Shit, Reid."

"Hey, if we can't get the door open, how are we supposed to get in? It's not like I haven't done it a few thousand times."

Her brothers. Total PITAs.

In this instance, Micki sided with Britt. Adding explosions to this insane mix could get someone hurt. "Please be careful. With the glass storefronts, Gage is probably hidden in a back room. Don't blow him up."

Reid turned to Grif and shoved a rifle, a handgun, and a holster at him. "All of a sudden everyone's an expert. Everyone grab a vest. We don't know what we're walking into."

"No," Micki said. "You guys wear them. If Phil sees me in a vest, he'll know we're planning something."

"Mikayla, don't fuck with me."

Jonah waggled his fingers. "Give me the nine millimeter. She's got a point. We'll be fine."

Reid handed over the weapon. "I don't like it."

"None of us do, bro."

"Give me a rifle," Britt said.

The Steele brothers. A four-man cavalry. This was what she'd missed in Vegas. The family loyalty, the binding ties, the willingness to risk everything. For each other.

"Guys," she said, "thank you."

The responses were as varied as the men.

Reid: "Whatever."

Grif: "Don't get mushy on us *now.*"

Brit: "We'll take care of this, Mikayla."

Jonah: "No. Thank *you*."

Her brothers in all their glory.

"Once we get Suds loose," Grif said, "we need to bug out fast. We don't know what kind of shape he'll be in, so I'll hop in the truck bed for the ride back."

Britt slid the strap of the rifle over his head. "If we have to blow the door, Phil will hear it."

"I've got him," Jonah said. "One of you take the other guy."

"Not a problem," Britt added. "Reid and Grif can get Suds out while I'm on Tomas."

Too many intangibles meant too many things going wrong. The only thing in Micki's control was her emotions and she owed it to Gage to stay calm and alert and focused. Plus, she couldn't think about this any longer.

"Let's do this. The idea of him in there, because of me, is making me insane."

Ready to free him, she started walking, her feet smacking against the wet pavement. At least the rain had passed. She'd take that as a good sign.

Hands in pockets, she drew a breath of cool air and let the oxygen sharpen her senses.

Jonah caught up, slinging his arm around her shoulders and giving her a squeeze. "We've got this. Trust me."

They made the turn at the front of the building and were met with intermittent overhead lights. It should have been comforting, but somehow total darkness would have been better. In total darkness she wouldn't have seen the disrepair, the abandonment of a once decent building.

But that was Phil's logic, wasn't it? Take something a little damaged and use it. Manipulate it until it works.

Just like her.

Now it was time to change all that. Finally.

They took the last few steps to unit 227, the one

Phil's car had been parked behind, and Micki grabbed the door handle. Locked.

Whoopsie. Hadn't anticipated that.

"Shit," Jonah said.

"That's all right."

Her foot crunched over shattered glass and she glanced up at the overhead light where half of a bulb remained. More than likely, Phil had used something to break the bulb. Given the other nonworking lamps, anyone driving along wouldn't think twice about it.

All the angles covered. Good old Phil.

She cupped her hands against the storefront's window and peered inside just as an interior door opened and spilled soft light into a narrow hallway. Phil stepped out and, as if sensing something, halted. Tomas plowed into the back of him, but Phil ignored him, did a half-turn and stopped.

Here we are...

Tomas straightened up and followed Phil's gaze, his mouth moving at the sight of Micki at the door.

Then the two of them smiled. *Smiled.*

These twisted fuckers had Gage tied up, hopefully here and not some other unknown spot, and they were smiling?

"I'm totally frying them," she said before banging on the door and putting a little mean into it. "Open up."

Phil strode to the door while Tomas kept watch from inside.

"We're alone," she said.

He flipped the lock on the door and pushed it open. "I'm only half surprised to see you. With your skills, I anticipated you'd do something. And look, you brought the rapist with you."

Micki met Jonah's eye, silently pleading with him not to take the bait. Her brother, knowing Tessa had agreed to clear him, only smirked.

"Tell me," Tomas said, "you sent that malware in the e-mail, didn't you?"

She wouldn't admit to that. Let them keep guessing. "Where's Gage?"

Phil waved one of his manicured hands. "I wanted to meet in town for this, but since you're here, why not? Let's finish it. He's fine. He'll stay that way as long as we come to an agreement."

Once she and Jonah were inside, Phil made a production of locking the door again.

"What agreement?"

"I've taken care of you all these years, haven't I? *I'm* the one you trust. Why you're suddenly doubting that, I can't fathom. But it is what it is."

Taken care of her? That was one way to put it.

"Micki, don't—"

Before Jonah could finish, she slapped her hand up, silencing him.

Phil clapped his hands together. "That's my girl. You know me. I wouldn't hurt you. I need you. Now that you're here, I'm going to reconsider. Call it a soft spot for you. With that in mind, I'm prepared to forgive all this nonsense."

Forgive it? The man was beyond unhinged. Truly psychotic.

"Come back to Vegas," he continued, "keep your mouth shut, and I'll let your boyfriend go. I'll even bury the evidence against your brother. I think that's more than fair, don't you?"

"Dude," Jonah said, "your evidence is bullshit."

What happened to her doing the talking?

Phil slid his gaze to Jonah, eyeing him up and down. "Do you *really* want to test me?"

Before Jonah did his I-am-a-Steele routine, Micki touched his arm, keeping her gaze on Phil. "No one is testing anything. Let Gage go and I'll come back to Vegas."

A lie, but Phil didn't know that. Didn't matter. All that mattered was Gage and his freedom.

Jonah swung his head, gawking at her.

"I'm sorry, Jonah. If it gets Gage out of this, I'll do it. I'll go back to Vegas."

Micki's voice. Coming from the front room.

What the fuck?

From what Gage could tell, there was a bathroom and another room outside the one where he was being held. So far he'd heard a toilet flush. On the left. From the right, muffled voices. Phil and Tomas talking. Kudos to the builder, because Gage couldn't make out what they were saying, and they'd obviously not heard him shuffling along that beam. Now, suddenly, Micki—and one of her brothers, Jonah maybe—added to the voices.

Dammit. *Work faster.* Gage had managed to chew the rope thin enough to rub it against the rough edge of the beam and snap the last bit of twine. Still on top of the workbench, he started on his ankle restraints, thanking whatever merciful angel had thrown him the bone of an easy knot.

Ten seconds and he'd be free.

Boom!

The door on the backside of the building exploded off its hinges, the sound loud enough to rattle the workbench. Way too much C-4. Friggin' Reid, always wanting the big bang. The door toppled over, landing with a crash in front of the open doorway as Reid burst into the room, weapon raised, his facial features like cut granite and carrying the intensity, the absolute no-fail determination he'd worn during missions. Britt and Grif shuffled in behind, the three of them wearing body armor and moving in perfect sync.

The other door flew open, the smack of the wood echoing off the walls as Tomas rushed in and lifted his weapon, pointing it straight ahead. At Reid. And then everything seemed to slow down and shouts were muffled as Gage's brain fired conflicting orders, all of them battling for his attention.

Every nerve ending fired, igniting that primal urge for war, and his vision tunneled. Right to Tomas and that man-stopper of a gun about to decimate Reid. Oblivious to Gage, Tomas didn't bother checking his right side, so Gage did the simplest thing.

He snatched up the hunk of vise that sat on the table and whipped it at Tomas. It wouldn't do much damage, but the distraction would buy Reid time.

The handle connected with Tomas's shoulder and he swiveled in Gage's direction, the gun moving with him.

"Drop it," Reid shouted. "Drop it, drop it, drop it!"

Reid moved fast, barreling into Tomas, knocking him to the ground and stomping on his hand, crushing all those tiny bones under his giant foot. Tomas howled while Britt closed in, using his boot to sweep the weapon across the floor.

With Britt on their prisoner, Reid looked up at Gage on the workbench. "What the hell? What are you standing around for?"

Riding the adrenaline high, Gage hopped down, sticking the landing and hauling ass into the hallway.

To Micki.

The explosion rocked the building. Even prepared for it—somewhat, anyway—Micki was shocked by the intensity as a mix of yelling voices collided with her ringing ears.

Phil reached under his jacket, revealing a holster and pulling a gun. "Move and I'll kill you both."

Gage appeared in the doorway, momentum bouncing his body off the far wall.

"Micki!"

Phil whipped sideways, the gun now on Gage, and

Jonah leaped, flying straight at him. But Phil had his finger locked on that trigger and...squeezed.

"No!" she roared.

Being the operator he was, Gage ducked left and the shot whizzed by him as Jonah plowed into Phil. *Gun.* Micki moved closer, her mind hyper-focused. Waiting.

Whap, whap, whap. Jonah slammed Phil's wrist against the wall and the gun fell free.

Get it.

In a move she'd seen Phil and Tomas practice, he got an elbow up, clocking Jonah on the forehead, sending his head snapping back. Micki lunged for the gun, her body bouncing against the hard tile and sending pain shooting up her ribs. She scooped the weapon up as she moved, and the warmth of the grip made her palm sweat, but she held on. Her mind tripped back to her father teaching her to shoot.

Guns, she didn't fear. People? They terrified her.

Still on the floor, she brought the gun up and a flash of metal in Phil's hand drew her gaze. *Knife.* His secondary weapon of choice.

"Drop it!"

Jonah pivoted and a hard thrust landed in the side of his abdomen.

"Jonah!"

Phil wrenched the knife free, drawing back again, ready to strike a second time.

At least until Micki squeezed the trigger.

CHAPTER TWENTY-THREE

THE SHOT RANG OUT.

An icy shiver gripped Micki and she locked her jaw, forced herself to concentrate. Phil's chest bloomed red and he stumbled back, the shock, the absolute horror, contorting his face. He backed into the wall and his body slid lower, sagging to the floor.

Her brother's shouting voices filled the small space, echoing off the walls, and Micki sat, the damned gun still in her hand, every inch of her frozen with fear and anger. Someone said something about checking the other one and zip-ties. What? She shook her head, confused by the shouting and merging voices.

Needing an anchor, she found Grif, on his phone relaying details to 911. Beside him a now shirtless Britt barked orders at Jonah, and Micki shivered again.

Jonah.

Her twin. On the floor, blood pouring from the side of his belly into Britt's shirt.

"Christ almighty, Tarzan," he said, "don't push that hard. That shit hurts."

Alive. *He's alive.*

"Quit your bitching, Baby Billionaire," Reid said from the other room. "Save your energy."

"Fuck off, Reid."

"Atta boy!"

What was *wrong* with them? Total morons. She'd just shot a man and they were screaming at each other.

"Micki."

Gage—*safe*—stood a foot to her right, out of the line of fire. He dropped to his knees. "Honey, put the gun down. On the floor. Right now."

He inched closer, sliding on his knees, his hands out in front of him.

"I...sh-sh-shot...shot him."

The reality of it hadn't quite sunk in, but she saw the evidence in front of her. A loud groan came from her throat and the room spun, the walls curving and swaying, and she rocked forward. And back. Forward and back.

"Ohmigod," she said.

"Honey." Gage again. "Look at me."

Forcing herself to move, she brought her head around. "What did I do?"

"You just saved your brother's life. You're okay. Just, please, put the gun down."

Gun. In her shaking hand. Lord, it could go off again.

Slowly, she lowered it, set it on the floor, and snatched her hands away. Gage wrapped his fingers around her arm, gently bringing her against him, holding her head to his chest. "Breathe. Nice and slow. You're okay."

The carnage in front of her brought on another bout of panic and she buried her forehead in his chest.

"Is he...dead?"

"Don't worry about it now."

"He had the knife," she said. "I had to."

"Yes. You did. He'd have killed you. And Jonah. All of us."

She nodded. He'd have done it. No matter what he said, all the years they'd been together, she knew, down deep, Phil wouldn't have walked away.

Too stubborn. Too driven. Too...competitive.

He had to win. Always. His reputation, his livelihood depended on it.

A wailing siren approached.

"Ambulance," Reid said. "I'm on it. Grif, keep an eye on that asshole back there."

Her brother ran to the door, holding it open with his foot while he waved his arms. "Hang on, Baby Billionaire. They're pulling in."

"Fuck you again, Reid."

"That's the spirit. You make me proud. Ooh, and would you look at this? You got yourself a pretty blond EMT. Lucky bastard."

"I just got stabbed," Jonah said to Britt. "I'm lucky?"

Micki shoved away from Gage, scrambling the few feet to Jonah because this was her chance. Before they took him. Just in case he didn't...no. She wouldn't put that out there.

She reached him and looked down at the stark white of his face, all that precious blood draining from him. She rested her head against his shoulder and stroked his hair. "I'm so sorry. Please forgive me."

"Pfft. For what? You didn't stab me. That fucking psycho did. Now shut up about it. This wasn't your fault."

Wasn't her fault.

"Ow, Britt. Shit. Take it easy. And Micki, don't make me say this again. What you sacrificed for me, what you gave up, I can't wrap my mind around it. You did all that. For me. Do you have any idea how humbling that is? To know my sister loved me that much? Girl, give yourself a break."

"Hey, sugar. Right in here."

Micki angled back to where Reid held the door for a female EMT and her partner rushing in wheeling a gurney. "My brother is the one on the ground. Stab wound, but he's pretty talkative right now. The other guy has a GSW to the chest."

CHAPTER TWENTY-FOUR

MICKI STOOD IN FRONT OF Saint Elizabeth's hospital, the bright morning sunshine blinding her. Beside her, Captain America, of course, had remembered his sunglasses and stood with his face tipped to the sun.

"Great day," he said.

Micki glanced at the hospital entrance where a nurse wheeled out a young mother cuddling a baby. A man carrying an armload of flowers and dragging a suitcase walked behind.

"It is a great day," Micki said. "Maybe when I'm done here, we can grab lunch."

He slid his arm over her shoulder and kissed the top of her head. "I'd like that. And, maybe tonight, after your meeting with Jonah, we'll go into Asheville. Wander around, grab a movie, listen to some live music. We'll get that date we haven't had yet."

A movie and music. How incredibly normal for a girl whose life had been anything but.

Two days ago she'd shot Phil. Self-defense. Owen, her crack lawyer, had made sure the State's Attorney went along with that and, given her testimony regarding the illegal dealings of Phil Flynn and Associates, it appeared she'd be granted immunity in the whole mess. Immunity and a chance to rebuild her life.

She needed time to make sense of all that they'd done,

the people they'd hurt. The ironic part? Phil had taught her, without question, that bad behavior came with consequences. Well, they had that by the truckload.

Last night, the shock of the past days had worn off and the full brunt of emotions socked her, left her reeling and terrified because everything she'd known her entire adult life was now gone. After her crying jag, she'd fallen asleep curled up with Gage while watching *All The President's Men*, apparently a favorite of Captain America's. Despite the sore neck this morning, the night had been all she'd really ever dreamed of.

Gage slid his sunglasses off and waved them at the hospital entrance. "You ready for this?"

She let out a sarcastic grunt. "No."

"You don't have to do it."

"I know, but I need to. I have to end it. Once I do, I'll finally be free."

"It's your call."

She gripped his hand still on her shoulder, pulling him along as she started toward the door. "Let's do this, Captain. I want that lunch you promised me."

Once inside, they rode the elevator to the fourth-floor surgical unit where doctors had plucked the bullet from Phil's chest and announced he'd survive.

As a result, he faced what looked like the next twenty years—at least—in prison. Tomas would be right there with him. He'd at least been smart and made a deal with the prosecutors for less time.

Outside room 412 stood an armed county sheriff's deputy. Micki checked in with him and turned to Gage.

"I'd like to go in alone."

Gage glanced at the partially open door. "You sure?"

"I am. I have things to say to him."

"If it's what you want. I'll wait right out here. Holler if you need me." He leaned in, ran one hand down the side of her cheek. "I'm here for you. Whatever you need, I'm here."

At that, she smiled. "I know."

She turned to the door and looked through the opening. Phil lay in bed, his head facing the window. If he wasn't asleep, he was simply ignoring his visitor. The silent treatment. One of his go-to forms of coercion.

Well, she had something to say and he'd hear it whether he wanted to or not.

She didn't bother knocking and stepped into the room. "Phil?"

When he didn't acknowledge her, she walked around the bed and peeked at him. Two days' worth of growth swathed his chin, an unusual occurrence for the manscaped Phil.

She moved closer, stepped around the rolling tray holding a small bouquet of flowers someone had cared enough to send. Probably a family member. Micki planted herself directly in his sightline. Still he stared straight ahead, absolutely refusing to acknowledge her. Well, too bad. A couple of weeks ago, it would have worked. She'd have rushed back to her desk and worked like a demon to please him. Anything to get out of the scary Phil doghouse.

How things changed with family support.

And Captain America.

"Look away," she said, "but I know you can hear me."

Still, he stared straight ahead as if she were a glass door. "We've been through a lot together, Phil, and we're not done yet. I came to tell you to, for once, do the right thing and plead guilty. Save your family the humiliation of a trial and give the taxpayers a break on the cost of prosecuting. They'll get you anyway, so why put the people you love through it?"

Finally, he slid his gaze up to her. "Never."

Ah, yes. The Phil she knew. The one with delusions about his indestructibility. "I know you think you've insulated yourself. And maybe, before all of this, you had. You've been careful all these years. Hiding or destroying evidence, offshore accounts, all of it in preparation for the day the feds would come knocking. You had it all figured out, didn't you?"

He didn't answer. She'd didn't expect him to.

"Well, there's one thing you didn't count on." She held up a flash drive and waggled it. "You didn't count on me helping myself to some of that precious evidence you tried to hide. I finally hacked into your server. Ironic, no?" She bent at the waist and met his eye. "Plead guilty, Phil, or I tell them everything. After what you did to Jonah and Gage, I will bleed myself dry to make sure you go to prison."

"I can still get to you from behind bars."

She shrugged. "Maybe. The difference now is that I'm not afraid of you anymore. I have my family back. You took them from me. I was a kid and you separated me from the only support system I had. I should hate you for that, but I forgive you."

He rolled his eyes. "Please. As if I care?"

"The forgiveness isn't for you. It's for me. I want to be done with you. Carrying anger and hatred takes way too much energy. There were kindnesses you showed me over the years. Thank you for that. Even if it was only to keep me in check, you still did it. Now it's over. Good-bye, Phil."

She stood tall, pushed her shoulders back, and headed for the door.

"You won't testify," he said. "I know you."

At the door, Micki stopped. She glanced back, found him staring right at her. Finally, he'd moved his head. Probably when he realized his old tricks no longer worked.

"You won't," he said again.

"Try me. This time, you won't win."

CHAPTER TWENTY-FIVE

GAGE KNOCKED ON REID'S OFFICE door and waited for the big man to look up from his laptop. "Hey," he said. "How'd it go?"

"I waited outside, but she said it was fine. Said what she had to say. Now she's done. Ready to move on."

"What a mess. It'll be good having her home. She's a pain in the ass, but I missed her."

Love. Steele style.

Apparently finished with that subject, Reid pointed at the computer. "Just got the inventory list for the hotel. Who the hell knew there was that much shit in a hotel?"

"It's a lot of soap, for sure."

"And really, do we need the fancy stuff? I mean, moisturizer? How many guys do you know who can't live without *that* for a few days? Aside from Danny B. from our old unit. He's a walking personal hygiene product."

Gage laughed. "The hope is the men will bring their families. If it's putting you over the edge, cut it. Just remember, it was Brynne's suggestion."

"Come on, man! Are you *kidding* me? I love her, but that's a lot of fucking moisturizer." He shook his head and swiveled his chair to face Gage. "I know you didn't come in here to talk moisturizer. What's up?"

What was up was today would be the day Gage came

clean to his bosses about his injury. In all the discussions with Micki about her secrets and having faith in her family to support her, Gage hadn't followed his own advice. True, Micki might be their own blood, but the Steeles had been good to him. They deserved the truth.

No matter the consequences.

In ten minutes Micki would meet with Jonah to pitch her software and Gage would be there as her test dummy. The day before, her need for distraction drove them to spending twelve freaking hours testing the program. It had some kinks, but he could see the use for it. Particularly in VA hospitals. Jonah, having launched a successful video game, knew the right people to make Micki's dream come true.

Gage waggled his hand. "I wanted to check in before this meeting with Jonah."

"*Jonah,*" Reid said, heavy on the sarcasm. "The Baby Billionaire is the only guy I know who can get stabbed and have the knife miss every major organ." Reid ran both hands over his face and blew out a breath. "Damn, that took a dozen years off my life. Scared the shit out of me."

"He's lucky he got out of it only needing stitches."

"Amen, brother. Am I in this meeting with you?"

"No. But, uh, I've been helping Micki with the software."

"I thought it was educational."

"It started out that way. She originally developed it with ADD kids in mind. She's tweaked it."

Reid sat back and propped one hand on the arm of his chair. Waiting. He narrowed his eyes, studying Gage as if, somehow, he knew what was coming. Still, an actual conversation needed to be had. He'd have to ask his friend to forgive him for concealing facts about his health. Facts that could have affected the business.

And really, that's what it came down to. Gage had been too caught up in proving he still had a right to carry a Man Club card to realize he'd jeopardized Jonah's money and Reid's future.

Now it was time to 'fess up. To admit that their president of operations suffered from a traumatic brain injury.

Sensing Gage's hesitation, Reid waved him off. "You don't have to say it. It's all good."

"No. It isn't."

"Look, dude, don't put yourself through this for me. We're men. We don't talk about shit like this. I know what you're gonna say. We don't need a conversation."

Yeah, they did. "I have a TBI."

There. He'd said it. After all these months of hiding it, damned if it didn't roll right off his tongue. No agony, no incompetence, no shame. Just...relief.

Settling in, Reid propped his giant feet on the desk. "I know. Which is why I said we don't have to talk about it."

"You knew-knew. Or you thought you knew?"

"God save me. What the hell does it matter? You hit your head. I saw changes in you. It's not rocket science. I kept it to myself, figuring you needed time to heal. And, for the record, I was right." He flashed his teeth. "As usual."

"Oh, fuck you."

Clearly enjoying himself, Reid raised his hands before Gage lit into him. "I'll admit there were a few things you missed. With all we had going on, it was minor. I fixed it and that was that. I got you, Suds. Always."

"Does Jonah know?"

"Not from me."

Damn. Now that was loyalty. The guy's brother had millions invested in this place and Reid had been covering Gage's ass while making sure his brother didn't lose his investment. The weight of Reid's responsibility hit him and the shame finally came. The superhero, because of his own ego, had put his friend in one hell of a corner. "Thank you. I didn't intend..."

"Stop." Reid said. "Please. We're all good and you're trying to piss me off by talking about this. I'm done analyzing. I suck at this sensitivity crap."

"Okay. We're done. I wanted you to hear it from me first. And I'm getting better. Every day."

"Once again, I know. I see the improvement. Chat over. *Bye-bye.*"

"Also—"

"Son of a bitch, why is it never over when I think it's over? Brynne does this to me all the time." He held up a finger. "'Are you okay?'" he said, mimicking Brynne's voice. "And then I say I'm fine. And then she says"—he cleared his throat to mimic his soon-to-be-bride again—"'you don't seem fine.'" Back to his regular voice. "I'm telling you, it never ends. It's like entering the gates of hell."

Wow. Dude needed to chill. "Jeez, take it easy. It's over. I'm just saying thanks for taking a chance when you knew my brain was scrambled."

"On your worst day, your scrambled brain is better than ninety percent of the brains out there. Hiring you was not a hard decision. Believe me. You could do this job in your sleep. With a scrambled brain. Now leave. Before I fire your ass."

Gage offered up a crisp salute. "Sir, yes, sir."

"Hey."

Gage turned back. "What?"

"My sister. You're sure she's okay?"

"She is. Getting settled in."

"Good. She deserves to be happy."

If the TBI thing wasn't all that awkward, why did this feel like a waterboarding session? "Uh, anything else you want to say? In regard to Micki?"

"No. But"—he circled one hand—"you know, all that other crap about if you hurt her, I'll kill you and I don't want to hear jack-shit about any problems. I told her and I'm telling you, I'm not gonna be in the middle."

"I wouldn't do that to you."

"Yeah, but you'd saddle me with five tons of moisturizer."

If it made their guests happy, yeah, he would. "Let's

see how the moisturizer goes over. If we need to, we'll ditch it."

Reid let out a long growl. "We can test it for a month. Now get the fuck out."

Gage held up his fist, waited for his friend to bump it. "Deal. By the way, if the moisturizer goes, so does that extra set of flash bangs you wanted."

With that, he left his boss alone and headed to the conference room to 'fess up to his other boss.

Micki checked the focus of the projector, then fiddled with the height adjustment so the screen would be centered on the whiteboard at the far end of the conference room wall.

All of it needed to be perfect. For her. For Jonah. And for Gage.

That's when it hit her. That this presentation, this demo of her software, for the first time, didn't need to be hidden. *This* project, the one good thing she'd done and which had kept her sane for months, gave her a long-missing sense of pride. For years she'd written code and lurked around the deep Web, scraping and dredging for any nibble of damning information that could be used as leverage.

Her career, until this point, had been centered on negativity. Career success meant destroying people.

How had she never seen that? Or at least admitted it.

Today, all of that changed. She checked the screen once more, where the home page of her program flashed. Not quite centered. She slid her notepad under the legs of the projector and—there—perfect.

"Good morning, Ms. Steele."

She swung back, found Gage in the doorway, one shoulder casually propped against the frame, his hair perfectly neat and orderly. He wore khakis and a white cotton shirt with the top button undone. Wisps of blond hair curled over the top button and she thought back to the night before, stretched out on his couch with her cheek and hands resting on his chest, her fingers, curling into the thin line of hair swirling down his torso. More perfection for her not-so-perfect existence.

Phil was out of her life and Gage, as much as he couldn't understand it, had let her cry. Let her mourn for a man who'd taken so much from her, but somehow still managed to make her care.

"Hello, Captain America. How are you this morning?"

"I'm good."

She held her hands wide. "Are you sure you're ready for this?"

"I am."

"I may have been gone a long time, but if I know my twin, he'll have a lot of questions. About the software and…"

"Cognitive function. I know, Micki. It's fine." He boosted off the wall and approached, sliding his arm around her and all at once dropping a quick kiss on her lips and a gentle pat on the butt. "We're good. I talked to Reid already. He's up to speed."

He did it. Admitted the one thing he thought made him weak. *Good for him.* "How was that? Reid isn't exactly in the running for president of the Sensitivity Club."

"He was an ace."

Oh, come on. Reid? Seriously? "Stop it."

He laughed. "Yep. He said he'd figured it out. My big reveal wasn't so big."

"But saying it, admitting it is harder. It feels good, doesn't it? To have it all out there."

"No more secrets."

She nodded. "No more secrets."

"In fact, I'm thinking I need some time off next month. For the holidays."

A jab of panic froze her in her spot. Time off. Why?

Maybe the ordeal with Phil had set him back on his recovery. She set her hands on his cheeks and the overhead light glinted off her skull ring. Some things she couldn't give up. "Are you okay? You can tell me."

He stepped back, gathered her hands in his, and squeezed. "I'm good. But please, you can't be checking on me all the time. If my head hurts, I'll tell you. Otherwise, I can't have it be a thing between us. It's…emasculating."

As if. The man was a Green Beret and about as manly as men could get. That history, years spent running toward danger rather than away from it, had conditioned him to think a certain way. To push through and never give in. For Captain America, being a man meant taking charge, protecting his loved ones, and not giving in to injury. "I'm sorry. I never thought about it that way."

"Now you know. We're learning here. Figuring out each other's hot buttons."

Yes they were. A relationship. The thought of it still amazed her. *Home.* "It's exciting. I've never had that before. I've always had to hide."

"That's over. Which is why, when I go to Iowa next month, I'd like you to come with me. To meet my family."

She opened her mouth, but her jaw simply hung there, refusing to move. Not just the fact that he'd finally decided to go home and face his family, but that he wanted to take her, the princess of darkness, with him. "You want…" She let out a gasp. "Oh."

"What you said to me the other day. About me needing my fix and you being the damsel in distress."

"I shouldn't have said that."

"You were right. It's why I haven't seen my family since my injury. I was afraid to face them. I thought if I couldn't be the fix-it guy, they'd be disappointed."

"Well," she said, "I can't imagine that."

"Now that you called me out on it, I've been thinking how incredibly stupid it is. It's time. They need to understand I'm not the guy I was when I left home. I can't fix all their problems. They'll have to adjust. You made me realize that. Thank you."

A burst of pride swarmed her chest. In her own twisted way, she'd helped. *Go, me.*

"You're welcome. I'm glad I could help. And that you want to see your family." She scrunched her nose. "Taking *me*, though? Are you sure about that?"

"Yep. If I have my way, you'll be around awhile and I want you to see where I come from. I'm thinking we'll drive. Maybe stop along the way and be tourists. But you don't have to answer me now. Think about it."

Damned Captain America comes into her life and now she's taking vacations and meeting his family.

Suddenly she's...normal.

And someone a man would want to take home to his parents.

Tears filled her eyes—and what was up with all the blubbering? She didn't fight them, just them fall. Let Gage see it. Why not? He'd seen everything else of her.

"Oh, ouch," he said. "I'm not all that experienced with this whole taking-a-girl-home thing, but no one has ever cried over the idea."

Micki cracked up. It came out as a disgusting half sob, half snort that was as humiliating as the tears. "I can't believe you want me."

"Well, babe, believe it."

Jonah swung into the room, caught them up close and personal and spun around, ready to head back in the direction he came from. "Whoopsie. Sorry. I'll go."

"No." Gage stepped back. "Micki has something important to talk to you about."

A wave of insecurity, that stomach-shredding doubt that she'd lived with for so long, ripped into her. *No.* She could do this. Wanted to do this. She faced Gage. "You ready?"

"I am. Let's do this," he said. "Together."

MORE STEELE RIDGE
COMING IN 2017

Roaming WILD

Stripping BARE

WWW.STEELERIDGESERIES.COM

ACKNOWLEDGMENTS

Although the physical act of writing a book is a solo endeavor, without the help of many people, I could not accomplish this job I love so much. Thank you to my readers for all the support and allowing my books into your worlds.

Special thanks to my pals and coauthors on this series, Tracey Devlyn and Kelsey Browning, for blessing me with the gift of Micki Steele. She's a character I've loved from the second I started writing her in *The Beginning*, and I'm grateful for the opportunity to bring her a happy ending. Misty Evans, thank you for always answering my e-mails when I've hit a wall and need to work through a scene with someone.

To Tony Iacullo, thank you for walking me through the intricacies of proffer agreements and for always giving me options to consider. Milton Grasle, I'm definitely running out of ways to say thank you. With each book, no matter what kind of situation I come up with, you are always there to help me brainstorm an action scene. Thank you!

A giant thanks also to our amazing editors, Deb Nemeth and Martha Trachtenberg for the guidance in bringing the complicated Micki Steele to the page.

As usual, thank you to my guys who inspire me and make me laugh every day. I love you.

ADRIENNE GIORDANO is a *USA Today* bestselling author of over twenty romantic suspense and mystery novels. She is a Jersey girl at heart, but now lives in the Midwest with her workaholic husband, sports-obsessed son and Buddy the Wheaten Terrorist (Terrier). She is a cofounder of Romance University blog and Lady Jane's Salon-Naperville, a reading series dedicated to romantic fiction.

www.AdrienneGiordano.com

Printed in Great Britain
by Amazon